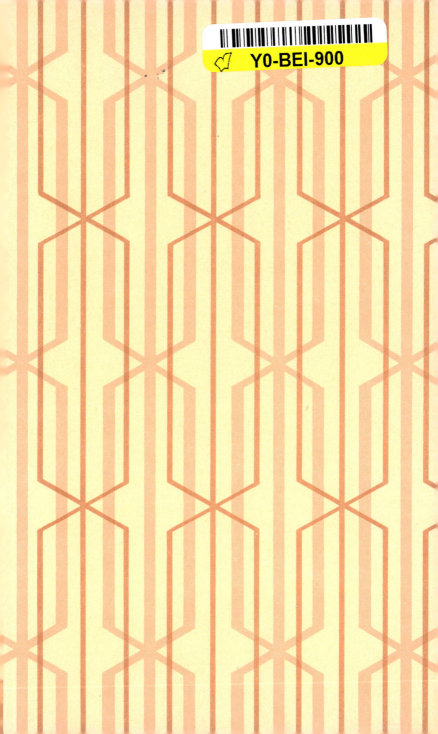

THE GREEN FLAG

AND OTHER STORIES

OF WAR AND SPORT

THE GREEN FLAG

AND

OTHER STORIES OF
WAR AND SPORT

By

SIR ARTHUR CONAN DOYLE

Short Story Index Reprint Series

BOOKS FOR LIBRARIES PRESS
FREEPORT, NEW YORK

First Published 1900
Reprinted 1969

STANDARD BOOK NUMBER:

8369-3201-3

LIBRARY OF CONGRESS CATALOG CARD NUMBER:
70-101468

MANUFACTURED
BY
HALLMARK LITHOGRAPHERS, INC.
IN THE U.S.A.

PREFACE

IT is difficult to make a volume of short stories homogeneous, but these have this in common: that they concern themselves with war and sport—a fact which may commend them to the temper of the times. Such as they are I have chosen them as the fittest survivors out of the tales which I have written during the last six years.

A. CONAN DOYLE.

Undershaw, Hindhead,
      February 18th, 1900.

64431

CONTENTS

THE GREEN FLAG

AND

OTHER STORIES

THE GREEN FLAG

WHEN Jack Conolly, of the Irish Shot-
gun Brigade, the Rory of the Hills
Inner Circle, and the extreme left wing of the
Land League, was incontinently shot by Sergeant Murdoch of the constabulary, in a little
moonlight frolic near Kanturk, his twin brother
Dennis joined the British Army. The countryside had become too hot for him; and, as
the seventy-five shillings were wanting which
might have carried him to America, he took
the only way handy of getting himself out of
the way. Seldom has Her Majesty had a less
promising recruit, for his hot Celtic blood
seethed with hatred against Britain and all
things British. The Sergeant, however, smiling
complacently over his six feet of brawn and
his forty-four-inch chest, whisked him off with
a dozen other of the boys to the depôt at Fer-
moy, whence in a few weeks they were sent on,
with the spade-work kinks taken out of their
backs, to the first battalion of the Royal Mallows, at the top of the roster for foreign service.

The Royal Mallows, at about that date, were as strange a lot of men as ever were paid by a great empire to fight its battles. It was the darkest hour of the land struggle, when the one side came out with crowbar and battering-ram by day, and the other with mask and with shot-gun by night. Men driven from their homes and potato-patches found their way even into the service of the Government, to which it seemed to them that they owed their troubles, and now and then they did wild things before they came. There were recruits in the Irish regiments who would forget to answer to their own names, so short had been their acquaintance with them. Of these the Royal Mallows had their full share ; and, while they still retained their fame as being one of the smartest corps in the Army, no one knew better than their officers that they were dry-rotted with treason and with bitter hatred of the flag under which they served.

And the centre of all the disaffection was C Company, in which Dennis Conolly found himself enrolled. They were Celts, Catholics, and men of the tenant class to a man ; and their whole experience of the British Government had been an inexorable landlord, and a constabulary who seemed to them to be always on the side of the rent-collector. Dennis was not the only moonlighter in the ranks, nor was he

alone in having an intolerable family blood-
feud to harden his heart. Savagery had be-
gotten savagery in that veiled civil war. A
landlord with an iron mortgage weighing down
upon him had small bowels for his tenantry.
He did but take what the law allowed ; and yet,
with men like Jim Holan, or Patrick McQuire,
or Peter Flynn, who had seen the roofs torn
from their cottages and their folk huddled
among their pitiable furniture upon the roadside, it was ill to argue about abstract law.
What matter that in that long and bitter struggle there was many another outrage on the part
of the tenant, and many another grievance on
the side of the landowner ! A stricken man
can only feel his own wound, and the rank
and file of the C Company of the Royal Mallows were sore and savage to the soul. There
were low whisperings in barrack-rooms and can-
teens, stealthy meetings in public-house par-
lours, bandying of passwords from mouth to
mouth, and many other signs which made their
officers right glad when the order came which
sent them to foreign, and better still to active,
service.

For Irish regiments have before now been
disaffected, and have at a distance looked upon
the foe as though he might, in truth, be the
friend ; but when they have been put face on
to him, and when their officers have dashed to

the front with a wave and a halloo, those rebel hearts have softened and their gallant Celtic blood has boiled with the mad joy of fight, until the slower Britons have marvelled that they ever could have doubted the loyalty of their Irish comrades. So it would be again, according to the officers, and so it would not be if Dennis Conolly and a few others could have their way.

It was a March morning upon the eastern fringe of the Nubian desert. The sun had not yet risen ; but a tinge of pink flushed up as far as the cloudless zenith, and the long strip of sea lay like a rosy ribbon across the horizon. From the coast inland stretched dreary sand-plains, dotted over with thick clumps of mimosa scrub and mottled patches of thorny bush. No tree broke the monotony of that vast desert. The dull, dusty hue of the thickets and the yellow glare of the sand were the only colours, save at one point where, from a distance, it seemed that a landslip of snow-white stones had shot itself across a low foot-hill. But as the traveller approached he saw, with a thrill, that these were no stones, but the bleaching bones of a slaughtered army. With its dull tints, its gnarled virous bushes, its arid, barren soil, and this death-streak trailed across it, it was indeed a nightmare country.

Some eight or ten miles inland the rolling
plain curved upwards with a steeper slope until
it ran into a line of red basaltic rock which zig-
zagged from north to south, heaping itself up at
one point into a fantastic knoll. On the summit of this there stood upon that March morning three Arab chieftains—the Sheik Kadra of
the Hadendowas, Moussa Wad Aburhegel, who
led the Berber dervishes, and Hamid Wad Hussein, who had come northward with his fighting
men from the land of the Baggaras. They had
all three just risen from their praying-carpets,
and were peering out, with fierce, high-nosed
faces thrust forwards, at the stretch of country
revealed by the spreading dawn.

The red rim of the sun was pushing itself
now above the distant sea, and the whole coast-
line stood out brilliantly yellow against the rich
deep blue beyond. At one spot lay a huddle
of white-walled houses, a mere splotch in the
distance ; while four tiny cock-boats, which lay
beyond, marked the position of three of Her
Majesty's ten-thousand-ton troopers and the
Admiral's flagship. But it was not upon the
distant town, nor upon the great vessels, nor
yet upon the sinister white litter which gleamed
in the plain beneath them, that the Arab chieftains gazed. Two miles from where they
stood, amid the sand-hills and the mimosa
scrub, a great parallelogram had been marked

7

by piled-up bushes. From the inside of this
dozens of tiny blue smoke-reeks curled up into
the still morning air; while there rose from it a
confused deep murmur, the voices of men and
the gruntings of camels blended into the same
insect buzz.

"The unbelievers have cooked their morning
food," said the Baggara chief, shading his eyes
with his tawny, sinewy hand. "Truly their
sleep has been but scanty; for Hamid and a
hundred of his men have fired upon them since
the rising of the moon."

"So it was with these others," answered the
Sheik Kadra, pointing with his sheathed sword
towards the old battle-field. "They also had
a day of little water and a night of little rest,
and the heart was gone out of them ere ever
the sons of the Prophet had looked them in
the eyes. This blade drank deep that day, and
will again before the sun has travelled from the
sea to the hill."

"And yet these are other men," remarked
the Berber dervish. "Well, I know that Allah
has placed them in the clutch of our fingers,
yet it may be that they with the big hats will
stand firmer than the cursed men of Egypt."

"Pray Allah that it may be so," cried the
fierce Baggara, with a flash of his black eyes.
"It was not to chase women that I brought
seven hundred men from the river to the coast.

See, my brother, already they are forming their array."

A fanfare of bugle-calls burst from the distant camp. At the same time the bank of bushes at one side had been thrown or trampled down, and the little army within began to move slowly out on to the plain. Once clear of the camp they halted, and the slant rays of the sun struck flashes from bayonet and from gun-barrel as the ranks closed up until the big pith helmets joined into a single long white ribbon. Two streaks of scarlet glowed on either side of the square, but elsewhere the fringe of fighting-men was of the dull yellow khaki tint which hardly shows against the desert sand. Inside their array was a dense mass of camels and mules bearing stores and ambulance needs. Outside a twinkling clump of cavalry was drawn up on each flank, and in front a thin scattered line of mounted infantry was already slowly advancing over the bush-strewn plain, halting on every eminence, and peering warily round as men might who have to pick their steps among the bones of those who have preceded them.

The three chieftains still lingered upon the knoll, looking down with hungry eyes and compressed lips at the dark steel-tipped patch.

" They are slower to start than the men of Egypt," the Sheik of the Hadendowas growled in his beard.

9

" Slower also to go back, perchance, my brother," murmured the dervish. "And yet they are not many—three thousand at the most."

" And we ten thousand, with the Prophet's grip upon our spear-hafts and his words upon our banner. See to their chieftain, how he rides upon the right and looks up at us with the glass that sees from afar! It may be that he sees this also." The Arab shook his sword at the small clump of horsemen who had spurred out from the square.

" Lo! he beckons," cried the dervish; "and see those others at the corner, how they bend and heave. Ha! by the Prophet, I had thought it."

As he spoke a little woolly puff of smoke spurted up at the corner of the square, and a seven-pound shell burst with a hard metallic smack just over their heads. The splinters knocked chips from the red rocks around them.

" Bismillah!" cried the Hadendowa; "if the gun can carry thus far, then ours can an-swer to it. Ride to the left, Moussa, and tell Ben Ali to cut the skin from the Egyptians if they cannot hit yonder mark. And you, Hamid, to the right, and see that three thou-sand men lie close in the wady that we have chosen. Let the others beat the drum and show the banner of the Prophet; for by the black stone their spears will have drunk deep ere they look upon the stars again."

A long, straggling, boulder-strewn plateau lay on the summit of the red hills, sloping very precipitously to the plain, save at one point, where a winding gully curved downwards, its mouth choked with sand-mounds and olive-hued scrub. Along the edge of this position lay the Arab host, a motley crew of shock-headed desert clansmen, fierce predatory slave-dealers of the interior, and wild dervishes from the Upper Nile, all blent together by their common fearlessness and fanaticism. Two races were there, as wide as the poles apart, the thin-lipped, straight-haired Arab, and the thick-lipped, curly negro; yet the faith of Islam had bound them closer than a blood tie. Squatting among the rocks, or lying thickly in the shadow, they peered out at the slow-moving square beneath them, while women with water-skins and bags of dhoora fluttered from group to group, calling out to each other those fighting texts from the Koran which in the hour of battle are maddening as wine to the true believer. A score of banners waved over the ragged, valiant crew, and among them, upon desert horses and white Bishareen camels, were the Emirs and Sheiks who were to lead them against the infidels.

As the Sheik Kadra sprang into his saddle and drew his sword there was a wild whoop and a clatter of waving spears, while the one-ended war-drums burst into a dull crash like a wave upon shingle. For a moment ten thousand men were up on the rocks with brandished arms and leaping figures; the next they were under cover, again waiting sternly and silently for their chieftain's orders. The square was less than half a mile from the ridge now, and shell after shell from the seven-pound guns were pitching over it. A deep roar on the right, and then a second one showed that the Egyptian Krupps were in action. Sheik Kadra's hawk eyes saw that the shells burst far beyond the mark, and he spurred his horse along to where a knot of mounted chiefs were gathered round the two guns, which were served by their captured crews.

"How is this, Ben Ali?" he cried. "It was not thus that the dogs fired when it was their own brothers in faith at whom they aimed!"

A chieftain reined his horse back, and thrust a blood-smeared sword into its sheath. Beside him two Egyptian artillerymen with their throats cut were sobbing out their lives upon the ground.

"Who lays the gun this time?" asked the fierce chief, glaring at the frightened gunners.

" Here, thou black-browed child of Shaitan, aim, and aim for thy life."

It may have been chance, or it may have been skill, but the third and fourth shells burst over the square. Sheik Kadra smiled grimly and galloped back to the left, where his spearmen were streaming down into the gully. As he joined them a deep growling rose from the plain beneath, like the snarling of a sullen wild beast, and a little knot of tribesmen fell in a struggling heap, caught in the blast of lead from a Gardner. Their comrades pressed on over them, and sprang down into the ravine. From all along the crest burst the hard sharp crackle of Remington fire.

The square had slowly advanced, rippling over the low sandhills, and halting every few minutes to rearrange its formation. Now, having made sure that there was no force of the enemy in the scrub, it changed its direction, and began to take a line parallel to the Arab position. It was too steep to assail from the front, and if they moved far enough to the right the General hoped that he might turn it. On the top of those ruddy hills lay a baronetcy for him, and a few extra hundreds in his pension, and he meant having them both that day. The Remington fire was annoying, and so were those two Krupp guns : already there were more cacolets full than he cared to see. But on the whole he thought it better to hold his fire until he had more to aim at than a few hundred of fuzzy heads peeping over a razor-back ridge. He was a bulky, red-faced man, a fine whist-player, and a soldier who knew his work. His men believed in him, and he had good reason to believe in them, for he had excellent stuff under him that day. Being an ardent champion of the short-service system, he took particular care to work with veteran first battalions, and his little force was the compressed essence of an army corps.

The left front of the square was formed by four companies of the Royal Wessex, and the right by four of the Royal Mallows. On either side the other halves of the same regiments marched in quarter column of companies. Behind them, on the right was a battalion of Guards, and on the left one of Marines, while the rear was closed in by a Rifle battalion. Two Royal Artillery seven-pound screw-guns kept pace with the square, and a dozen white-bloused sailors, under their blue-coated, tight-waisted officers, trailed their Gardner in front, turning every now and then to spit up at the draggled banners which waved over the cragged ridge. Hussars and Lancers scouted in the scrub at each side, and within moved the clump of camels, with humorous eyes and supercilious lips, their comic faces a contrast to the blood-stained men who already lay huddled in the cacolets on either side.

The square was now moving slowly on a line parallel with the rocks, stopping every few minutes to pick up wounded, and to allow the screw-guns and Gardner to make themselves felt. The men looked serious, for that spring on to the rocks of the Arab army had given them a vague glimpse of the number and ferocity of their foes; but their faces were set like stone, for they knew to a man that they must win or they must die—and die, too, in a particularly unlovely fashion. But most serious of all was the General, for he had seen that which brought a flush to his cheeks and a frown to his brow.

"I say, Stephen," said he to his galloper, "those Mallows seems a trifle jumpy. The right flank company bulged a bit when the niggers showed on the hill."

"Youngest troops in the square, sir," murmured the aide, looking at them critically through his eyeglass.

"Tell Colonel Flanagan to see to it, Stephen," said the General; and the galloper sped upon his way. The Colonel, a fine old Celtic warrior, was over at C Company in an instant.

"How are the men, Captain Foley?"

"Never better, sir," answered the senior captain in the spirit that makes a Madras officer look murder if you suggest recruiting his regiment from the Punjaub.

"Stiffen them up!" cried the Colonel. As he rode away a colour-sergeant seemed to trip, and fell forward into a mimosa bush.

He made no effort to rise, but lay in a heap among the thorns.

"Sergeant O'Rooke's gone, sorr," cried a voice.

"Never mind, lads," said Captain Foley. "He's died like a soldier, fighting for his Queen."

"To hell with the Queen!" shouted a hoarse voice from the ranks.

But the roar of the Gardner and the typewriter-like clicking of the hopper burst in at the tail of the words. Captain Foley heard them, and Subalterns Grice and Murphy heard them; but there are times when a deaf ear is a gift from the gods.

"Steady, Mallows!" cried the Captain, in a pause of the grunting machine-gun. "We have the honour of Ireland to guard this day."

"And well we know how to guard it, Captin!" cried the same ominous voice; and there was a buzz from the length of the company.

The Captain and the two subs. came together behind the marching line.

"They seem a bit out of hand," murmured the Captain.

" Bedad," said the Galway boy, " they mean to scoot like redshanks."

" They nearly broke when the blacks showed on the hill," said Grice.

" The first man that turns, my sword is through him," cried Foley, loud enough to be heard by five files on either side of him. Then, in a lower voice, " It's a bitter drop to swallow, but it's my duty to report what you think to the Chief and have a company of Jollies put behind us." He turned away with the safety of the square upon his mind, and before he had reached his goal the square had ceased to exist.

In their march in front of what looked like a face of cliff, they had come opposite to the mouth of the gully, in which, screened by scrub and boulders, three thousand chosen dervishes, under Hamid Wad Hussein of the Bagarras, were crouching. Tat, tat, tat, went the rifles of three mounted infantrymen in front of the left shoulder of the square, and an instant later they were spurring it for their lives, crouching over the manes of their horses, and pelting over the sandhills with thirty or forty galloping chieftains at their heels. Rocks and scrub and mimosa swarmed suddenly into life. Rushing black figures came and went in the gaps of the bushes. A howl that drowned the shouts of the officers, a long quavering yell, burst from

17

the ambuscade. Two rolling volleys from the Royal Wessex, one crash from the screw-gun firing shrapnel, and then before a second cart-ridge could be rammed in, a living, glistening black wave tipped with steel, had rolled over the gun, the Royal Wessex had been dashed back among the camels, and a thousand fanat-ics were hewing and hacking in the heart of what had been the square.

The camels and mules in the centre, jammed more and more together as their leaders flinched from the rush of the tribesmen, shut out the view of the other three faces, who could only tell that the Arabs had got in by the yells upon Allah, which rose ever nearer and nearer amid the clouds of sand-dust, the struggling animals, and the dense mass of swaying, cursing men. Some of the Wessex fired back at the Arabs who had passed them, as excited Tommies will, and it is whispered among doctors that it was not always a Remington bullet which was cut from a wound that day. Some rallied in little knots, stabbing furiously with their bayonets at the rushing spearmen. Others turned at bay with their backs against the camels, and others round the General and his staff, who, revolver in hand, had flung themselves into the heart of it. But the whole square was sidling slowly away from the gorge, pushed back by the pres-sure at the shattered corner.

The officers and men at the other faces were glancing nervously to their rear, uncertain what was going on, and unable to take help to their comrades without breaking the formation.

" By Jove, they've got through the Wessex!" cried Grice of the Mallows.

" The divils have hurrooshed us, Ted," said his brother subaltern, cocking his revolver.

The ranks were breaking and crowding towards Private Conolly, all talking together as the officers peered back through the veil of dust. The sailors had run their Gardner out, and she was squirting death out of her five barrels into the flank of the rushing stream of savages.

" Oh, this bloody gun!" shouted a voice. " She's jammed again." The fierce metallic grunting had ceased, and her crew were straining and hauling at the breech.

" This damned vertical feed!" cried an officer. " The spanner, Wilson, the spanner! Stand to your cutlasses, boys, or they're into us."

His voice rose into a shriek as he ended, for a shovel-headed spear had been buried in his chest. A second wave of dervishes lapped over the hillocks, and burst upon the machine-gun and the right front of the line. The sailors were overborne in an instant, but the Mallows, with their fighting blood aflame, met the yell of the Moslem with an even wilder, fiercer cry, and dropped two hundred of them with a single point-blank volley. The howling, leaping crew swerved away to the right, and dashed on into the gap which had already been made for them.

But C Company had drawn no trigger to stop that fiery rush. The men leaned moodily upon their Martinis. Some had even thrown them upon the ground. Conolly was talking fiercely to those about him. Captain Foley, thrusting his way through the press, rushed up to him with a revolver in his hand.

" This is your doing, you villain ! " he cried.

" If you raise your pistol, Captin, your brains will be over your coat," said a low voice at his side.

He saw that several rifles were turned on him. The two subs. had pressed forward, and were by his side.

" What is it, then ? " he cried, looking round from one fierce mutinous face to another. " Are you Irishmen ? Are you soldiers ? What are you here for but to fight for your country ? "

" England is no country of ours," cried several.

" You are not fighting for England. You are fighting for Ireland, and for the Empire of which it is part."

" A black curse on the Impire ! " shouted Private McQuire, throwing down his rifle.

" 'Twas the Impire that backed the man that druv me onto the roadside. May me hand stiffen before I draw thrigger for it."

" What's the Impire to us, Captain Foley, and what's the Widdy to us ayther?" cried a voice.

" Let the constabulary foight for her."

" Ay, be God, they'd be better imployed than pullin' a poor man's thatch about his ears."

" Or shootin' his brother, as they did mine."

" It was the Impire laid my groanin' mother by the wayside. Her son will rot before he upholds it, and ye can put that in the charge-sheet in the next coort-martial."

In vain the three officers begged, menaced, persuaded. The square was still moving, ever moving, with the same bloody fight raging in its entrails. Even while they had been speaking they had been shuffling backwards, and the useless Gardner, with her slaughtered crew, was already a good hundred yards from them. And the pace was accelerating. The mass of men, tormented and writhing, was trying, by a common instinct, to reach some clearer ground where they could re-form. Three faces were still intact, but the fourth had been caved in, and badly mauled, without its comrades being able to help it. The Guards had met a fresh rush of the Hadendowas, and had blown back the tribesmen with a volley, and the Cavalry had ridden over another stream of them, as they welled out of the gully. A litter of hamstrung horses, and haggled men behind them, showed that a spearman on his face among the bushes can show some sport to the man who charges him. But, in spite of all, the square was still reeling swiftly backwards trying to shake itself clear of this torment which clung to its heart. Would it break, or would it re-form? The lives of five regiments and the honour of the flag hung upon the answer.

Some, at least, were breaking. The C Company of the Mallows had lost all military order and was pushing back in spite of the haggard officers, who cursed and shoved and prayed in the vain attempt to hold them. Their Captain and the subs. were elbowed and jostled, while the men crowded towards Private Conolly for their orders. The confusion had not spread, for the other companies, in the dust and smoke and turmoil, had lost touch with their mutinous comrades. Captain Foley saw that even now there might be time to avert a disaster.

" Think what you are doing, man," he yelled, rushing towards the ringleader. " There are a thousand Irish in the square, and they are dead men if we break."

The words alone might have had little effect on the old moonlighter. It is possible that, in his scheming brain, he had already planned how

he was to club his Irish together and lead them
to the sea. But at that moment the Arabs
broke through the screen of camels which had
fended them off. There was a struggle, a
screaming, a mule rolled over, a wounded man
sprang up in a cacolet with a spear through
him, and then through the narrow gap surged
a stream of naked savages, mad with battle,
drunk with slaughter, spotted and splashed with
blood—blood dripping from their spears, their
arms, their faces. Their yells, their bounds,
their crouching, darting figures, the horrid energy of their spear-thrusts, made them look
like a blast of fiends from the pit. And were
these the Allies of Ireland? Were these the
men who were to strike for her against her enemies? Conolly's soul rose up in loathing at
the thought.

He was a man of firm purpose, and yet at
the first sight of those howling fiends that purpose faltered, and at the second it was blown to
the winds. He saw a huge coal-black negro
seize a shrieking camel-driver and saw at his
throat with a knife. He saw a shock-headed
tribesman plunge his great spear through the
back of their own little bugler from Millstreet.
He saw a dozen deeds of blood—the murder of
the wounded, the hacking of the unarmed—
and caught, too, in a glance, the good whole-
some faces of the faced-about rear rank of the

Marines. The Mallows, too, had faced about, and in an instant Conolly had thrown himself into the heart of C Company, striving with the officers to form the men up with their comrades.

But the mischief had gone too far. The rank and file had no heart in their work. They had broken before, and this last rush of murderous savages was a hard thing for broken men to stand against. They flinched from the furious faces and dripping forearms. Why should they throw away their lives for a flag for which they cared nothing? Why should their leader urge them to break, and now shriek to them to re-form? They would not re-form. They wanted to get to the sea and to safety. He flung himself among them with outstretched arms, with words of reason, with shouts, with gaspings. It was useless; the tide was beyond his control. They were shredding out into the desert with their faces set for the coast.

" Bhoys, will ye stand for this?" screamed a voice. It was so ringing, so strenuous, that the breaking Mallows glanced backwards. They were held by what they saw. Private Conolly had planted his rifle-stock downwards in a mimosa bush. From the fixed bayonet there fluttered a little green flag with the crownless harp. God knows for what black mutiny, for what signal of revolt, that flag had been

treasured up within the Corporal's tunic! Now
its green wisp stood amid the rush, while three
proud regimental colours were reeling slowly
backwards.

" What for the flag?" yelled the private.

" My heart's blood for it! and mine! and
mine!" cried a score of voices. " God bless
it! The flag, boys—the flag!"

C Company were rallying upon it. The
stragglers clutched at each other, and pointed.
" Here, McQuire, Flynn, O'Hara," ran the
shoutings. " Close on the flag! Back to the
flag!" The three standards reeled backwards,
and the seething square strove for a clearer
space where they could form their shattered
ranks; but C company, grim and powder-
stained, choked with enemies and falling fast,
still closed in on the little rebel ensign that
flapped from the mimosa bush.

It was a good half-hour before the square,
having disentangled itself from its difficulties
and dressed its ranks, began to slowly move
forwards over the ground, across which in its
labor and anguish it had been driven. The
long trail of Wessex men and Arabs showed
but too clearly the path they had come.

" How many got into us, Stephen?" asked
the General, tapping his snuff-box.

" I should put them down at a thousand or
twelve hundred, sir."

25

" I did not see any get out again. What the devil were the Wessex thinking about? The Guards stood well, though; so did the Mallows."

" Colonel Flanagan reports that his front flank company was cut off, sir."

" Why, that's the Company that was out of hand when we advanced ! "

" Colonel Flanagan reports, sir, that the Company took the whole brunt of the attack, and gave the square time to re-form."

" Tell the Hussars to ride forward, Stephen," said the General, " and try if they can see anything of them. There's no firing, and I fear that the Mallows will want to do some recruiting. Let the square take ground by the right, and then advance ! "

But the Sheik Kadra of the Hadendowas saw from his knoll that the men with the big hats had rallied, and that they were coming back in the quiet business fashion of men whose work was before them. He took counsel with Moussa the Dervish and Hussein the Bagarra, and a woestruck man was he when he learned that the third of his men were safe in the Moslem Paradise. So, having still some signs of victory to show, he gave the word, and the desert warriors flitted off unseen and unheard, even as they had come.

A red rock plateau, a few hundred spears and

Remingtons, and a plain which for the second time was strewn with slaughtered men, was all that his day's fighting gave to the English General.

It was a squadron of Hussars which came first to the spot where the rebel flag had waved. A dense litter of Arab dead marked the place. Within the flag waved no longer, but the rifle still stood in the mimosa bush, and round it, with their wounds in front, lay the Fenian private and the silent ranks of his Irishry. Sentiment is not an English failing, but the Hussar Captain raised his hilt in a salute as he rode past the blood-soaked ring.

The British General sent home dispatches to his Government, and so did the Chief of the Hadendowas to his, though the style and manner differed somewhat in each. " The Sheik Kadra of the Hadendowa people to Mohammed Ahmed, the chosen of Allah, homage and greeting," began the latter. " Know by this that on the fourth day of this moon we gave battle to the Kaffirs who call themselves Inglees, having with us the Chief Hussein with ten thousand of the faithful. By the blessing of Allah we have broken them, and chased them for a mile, though indeed these infidels are different from the dogs of Egypt, and have slain very many of our men. Yet we hope to smite them

27

again ere the new moon be come, to which end I trust that thou wilt send us a thousand Dervishes from Omdurman. In token of our victory I send you by this messenger a flag which we have taken. By the colour it might well seem to have belonged to those of the true faith, but the Kaffirs gave their blood freely to save it, and so we think that, though small, it is very dear to them."

CAPTAIN SHARKEY

I

HOW THE GOVERNOR OF SAINT KITT'S CAME HOME

WHEN the great wars of the Spanish Succession had been brought to an end by the Treaty of Utrecht, the vast number of privateers which had been fitted out by the contending parties found their occupation gone. Some took to the more peaceful but less lucrative ways of ordinary commerce, others were absorbed into the fishing-fleets, and a few of the more reckless hoisted the Jolly Rodger at the mizzen and the bloody flag at the main, declaring a private war upon their own account against the whole human race.

With mixed crews, recruited from every nation, they scoured the seas, disappearing occasionally to careen in some lonely inlet, or putting in for a debauch at some outlying port, where they dazzled the inhabitants by their lavishness and horrified them by their brutalities.

On the Coromandel Coast, at Madagascar, in the African waters, and above all in the West Indian and American seas, the pirates were a constant menace. With an insolent luxury they would regulate their depredations by the comfort of the seasons, harrying New England in the summer and dropping south again to the tropical islands in the winter.

They were the more to be dreaded because they had none of that discipline and restraint which made their predecessors, the Buccaneers, both formidable and respectable. These Ishmaels of the sea rendered an account to no man, and treated their prisoners according to the drunken whim of the moment. Flashes of grotesque generosity alternated with longer stretches of inconceivable ferocity, and the skipper who fell into their hands might find himself dismissed with his cargo, after serving as boon companion in some hideous debauch, or might sit at his cabin table with his own nose and his lips served up with pepper and salt in front of him. It took a stout seaman in those days to ply his calling in the Caribbean Gulf.

Such a man was Captain John Scarrow, of the ship *Morning Star*, and yet he breathed a long sigh of relief when he heard the splash of the falling anchor and swung at his moorings within a hundred yards of the guns of the citadel of Basseterre. St. Kitt's was his final port of call, and early next morning his bowsprit would be pointed for Old England. He had had enough of those robber-haunted seas. Ever since he had left Maracaibo upon the Main, with his full lading of sugar and red pepper, he had winced at every topsail which glimmered over the violet edge of the tropical sea. He had coasted up the Windward Islands, touching here and there, and assailed continually by stories of villainy and outrage.

Captain Sharkey, of the 20-gun pirate barque, *Happy Delivery*, had passed down the coast, and had littered it with gutted vessels and with murdered men. Dreadful anecdotes were current of his grim pleasantries and of his inflexible ferocity. From the Bahamas to the Main his coal black barque, with the ambiguous name, had been freighted with death and many things which are worse than death. So nervous was Captain Scarrow, with his new full-rigged ship and her full and valuable lading that he struck out to the west as far as Bird's Island to be out of the usual track of commerce. And yet even in those solitary waters he had been unable to shake off sinister traces of Captain Sharkey.

One morning they had raised a single skiff adrift upon the face of the ocean. Its only occupant was a delirious seaman, who yelled hoarsely as they hoisted him aboard, and showed a dried-up tongue like a black and wrinkled fungus at the back of his mouth. Water and nursing soon transformed him into the strongest and smartest sailor on the ship. He was from Marblehead, in New England, it seemed, and was the sole survivor of a schooner which had been scuttled by the dreadful Sharkey.

For a week Hiram Evanson, for that was his name, had been adrift beneath a tropical sun. Sharkey had ordered the mangled remains of his late captain to be thrown into the boat, "as provisions for the voyage," but the seaman had at once committed it to the deep, lest the temptation should be more than he could bear. He had lived upon his own huge frame, until, at the last moment, the *Morning Star* had found him in that madness which is the precursor of such a death. It was no bad find for Captain Scarrow, for, with a short-handed crew, such a seaman as this big New Englander was a prize worth having. He vowed that he was the only man whom Captain Sharkey had ever placed under an obligation.

Now that they lay under the guns of Basse-terre, all danger from the pirate was at an end, and yet the thought of him lay heavily upon the seaman's mind as he watched the agent's boat shooting out from the custom-house quay.

"I'll lay you a wager, Morgan," said he to the first mate, "that the agent will speak of

Sharkey in the first hundred words that pass his lips."

"Well, captain, I'll have you a silver dollar, and chance it," said the rough old Bristol man beside him.

The negro rowers shot the boat alongside, and the linen-clad steersman sprang up the ladder.

"Welcome, Captain Scarrow!" he cried. "Have you heard about Sharkey?"

The captain grinned at the mate.

"What devilry has he been up to now?" he asked.

"Devilry! You've not heard, then! Why, we've got him safe under lock and key here at Basseterre. He was tried last Wednesday, and he is to be hanged to-morrow morning."

Captain and mate gave a shout of joy, which an instant later was taken up by the crew. Discipline was forgotten as they scrambled up through the break of the poop to hear the news. The New Englander was in the front of them with a radiant face turned up to heaven, for he came of the Puritan stock.

"Sharkey to be hanged!" he cried. "You don't know, Master Agent, if they lack a hangman, do you?"

"Stand back!" cried the mate, whose outraged sense of discipline was even stronger than his interest at the news. "I'll pay that dollar, Captain Scarrow, with the lightest heart that ever I paid a wager yet. How came the villain to be taken?"

"Why, as to that, he became more than his own comrades could abide, and they took such a horror of him that they would not have him on the ship. So they marooned him upon the Little Mangles to the south of the Mysteriosa Bank, and there he was found by a Portobello trader, who brought him in. There was talk of sending him to Jamaica to be tried, but our good little governor, Sir Charles Ewan, would not hear of it. 'He's my meat,' said he, 'and I claim the cooking of it.' If you can stay till to-morrow morning at ten, you'll see the joint swinging."

"I wish I could," said the captain, wistfully, "but I am sadly behind time now. I should start with the evening tide."

"That you can't do," said the agent with decision. "The governor is going back with you."

"The Governor!"

"Yes. He's had a dispatch from Government to return without delay. The fly-boat that brought it has gone on to Virginia. So Sir Charles has been waiting for you, as I told him you were due before the rains."

"Well, well!" cried the captain in some perplexity, "I'm a plain seaman, and I don't know

much of governors and baronets and their
ways. I don't remember that I ever so much
as spoke to one. But if it's in King George's
service, and he asks a cast in the *Morning Star*
as far as London, I'll do what I can for him.
There's my own cabin he can have and welcome. As to the cooking, it's lobscouse and
salmagundy six days in the week; but he can
bring his own cook aboard with him if he
thinks our galley too rough for his taste."

"You need not trouble your mind, Captain
Scarrow," said the agent. "Sir Charles is in
weak health just now, only clear of a quartan
ague, and it is likely he will keep his cabin most
of the voyage. Dr. Larousse said that he
would have sunk had the hanging of Sharkey
not put fresh life into him. He has a great
spirit in him, though, and you must not blame
him if he is somewhat short in his speech."

"He may say what he likes and do what he
likes so long as he does not come athwart my
hawse when I am working the ship," said the
captain. "He is Governor of St. Kitt's, but I
am Governor of the *Morning Star*. And, by
his leave, I must weigh with the first tide, for I
owe a duty to my employer, just as he does to
King George."

"He can scarce be ready to-night, for he
has many things to set in order before he
leaves."

" The early morning tide, then."

" Very good. I shall send his things aboard to-night, and he will follow them to-morrow early if I can prevail upon him to leave St. Kitt's without seeing Sharkey do the rogue's hornpipe. His own orders were instant, so it may be that he will come at once. It is likely that Dr. Larousse may attend him upon the journey."

Left to themselves, the captain and mate made the best preparations which they could for their illustrious passenger. The largest cabin was turned out and adorned in his honor, and orders were given by which barrels of fruit and some cases of wine should be brought off to vary the plain food of an ocean-going trader. In the evening the Governor's baggage began to arrive—great iron-bound ant-proof trunks, and official tin packing-cases, with other strange-shaped packages, which suggested the cocked hat or the sword within. And then there came a note, with a heraldic device upon the big red seal, to say that Sir Charles Ewan made his compliments to Captain Scarrow, and that he hoped to be with him in the morning as early as his duties and his infirmities would permit.

He was as good as his word, for the first gray of dawn had hardly begun to deepen into pink when he was brought alongside, and climbed with some difficulty up the ladder.

The captain had heard that the Governor was an eccentric, but he was hardly prepared for the curious figure who came limping feebly down his quarter-deck, his steps supported by a thick bamboo cane. He wore a Ramillies wig, all twisted into little tails like a poodle's coat, and cut so low across the brow that the large green glasses which covered his eyes looked as if they were hung from it. A fierce beak of a nose, very long and very thin, cut the air in front of him. His ague had caused him to swathe his throat and chin with a broad linen cravat, and he wore a loose damask powdering-gown secured by a cord round the waist. As he advanced he carried his masterful nose high in the air, but his head turned slowly from side to side in the helpless manner of the purblind, and he called in a high, querulous voice for the captain.

"You have my things?" he asked.

"Yes, Sir Charles."

"Have you wine aboard?"

"I have ordered five cases, sir."

"And tobacco?"

"There is a keg of Trinidad."

"You play a hand at picquet?"

"Passably well, sir."

"Then up anchor, and to sea!"

There was a fresh westerly wind, so by the time the sun was fairly through the morning haze, the ship was hull down from the islands. The decrepit Governor still limped the deck, with one guiding hand upon the quarter-rail.

"You are on Government service now, captain," said he. "They are counting the days till I come to Westminster, I promise you. Have you all that she will carry?"

"Every inch, Sir Charles."

"Keep her so if you blow the sails out of her. I fear, Captain Scarrow, that you will find a blind and broken man a poor companion for your voyage."

"I am honored in enjoying your Excellency's society," said the captain. "But I am sorry that your eyes should be so afflicted."

"Yes, indeed. It is the cursed glare of the sun on the white streets of Basseterre which has gone far to burn them out."

"I had heard also that you had been plagued by a quartan ague."

"Yes; I have had a pyrexy, which has reduced me much."

"We had set aside a cabin for your surgeon."

"Ah, the rascal! There was no budging him, for he has a snug business amongst the merchants. But hark!"

He raised his ring-covered hand in the air. From far astern there came the low deep thunder of cannon.

"It is from the island!" cried the captain in

astonishment. "Can it be a signal for us to put back?"

The Governor laughed.

"You have heard that Sharkey, the pirate, is to be hanged this morning. I ordered the batteries to salute when the rascal was kicking his last, so that I might know of it out at sea. There's an end of Sharkey!"

"There's an end of Sharkey!" cried the captain; and the crew took up the cry as they gathered in little knots upon the deck and stared back at the low, purple line of the vanishing land.

It was a cheering omen for their start across the Western Ocean, and the invalid Governor found himself a popular man on board, for it was generally understood that but for his insistence upon an immediate trial and sentence, the villain might have played upon some more venal judge and so escaped. At dinner that day Sir Charles gave many anecdotes of the deceased pirate; and so affable was he, and so skilful in adapting his conversation to men of lower degree, that captain, mate, and Governor smoked their long pipes and drank their claret as three good comrades should.

"And what figure did Sharkey cut in the dock?" asked the captain.

"He is a man of some presence," said the Governor.

"I had always understood that he was an ugly, sneering devil," remarked the mate.

"Well, I dare say he could look ugly upon occasions," said the Governor.

"I have heard a New Bedford whaleman say that he could not forget his eyes," said Captain Scarrow. "They were of the lightest filmy blue, with red-rimmed lids. Was that not so, Sir Charles?"

"Alas, my own eyes will not permit me to know much of those of others! But I remember now that the Adjutant-General said that he had such an eye as you describe, and added that the jury were so foolish as to be visibly discomposed when it was turned upon them. It is well for them that he is dead, for he was a man who would never forget an injury, and if he had laid hands upon any one of them he would have stuffed him with straw and hung him for a figure-head."

The idea seemed to amuse the Governor, for he broke suddenly into a high, neighing laugh, and the two seamen laughed also, but not so heartily, for they remembered that Sharkey was not the last pirate who sailed the western seas, and that as grotesque a fate might come to be their own. Another bottle was broached to drink to a pleasant voyage, and the Governor would drink just one other on the top of it, so that the seamen were glad at last to stagger off—

the one to his watch and the other to his bunk.
But when after his four hours' spell the mate came
down again, he was amazed to see the Governor in his Ramillies wig, his glasses, and his
powdering-gown still seated sedately at the
lonely table with his reeking pipe and six black
bottles by his side.

"I have drunk with the Governor of St.
Kitt's when he was sick," said he, "and God
forbid that I should ever try to keep pace with
him when he is well."

The voyage of the *Morning Star* was a successful one, and in about three weeks she was
at the mouth of the British Channel. From
the first day the infirm Governor had begun to
recover his strength, and before they were half-
way across the Atlantic he was, save only for his
eyes, as well as any man upon the ship. Those
who uphold the nourishing qualities of wine
might point to him in triumph, for never a night
passed that he did not repeat the performance
of his first one. And yet he would be out upon
deck in the early morning as fresh and brisk as
the best of them, peering about with his weak
eyes, and asking questions about the sails and
the rigging, for he was anxious to learn the ways
of the sea. And he made up for the deficiency
of his eyes by obtaining leave from the captain
that the New England seaman—he who had
been cast away in the boat—should lead him

about, and above all that he should sit beside him when he played cards and count the number of the pips, for unaided he could not tell the king from the knave.

It was natural that this Evanson should do the Governor willing service, since the one was the victim of the vile Sharkey, and the other was his avenger. One could see that it was a pleasure to the big American to lend his arm to the invalid, and at night he would stand with all respect behind his chair in the cabin and lay his great stub-nailed forefinger upon the card which he should play. Between them there was little in the pockets either of Captain Scarrow or of Morgan, the first mate, by the time they sighted the Lizard.

And it was not long before they found that all they had heard of the high temper of Sir Charles Ewan fell short of the mark. At a sign of opposition or a word of argument his chin would shoot out from his cravat, his masterful nose would be cocked at a higher and more insolent angle, and his bamboo cane would whistle up over his shoulder. He cracked it once over the head of the carpenter when the man had accidentally jostled him upon the deck. Once, too, when there was some grumbling and talk of a mutiny over the state of the provisions, he was of opinion that they should not wait for the dogs to rise, but that they should march for-

ward and set upon them until they had trounced
the devilment out of them. " Give me a knife
and a bucket ! " he cried with an oath, and could
hardly be withheld from setting forth alone to
deal with the spokesman of the seamen.

Captain Scarrow had to remind him that
though he might be only answerable to himself
at St. Kitt's, killing became murder upon the
high seas. In politics he was, as became his
official position, a stout prop of the House of
Hanover, and he swore in his cups that he had
never met a Jacobite without pistolling him
where he stood. Yet for all his vapouring and
his violence he was so good a companion, with
such a stream of strange anecdote and reminis-
cence, that Scarrow and Morgan had never
known a voyage pass so pleasantly.

And then at length came the last day, when,
after passing the island, they had struck land
again at the high white cliffs at Beachy Head.
As evening fell the ship lay rolling in an oily
calm, a league off from Winchelsea, with the
long dark snout of Dungeness jutting out in
front of her. Next morning they would pick
up their pilot at the Foreland, and Sir Charles
might meet the king's ministers at Westminster
before the evening. The boatswain had the
watch, and the three friends were met for a last
turn of cards in the cabin, the faithful American still serving as eyes to the Governor. There

was a good stake upon the table, for the sailors had tried on this last night to win their losses back from their passenger. Suddenly he threw his cards down, and swept all the money into the pocket of his long-flapped silken waistcoat.

" The game's mine ! " said he.

" Heh, Sir Charles, not so fast ! " cried Captain Scarrow ; " you have not played out the hand, and we are not the losers."

" Sink you for a liar ! " said the Governor. " I tell you that I *have* played out the hand, and that you *are* a loser." He whipped off his wig and his glasses as he spoke, and there was a high, bald forehead, and a pair of shifty blue eyes with the red rims of a bull terrier.

" Good God ! " cried the mate. " It's Sharkey ! "

The two sailors sprang from their seats, but the big American castaway had put his huge back against the cabin door, and he held a pistol in each of his hands. The passenger had also laid a pistol upon the scattered cards in front of him, and he burst into his high, neighing laugh.

" Captain Sharkey is the name, gentlemen," said he, " and this is Roaring Ned Galloway, the quartermaster of the *Happy Delivery*. We made it hot, so they marooned us : me on a dry Tortuga cay, and him in an oarless boat.

You dogs—you poor, fond, water-hearted dogs
—we hold you at the end of our pistols!"

"You may shoot, or you may not!" cried
Scarrow, striking his hand upon the breast of
his frieze jacket. "If it's my last breath,
Sharkey, I tell you that you are a bloody rogue
and miscreant, with a halter and hell-fire in
store for you!"

"There's a man of spirit, and one of my
own kidney, and he's going to make a very
pretty death of it!" cried Sharkey. "There's
no one aft save the man at the wheel, so you
may keep your breath, for you'll need it soon.
Is the dingey astern, Ned?"

"Ay, ay, captain!"

"And the other boats scuttled?"

"I bored them all in three places."

"Then we shall have to leave you, Captain
Scarrow. You look as if you hadn't quite got
your bearings yet. Is there anything you'd
like to ask me?"

"I believe you're the devil himself!" cried
the captain. "Where is the Governor of St.
Kitt's?"

"When last I saw him his Excellency was
in bed with his throat cut. When I broke
prison I learnt from my friends—for Captain
Sharkey has those who love him in every port
—that the Governor was starting for Europe
under a master who had never seen him. I

climbed his verandah, and I paid him the little debt that I owed him. Then I came aboard you with such of his things as I had need of, and a pair of glasses to hide these tell-tale eyes of mine, and I have ruffled it as a governor should. Now, Ned, you can get to work upon them."

"Help! Help! Watch ahoy!" yelled the mate; but the butt of the pirate's pistol crashed down on to his head, and he dropped like a pithed ox. Scarrow rushed for the door, but the sentinel clapped his hand over his mouth, and threw his other arm around his waist.

"No use, Master Scarrow," said Sharkey. "Let us see you go down on your knees and beg for your life."

"I'll see you ———" cried Scarrow, shaking his mouth clear.

"Twist his arm round, Ned. Now will you?"

"No; not if you twist it off."

"Put an inch of your knife into him."

"You may put six inches, and then I won't."

"Sink me, but I like his spirit!" cried Sharkey. "Put your knife in your pocket, Ned. You've saved your skin, Scarrow, and it's a pity so stout a man should not take to the only trade where a pretty fellow can pick up a living. You must be born for no common death, Scarrow, since you have lain at my mercy and lived to tell the story. Tie him up, Ned."

" To the stove, captain ? "

" Tut, tut ! there's a fire in the stove. None of your rover tricks, Ned Galloway, unless they are called for, or I'll let you know which of us two is captain and which is quartermaster. Make him fast to the table."

" Nay, I thought you meant to roast him ! " said the quartermaster. " You surely do not mean to let him go ? "

" If you and I were marooned on a Bahama cay, Ned Galloway, it is still for me to command and for you to obey. Sink you for a villain, do you dare to question my orders ? "

" Nay, nay, Captain Sharkey, not so hot, sir ! " said the quartermaster, and, lifting Scarrow like a child, he laid him on the table. With the quick dexterity of a seaman, he tied his spreadeagled hands and feet with a rope which was passed underneath, and gagged him securely with the long cravat which used to adorn the chin of the Governor of St. Kitt's.

" Now, Captain Scarrow, we must take our leave of you," said the pirate. " If I had half a dozen of my brisk boys at my heels I should have had your cargo and your ship, but Roaring Ned could not find a foremast hand with the spirit of a mouse. I see there are some small craft about, and we shall get one of them.

When Captain Sharkey has a boat he can get a smack, when he has a smack he can get a brig, when he has a brig he can get a barque, and when he has a barque he'll soon have a full-rigged ship of his own—so make haste into London town, or I may be coming back, after all, for the *Morning Star*."

Captain Scarrow heard the key turn in the lock as they left the cabin. Then, as he strained at his bonds, he heard their footsteps pass up the companion and along the quarter-deck to where the dingey hung in the stern. Then, still struggling and writhing, he heard the creak of the falls and the splash of the boat in the water. In a mad fury he tore and dragged at his ropes, until at last, with flayed wrists and ankles, he rolled from the table, sprang over the dead mate, kicked his way through the closed door, and rushed hatless on to the deck.

" Ahoy ! Peterson, Armitage, Wilson ! " he screamed. " Cutlasses and pistols ! Clear away the long-boat ! Clear away the gig ! Sharkey, the pirate, is in yonder dingey. Whistle up the larboard watch, bo'sun, and tumble into the boats all hands."

Down splashed the long-boat and down splashed the gig, but in an instant the coxswains and crews were swarming up the falls on to the deck once more.

" The boats are scuttled ! "they cried. " They are leaking like a sieve."

The captain gave a bitter curse. He had been beaten and outwitted at every point. Above was a cloudless, starlit sky, with neither wind nor the promise of it. The sails flapped idly in the moonlight. Far away lay a fishing-smack, with the men clustering over their net.

Close to them was the little dingey, dipping and lifting over the shining swell.

" They are dead men ! " cried the captain. " A shout all together, boys, to warn them of their danger."

But it was too late.

At that very moment the dingey shot into the shadow of the fishing-boat. There were two rapid pistol-shots, a scream, and then another pistol-shot, followed by silence. The clustering fishermen had disappeared. And then, suddenly, as the first puffs of a land-breeze came out from the Sussex shore, the boom swung out, the mainsail filled, and the little craft crept out with her nose to the Atlantic.

II

THE DEALINGS OF CAPTAIN SHARKEY WITH
STEPHEN CRADDOCK

CAREENING was a very necessary opera-
tion for the old pirate. On his superior
speed he depended both for overhauling the
trader and escaping the man-of-war. But it
was impossible to retain his sailing qualities unless he periodically—once a year, at the least—
cleared his vessel's bottom from the long, trailing plants and crusting barnacles which gather
so rapidly in the tropical seas.

For this purpose he lightened his vessel,
thrust her into some narrow inlet where she
would be left high and dry at low water, fastened blocks and tackles to her masts to pull
her over on to her bilge, and then scraped her
thoroughly from rudder-post to cutwater.

During the weeks which were thus occupied
the ship was, of course, defenceless; but, on
the other hand, she was unapproachable by
anything heavier than an empty hull, and the
place for careening was chosen with an eye to
secresy, so that there was no great danger.

So secure did the captains feel, that it was not
uncommon for them, at such times, to leave
their ships under a sufficient guard and to start
off in the long-boat, either upon a sporting expedition or, more frequently, upon a visit to
some outlying town, where they turned the
heads of the women by their swaggering gal-
lantry, or broached pipes of wine in the market square, with a threat to pistol all who
would not drink with them.

Sometimes they would even appear in cities
of the size of Charleston, and walk the streets
with their clattering sidearms—an open scandal
to the whole law-abiding colony. Such visits
are not always paid with impunity. It was one
of them, for example, which provoked Lieutenant Maynard to hack off Blackbeard's head,
and to spear it upon the end of his bowsprit.
But, as a rule, the pirate ruffled and bullied
and drabbed without let or hindrance until it
was time for him to go back to his ship once
more.

There was one pirate, however, who never
crossed even the skirts of civilization, and that
was the sinister Sharkey, of the barque *Happy
Delivery*. It may have been from his morose
and solitary temper, or, as is more probable,
that he knew that his name upon the coast was
such that outraged humanity would, against
all odds, have thrown themselves upon him,

but never once did he show his face in a settlement.

When his ship was laid up he would leave her under the charge of Ned Galloway—her New England quartermaster—and would take long voyages in his boat, sometimes, it was said, for the purpose of burying his share of the plunder, and sometimes to shoot the wild oxen of Hispaniola, which, when dressed and barbecued, provided provisions for his next voyage. In the latter case the barque would come round to some prearranged spot to pick him up and take on board what he had shot.

There had always been a hope in the islands that Sharkey might be taken on one of these occasions; and at last there came news to Kingston which seemed to justify an attempt upon him. It was brought by an elderly logwood-cutter who had fallen into the pirate's hands, and in some freak of drunken benevolence had been allowed to get away with nothing worse than a slit nose and a drubbing. His account was recent and definite. The *Happy Delivery* was careening at Torbec on the south-west of Hispaniola. Sharkey, with four men, was buccaneering on the outlying island of La Vache. The blood of a hundred murdered crews was calling out for vengeance, and now at last it seemed as if it might not call in vain.

Sir Edward Compton, the high-nosed, red-faced Governor, sitting in solemn conclave with the commandant and the head of the council, was sorely puzzled in his mind as to how he should use this chance. There was no man-of-war nearer than Jamestown, and she was a clumsy old fly-boat, which could neither overhaul the pirate on the seas, nor reach her in a shallow inlet. There were forts and artillerymen both at Kingston and Port Royal, but no soldiers available for an expedition.

A private venture might be fitted out—and there were many who had a blood-feud with Sharkey,—but what could a private venture do? The pirates were numerous and desperate. As to taking Sharkey and his four companions, that, of course, would be easy if they could get at them; but how were they to get at them on a large well-wooded island like La Vache, full of wild hills and impenetrable jungles? A reward was offered to whoever could find a solution, and that brought a man to the front who had a singular plan, and was himself prepared to carry it out.

Stephen Craddock had been that most formidable person, the Puritan gone wrong. Sprung from a decent Salem family, his ill-doing seemed to be a recoil from the austerity of their religion, and he brought to vice all the physical strength and energy with which the virtues of his ancestors had endowed him. He was ingenious, fearless, and exceedingly tenacious of purpose, so that when he was still young his name became notorious upon the American coast.

He was the same Craddock who was tried for his life in Virginia for the slaying of the Seminole Chief, and, though he escaped, it was well known that he had corrupted the witnesses and bribed the judge.

Afterwards, as a slaver, and even, as it was hinted, as a pirate, he had left an evil name behind him in the Bight of Benin. Finally he had returned to Jamaica with a considerable fortune, and had settled down to a life of sombre dissipation. This was the man, gaunt, austere, and dangerous, who now waited upon the Governor with a plan for the extirpation of Sharkey.

Sir Edward received him with little enthusiasm, for in spite of some rumours of conversion and reformation, he had always regarded him as an infected sheep who might taint the whole of his little flock. Craddock saw the Governor's mistrust under his thin veil of formal and restrained courtesy.

"You've no call to fear me, sir," said he; "I'm a changed man from what you've known. I've seen the light again, of late, after losing sight of it for many a black year. It was through the ministration of the Rev. John Simons, of our own people. Sir, if your spirit should be in need of quickening, you would find a very sweet savor in his discourse."

The Governor cocked his Episcopalian nose at him.

"You came here to speak of Sharkey, Master Craddock," said he.

" The man Sharkey is a vessel of wrath," said Craddock. " His wicked horn has been exalted over long, and it is borne in upon me that if I can cut him off and utterly destroy him, it will be a goodly deed, and one which may atone for many backslidings in the past. A plan has been given to me whereby I may encompass his destruction."

The Governor was keenly interested, for there was a grim and practical air about the man's freckled face which showed that he was in earnest. After all, he was a seaman and a fighter, and, if it were true that he was eager to atone for his past, no better man could be chosen for the business.

" This will be a dangerous task, Master Craddock," said he.

" If I meet my death at it, it may be that it will cleanse the memory of an ill-spent life. I have much to atone for."

The Governor did not see his way to contradict him.

" What was your plan ? " he asked.

" You have heard that Sharkey's barque, the

Happy Delivery, came from this very port of Kingston?"

"It belonged to Mr. Codrington, and it was taken by Sharkey, who scuttled his own sloop and moved into her because she was faster," said Sir Edward.

"Yes; but it may be that you have never heard that Mr. Codrington has a sister ship, the *White Rose*, which lies even now in the harbor, and which is so like the pirate, that, if it were not for a white paint line, none could tell them apart."

"Ah! and what of that?" asked the Governor keenly, with the air of one who is just on the edge of an idea.

"By the help of it this man shall be delivered into our hands."

"And how?"

"I will paint out the streak upon the *White Rose*, and make it in all things like the *Happy Delivery*. Then I will set sail for the Island of La Vache, where this man is slaying the wild oxen. When he sees me he will surely mistake me for his own vessel which he is awaiting, and he will come on board to his own undoing."

It was a simple plan, and yet it seemed to the Governor that it might be effective. Without hesitation he gave Craddock permission to carry it out, and to take any steps he liked in order to further the object which he had in view. Sir Edward was not very sanguine, for many attempts had been made upon Sharkey, and their results had shown that he was as cunning as he was ruthless. But this gaunt Puritan with the evil record was cunning and ruthless also.

The contest of wits between two such men as Sharkey and Craddock appealed to the Governor's acute sense of sport, and though he was inwardly convinced that the chances were against him, he backed his man with the same loyalty which he would have shown to his horse or his cock.

Haste was, above all things, necessary, for upon any day the careening might be finished, and the pirates out at sea once more. But there was not very much to do, and there were many willing hands to do it, so the second day saw the *White Rose* beating out for the open sea. There were many seamen in the port who knew the lines and rig of the pirate barque, and not one of them could see the slightest difference in this counterfeit. Her white side line had been painted out, her masts and yards were smoked, to give them the dingy appearance of the weather-beaten rover, and a large diamond-shaped patch was let into her foretopsail.

Her crew were volunteers, many of them being men who had sailed with Stephen Craddock before—the mate, Joshua Hird, an old slaver, had been his accomplice in many voyages, and came now at the bidding of his chief.

The avenging barque sped across the Caribbean Sea, and, at the sight of that patched topsail, the little craft which they met flew left and right like frightened trout in a pool. On the fourth evening Point Abacou bore five miles to the north and east of them.

On the fifth they were at anchor in the Bay of Tortoises at the Island of La Vache, where Sharkey and his four men had been hunting. It was a well-wooded place, with the palms and underwood growing down to the thin crescent of silver sand which skirted the shore. They had hoisted the black flag and the red pennant, but no answer came from the shore. Craddock strained his eyes, hoping every instant to see a boat shoot out to them with Sharkey seated in the sheets. But the night passed away, and a day and yet another night, without any sign of the men whom they were endeavouring to trap. It looked as if they were already gone.

On the second morning Craddock went ashore in search of some proof whether Sharkey and his men were still upon the island. What he found reassured him greatly. Close to the shore was a boucan of green wood, such as was used for preserving the meat, and a great store of barbecued strips of ox-flesh was hung upon lines all round it. The pirate ship had not taken off her provisions, and therefore the hunters were still upon the island.

Why had they not shown themselves? Was it that they had detected that this was not their own ship? Or was it that they were hunting in the interior of the island, and were not on the lookout for a ship yet? Craddock was still hesitating between the two alternatives, when a Carib Indian came down with information. The pirates were in the island, he said, and their camp was a day's march from the sea. They had stolen his wife, and the marks of their stripes were still pink upon his brown back. Their enemies were his friends, and he would lead them to where they lay.

Craddock could not have asked for anything better; so early next morning, with a small party armed to the teeth, he set off under the guidance of the Carib. All day they struggled through brushwood and clambered over rocks, pushing their way further and further into the desolate heart of the island. Here and there they found traces of the hunters, the bones of a slain ox, or the marks of feet in a morass, and once, towards evening, it seemed to some of them that they heard the distant rattle of guns.

That night they spent under the trees, and pushed on again with the earliest light. About noon they came to the huts of bark, which, the Carib told them, were the camp of the hunters, but they were silent and deserted. No doubt their occupants were away at the hunt and would return in the evening, so Craddock and his men lay in ambush in the brushwood around them. But no one came, and another night was spent in the forest. Nothing more could be done, and it seemed to Craddock that after the two days' absence it was time that he returned to his ship once more.

The return journey was less difficult, as they had already blazed a path for themselves. Before evening they found themselves once more at the Bay of Palms, and saw their ship riding at anchor where they had left her. Their boat and oars had been hauled up among the bushes, so they launched it and pulled out to the barque.

" No luck, then ! " cried Joshua Hird, the mate, looking down with a pale face from the poop.

" His camp was empty, but he may come down to us yet," said Craddock, with his hand on the ladder.

Somebody upon deck began to laugh. " I think," said the mate, " that these men had better stay in the boat."

" Why so ? "

" If you will come aboard, sir, you will understand it." He spoke in a curious hesitating fashion.

The blood flushed to Craddock's gaunt face.

"How is this, Master Hird?" he cried, springing up the side. "What mean you by giving orders to my boat's crew?"

But as he passed over the bulwarks, with one foot upon the deck and one knee upon the rail, a tow-bearded man, whom he had never before observed aboard his vessel, grabbed suddenly at his pistol. Craddock clutched at the fellow's wrist, but at the same instant his mate snatched the cutlass from his side.

"What roguery is this?" shouted Craddock, looking furiously around him. But the crew stood in little knots about the deck, laughing and whispering amongst themselves without showing any desire to go to his assistance. Even in that hurried glance Craddock noticed that they were dressed in the most singular manner, with long riding-coats, full-skirted velvet gowns and coloured ribands at their knees, more like men of fashion than seamen.

As he looked at their grotesque figures he struck his brow with his clenched fist to be sure that he was awake. The deck seemed to be much dirtier than when he had left it, and there were strange, sun-blackened faces turned upon him from every side. Not one of them did he know save only Joshua Hird. Had the ship been captured in his absence? Were these Sharkey's men who were around him? At the thought he broke furiously away and tried to climb over to his boat, but a dozen hands were on him in an instant, and he was pushed aft through the open door of his own cabin.

And it was all different to the cabin which he had left. The floor was different, the ceiling was different, the furniture was different. His had been plain and austere. This was sumptuous and yet dirty, hung with rare velvet curtains splashed with wine-stains, and paneled with costly woods which were pocked with pistol-marks.

On the table was a great chart of the Caribbean Sea, and beside it, with compasses in his hand, sat a clean-shaven, pale-faced man with a fur cap and a claret-coloured coat of damask. Craddock turned white under his freckles as he looked upon the long, thin, high-nostrilled nose and the red-rimmed eyes which were turned upon him with the fixed, humourous gaze of the master player who has left his opponent without a move.

" Sharkey !" cried Craddock.

Sharkey's thin lips opened and he broke into his high, sniggering laugh.

" You fool !" he cried, and, leaning over, he stabbed Craddock's shoulder again and again with his compasses. "You poor, dull-witted fool, would you match yourself against me?"

It was not the pain of the wounds, but it was the contempt in Sharkey's voice which turned Craddock into a savage madman. He flew at the pirate, roaring with rage, striking, kicking, writhing, and foaming. It took six men to drag him down on to the floor amidst the splintered remains of the table—and not one of the six who did not bear the prisoner's mark upon him. But Sharkey still surveyed him with the same contemptuous eye. From outside there came the crash of breaking wood and the clamour of startled voices.

" What is that ? " asked Sharkey.

" They have stove the boat with cold shot, and the men are in the water."

" Let them stay there," said the pirate. " Now, Craddock, you know where you are. You are aboard my ship the *Happy Delivery*, and you lie at my mercy. I knew you for a stout seaman, you rogue, before you took to this long-shore canting. Your hands then were no cleaner than my own. Will you sign articles, as your mate has done, and join us, or shall I heave you over to follow your ship's company ? "

" Where is my ship ? " asked Craddock.

" Scuttled in the bay."

" And the hands? "

" In the bay, too."

" Then, I'm for the bay also."

" Hock him and heave him over," said Sharkey.

Many rough hands had dragged Craddock out upon deck, and Galloway, the quartermaster, had already drawn his hanger to cripple him, when Sharkey came hurrying from his cabin with an eager face.

" We can do better with the hound! " he cried. " Sink me if it is not a rare plan. Throw him into the sail-room with the irons on, and do you come here, quartermaster, that I may tell you what I have in my mind."

So Craddock, bruised and wounded in soul and body, was thrown into the dark sail-room, so fettered that he could not stir hand or foot, but his Northern blood was running strong in his veins, and his grim spirit aspired only to make such an ending as might go some way towards atoning for the evil of his life. All night he lay in the curve of the bilge listening to the rush of the water and the straining of the timbers which told him that the ship was at sea, and driving fast. In the early morning some one came crawling to him in the darkness over the heaps of sails.

" Here's rum and biscuits," said the voice of his late mate. " It's at the risk of my life, Master Craddock, that I bring them to you."

" It was you who trapped me and caught me as in a snare ! " cried Craddock. " How shall you answer for what you have done ? "

" What I did I did with the point of a knife betwixt my blade-bones."

" God forgive you for a coward, Joshua Hird. How came you into their hands ?"

" Why, Master Craddock, the pirate ship came back from its careening upon the very day that you left us. They laid us aboard, and, short-handed as we were, with the best of the men ashore with you, we could offer but a poor defence. Some were cut down, and they were the happiest. The others were killed afterwards. As to me, I saved my life by signing on with them."

" And they scuttled my ship ?"

" They scuttled her, and then Sharkey and his men, who had been watching us from the brushwood, came off to the ship. His mainyard had been cracked and fished last voyage, so he had suspicions of us, seeing that ours was whole. Then he thought of laying the same trap for you which you had set for him."

Craddock groaned.

" How came I not to see that fished mainyard ?" he muttered. " But whither are we bound ? "

" We are running north and west."

"North and west! Then we are heading back towards Jamaica."

"With an eight-knot wind."

"Have you heard what they mean to do with me?"

"I have not heard. If you would but sign the articles——"

"Enough, Joshua Hird! I have risked my soul too often."

"As you wish! I have done what I could. Farewell!"

All that night and the next day the *Happy Delivery* ran before the easterly trades, and Stephen Craddock lay in the dark of the sail-room working patiently at his wrist-irons. One he had slipped off at the cost of a row of broken and bleeding knuckles, but, do what he would, he could not free the other, and his ankles were securely fastened.

From hour to hour he heard the swish of the water, and knew that the barque must be driving with all set in front of the trade wind. In that case they must be nearly back again to Jamaica by now. What plan could Sharkey have in his head, and what use did he hope to make of him? Craddock set his teeth, and vowed that if he had once been a villain from choice he would, at least, never be one by compulsion.

On the second morning Craddock became

aware that sail had been reduced in the vessel, and that she was tacking slowly, with a light breeze on her beam. The varying slope of the sail-room and the sounds from the deck told his practised senses exactly what she was doing. The short reaches showed him that she was manœuvring near shore, and making for some definite point. If so, she must have reached Jamaica. But what could she be doing there?

And then suddenly there was a burst of hearty cheering from the deck, and then the crash of a gun above his head, and then the answering booming of guns from far over the water. Craddock sat up and strained his ears. Was the ship in action? Only the one gun had been fired, and though many had answered, there were none of the crashings which told of a shot coming home.

Then, if it was not an action, it must be a salute. But who would salute Sharkey, the pirate? It could only be another pirate ship which would do so. So Craddock lay back again with a groan, and continued to work at the manacle which still held his right wrist.

But suddenly there came the shuffling of steps outside, and he had hardly time to wrap the loose links round his free hand, when the door was unbolted and two pirates came in.

" Got your hammer, carpenter ? " asked one,

whom Craddock recognized as the big quarter-master. "Knock off his leg shackles, then. Better leave the bracelets—he's safer with them on."

With hammer and chisel the carpenter loosened the irons.

"What are you going to do with me?" asked Craddock.

"Come on deck and you'll see."

The sailor seized him by the arm and dragged him roughly to the foot of the companion. Above him was a square of blue sky cut across by the mizzen gaff, with the colours flying at the peak. But it was the sight of those colours which struck the breath from Stephen Craddock's lips. For there were two of them, and the British ensign was flying above the Jolly Rodger—the honest flag above that of the rogue.

For an instant Craddock stopped in amazement, but a brutal push from the pirates behind drove him up the companion ladder. As he stepped out upon deck, his eyes turned up to the main, and there again were the British colours flying above the red pennant, and all the shrouds and rigging were garlanded with streamers

Had the ship been taken, then? But that was impossible, for there were the pirates clustering in swarms along the port bulwarks, and waving their hats joyously in the air. Most prominent of all was the renegade mate, standing on the foc'sle head, and gesticulating wildly. Craddock looked over the side to see what they were cheering at, and then in a flash he saw how critical was the moment.

On the port bow, and about a mile off, lay the white houses and forts of Port Royal, with flags breaking out everywhere over their roofs. Right ahead was the opening of the palisades leading to the town of Kingston. Not more than a quarter of a mile off was a small sloop working out against the very slight wind. The British ensign was at her peak, and her rigging was all decorated. On her deck could be seen a dense crowd of people cheering and waving their hats, and the gleam of scarlet told that there were officers of the garrison among them.

In an instant, with the quick perception of a man of action, Craddock saw through it all. Sharkey, with that diabolical cunning and audacity which were among his main characteristics, was simulating the part which Craddock would himself have played, had he come back victorious. It was in *his* honour that the salutes were firing and the flags flying. It was to welcome *him* that this ship with the Governor, the commandant, and the chiefs of the island were approaching. In another ten minutes they would all be under the guns of the *Happy De-*

livery, and Sharkey would have won the greatest stake that ever a pirate played for yet.

" Bring him forward," cried the pirate captain, as Craddock appeared between the carpenter and the quartermaster. " Keep the ports closed, but clear away the port guns, and stand by for a broadside. Another two cable lengths and we have them."

" They are edging away," said the boatswain. " I think they smell us."

" That's soon set right," said Sharkey, turning his filmy eyes upon Craddock. " Stand there, you—right there, where they can recognize you, with your hand on the guy, and wave your hat to them. Quick, or your brains will be over your coat. Put an inch of your knife into him, Ned. Now, will you wave your hat? Try him again, then. Hey, shoot him! stop him !"

But it was too late. Relying upon the manacles, the quartermaster had taken his hands for a moment off Craddock's arm. In that instant he had flung off the carpenter and, amid a spatter of pistol bullets, had sprung the bulwarks and was swimming for his life. He had been hit and hit again, but it takes many pistols to kill a resolute and powerful man who has his mind set upon doing something before he dies. He was a strong swimmer, and, in spite of the red trail which he left in the water behind him, he was rapidly increasing his distance from the pirate.

"Give me a musket!" cried Sharkey, with a savage oath.

He was a famous shot, and his iron nerves never failed him in an emergency. The dark head appearing on the crest of a roller, and then swooping down on the other side, was already half-way to the sloop. Sharkey dwelt long upon his aim before he fired. With the crack of the gun the swimmer reared himself up in the water, waved his hands in a gesture of warning, and roared out in a voice which rang over the bay. Then, as the sloop swung round her head-sails, and the pirate fired an impotent broadside, Stephen Craddock, smiling grimly in his death agony, sank slowly down to that golden couch which glimmered far beneath him.

III

HOW COPLEY BANKS SLEW CAPTAIN SHARKEY

THE Buccaneers were something higher than a mere band of marauders. They were a floating republic, with laws, usages, and discipline of their own. In their endless and remorseless quarrel with the Spaniards they had some semblance of right upon their side. Their bloody harryings of the cities of the Main were not more barbarous than the inroads of Spain upon the Netherlands—or upon the Caribs in these same American lands.

The chief of the Buccaneers, were he English or French, a Morgan or a Granmont, was still a responsible person, whose country might countenance him, or even praise him, so long as he refrained from any deed which might shock the leathery seventeenth-century conscience too outrageously. Some of them were touched with religion, and it is still remembered how Sawkins threw the dice overboard upon the Sabbath, and Daniel pistoled a man before the altar for irreverence.

But there came a day when the fleets of the

Buccaneers no longer mustered at the Tortugas, and the solitary and outlawed pirate took their place. Yet even with him the tradition of restraint and of discipline still lingered; and among the early pirates, the Avorys, the Englands, and the Robertses, there remained some respect for human sentiment. They were more dangerous to the merchant than to the seaman.

But they in turn were replaced by more savage and desperate men, who frankly recognized that they would get no quarter in their war with the human race, and who swore that they would give as little as they got. Of their histories we know little that is trustworthy. They wrote no memoirs and left no trace, save an occasional blackened and bloodstained derelict adrift upon the face of the Atlantic. Their deeds could only be surmised from the long roll of ships who never made their port.

Searching the records of history, it is only here and there in an old-world trial that the veil that shrouds them seems for an instant to be lifted, and we catch a glimpse of some amazing and grotesque brutality behind. Such was the breed of Ned Low, of Gow the Scotchman, and of the infamous Sharkey, whose coal-black barque, the *Happy Delivery*, was known from the Newfoundland Banks to the mouths of the Orinoco as the dark forerunner of misery and of death.

There were many men, both among tne islands and on the main, who had a blood feud with Sharkey, but not one who had suffered more bitterly than Copley Banks, of Kingston. Banks had been one of the leading sugar merchants of the West Indies. He was a man of position, a member of the Council, the husband of a Percival, and the cousin of the Governor of Virginia. His two sons had been sent to London to be educated, and their mother had gone over to bring them back. On their return voyage the ship, the *Duchess of Cornwall*, fell into the hands of Sharkey, and the whole family met with an infamous death.

Copley Banks said little when he heard the news, but he sank into a morose and enduring melancholy. He neglected his business, avoided his friends, and spent much of his time in the low taverns of the fishermen and seamen. There, amidst riot and devilry, he sat silently puffing at his pipe, with a set face and a smouldering eye. It was generally supposed that his misfortunes had shaken his wits, and his old friends looked at him askance, for the company which he kept was enough to bar him from honest men.

From time to time there came rumours of Sharkey over the sea. Sometimes it was from some schooner which had seen a great flame upon the horizon, and approaching to offer help to the burning ship, had fled away at the sight of the sleek, black barque, lurking like a wolf near a mangled sheep. Sometimes it was a frightened trader, which had come tearing in with her canvas curved like a lady's bodice, because she had seen a patched fore-topsail rising slowly above the violet water-line. Sometimes it was from a Coaster, which had found a waterless Bahama Cay littered with sun-dried bodies.

Once there came a man who had been mate cf a Guineaman, and who had escaped from the pirate's hands. He could not speak—for reasons which Sharkey could best supply—but he could write, and he did write, to the very great interest of Copley Banks. For hours they sat together over the map, and the dumb man pointed here and there to outlying reefs and tortuous inlets, while his companion sat smoking in silence, with his unvarying face and his fiery eyes.

One morning, some two years after his misfortune, Mr. Copley Banks strode into his own office with his old air of energy and alertness. The manager stared at him in surprise, for it was months since he had shown any interest in business.

"Good morning, Mr. Banks!" said he.

"Good morning, Freeman. I see that *Ruffling Harry* is in the Bay."

"Yes, sir; she clears for the Windward Islands on Wednesday."

"I have other plans for her, Freeman. I have determined upon a slaving venture to Whydah."

"But her cargo is ready, sir."

"Then it must come out again, Freeman. My mind is made up, and the *Ruffling Harry* must go slaving to Whydah."

All argument and persuasion were vain, so the manager had dolefully to clear the ship once more.

And then Copley Banks began to make preparations for his African voyage. It appeared that he relied upon force rather than barter for the filling of his hold, for he carried none of those showy trinkets which savages love, but the brig was fitted with eight nine-pounder guns and racks full of muskets and cutlasses. The after sailroom next the cabin was transformed into a powder magazine, and she carried as many round shot as a well-found privateer. Water and provisions were shipped for a long voyage.

But the preparation of his ship's company was most surprising. It made Freeman, the manager, realize that there was truth in the rumour that his master had taken leave of his senses. For, under one pretext or another, he began to dismiss the old and tried hands, who had served the firm for years, and in their place he embarked the scum of the port — men whose reputations were so vile that the lowest crimp would have been ashamed to furnish them.

There was Birthmark Sweetlocks, who was known to have been present at the killing of the logwood cutters, so that his hideous scarlet disfigurement was put down by the fanciful as being a red afterglow from that great crime. He was first mate, and under him was Israel Martin, a little sun-wilted fellow who had served with Howell Davies at the taking of Cape Coast Castle.

The crew were chosen from amongst those whom Banks had met and known in their own infamous haunts, and his own table-steward was a haggard-faced man, who gobbled at you when he tried to talk. His beard had been shaved, and it was impossible to recognize him as the same man whom Sharkey had placed under the knife, and who had escaped to tell his experiences to Copley Banks.

These doings were not unnoticed, nor yet uncommented upon in the town of Kingston. The Commandant of the troops—Major Harvey, of the Artillery—made serious representations to the Governor.

" She is not a trader, but a small warship," said he. " I think it would be as well to arrest Copley Banks and to seize the vessel."

"What do you suspect?" asked the Governor, who was a slow-witted man, broken down with fevers and port wine.

"I suspect," said the soldier, "that it is Stede Bonnet over again."

Now, Stede Bonnet was a planter of high reputation and religious character, who, from some sudden and overpowering freshet of wildness in his blood, had given up everything in order to start off pirating in the Caribbean Sea. The example was a recent one, and it had caused the utmost consternation in the islands. Governors had before now been accused of being in league with pirates, and of receiving commissions upon their plunder, so that any want of vigilance was open to a sinister construction.

"Well, Major Harvey," said he, "I am vastly sorry to do anything which may offend my friend Copley Banks, for many a time have my knees been under his mahogany, but in face of what you say there is no choice for me but to order you to board the vessel and to satisfy yourself as to her character and destination."

So at one in the morning Major Harvey, with a launchful of his soldiers, paid a surprise visit to the *Ruffling Harry*, with the result that they picked up nothing more solid than a hempen cable floating at the moorings. It had been slipped by the brig, whose owner had scented danger. She had already passed the Palisades, and was beating out against the northeast trades on a course for the Windward Passage.

When upon the next morning the brig had left Morant Point a mere haze upon the Southern horizon, the men were called aft, and Copley Bangs revealed his plans to them. He had chosen them, he said, as brisk boys and lads of spirit, who would rather run some risk upon the sea than starve for a living upon the shore. King's ships were few and weak, and they could master any trader who might come their way. Others had done well at the business, and with a handy, well-found vessel, there was no reason why they should not turn their tarry jackets into velvet coats. If they were prepared to sail under the black flag, he was ready to command them; but if any wished to withdraw, they might have the gig and row back to Jamaica.

Four men out of six-and-forty asked for their discharge, went over the ship's side into the boat, and rowed away amidst the jeers and howlings of the crew. The rest assembled aft, and drew up the articles of their association. A square of black tarpaulin had the white skull painted upon it, and was hoisted amidst cheering at the main.

Officers were elected, and the limits of their authority fixed. Copley Banks was chosen Captain, but, as there are no mates upon a pirate craft, Birthmark Sweetlocks became quartermaster, and Israel Martin the boatswain. There was no difficulty in knowing what was the custom of the brotherhood, for half the men at least had served upon pirates before. Food should be the same for all, and no man should interfere with another man's drink! The Captain should have a cabin, but all hands should be welcome to enter it when they chose.

All should share and share alike, save only the captain, quartermaster, boatswain, carpenter, and master-gunner, who had from a quarter to a whole share extra. He who saw a prize first should have the best weapon taken out of her. He who boarded her first should have the richest suit of clothes aboard of her. Every man might treat his own prisoner, be it man or woman, after his own fashion. If a man flinched from his gun, the quartermaster should pistol him. These were some of the rules which the crew of the *Ruffling Harry* subscribed by putting forty-two crosses at the foot of the paper upon which they had been drawn.

So a new rover was afloat upon the seas, and her name before a year was over became as well known as that of the *Happy Delivery*. From the Bahamas to the Leewards, and from the Leewards to the Windwards, Copley Banks became the rival of Sharkey and the terror of traders. For a long time the barque and the brig never met, which was the more singular, as the *Ruffling Harry* was forever looking in at Sharkey's resorts; but at last one day, when she was passing down the inlet of Coxon's Hole, at the east end of Cuba, with the intention of careening, there was the *Happy Delivery*, with her blocks and tackle-falls already rigged for the same purpose.

Copley Banks fired a shotted salute and hoisted the green trumpeter ensign, as the custom was among gentlemen of the sea. Then he dropped his boat and went aboard.

Captain Sharkey was not a man of a genial mood, nor had he any kindly sympathy for those who were of the same trade as himself. Copley Banks found him seated astride upon one of the after guns, with his New England quartermaster, Ned Galloway, and a crowd of roaring ruffians standing about him. Yet none of them roared with quite such assurance when Sharkey's pale face and filmy blue eyes were turned upon him.

He was in his shirt-sleeves, with his cambric frills breaking through his open red satin long-flapped vest. The scorching sun seemed to have no power upon his fleshless frame, for he wore a low fur cap, as though it had been winter. A many-coloured band of silk passed across his body and supported a short murderous sword, while his broad, brass-buckled belt was stuffed with pistols.

" Sink you for a poacher ! " he cried as Copley Banks passed over the bulwarks. " I will drub you within an inch of your life, and that inch also ! What mean you by fishing in my waters ? "

Copley Banks looked at him, and his eyes were like those of a traveller who sees his home at last.

" I am glad that we are of one mind," said he, " for I am myself of opinion that the seas are not large enough for the two of us. But if you will take your sword and pistols and come upon a sand-bank with me, then the world will be rid of a damned villain whichever way it goes."

" Now, this is talking ! " cried Sharkey, jumping off the gun and holding out his hand. " I have not met many who could look John Sharkey in the eyes and speak with a full breath. May the devil seize me if I do not choose you as a consort ! But if you play me false, then I will come aboard of you and gut you upon your own poop."

" And I pledge you the same ! " said Copley Banks, and so the two pirates became sworn comrades to each other.

That summer they went north as far as the Newfoundland Banks, and harried the New York traders and the whale-ships from New England. It was Copley Banks who captured the Liverpool ship, *House of Hanover*, but it was Sharkey who fastened her master to the windlass and pelted him to death with empty claret-bottles.

Together they engaged the King's ship, *Royal Fortune*, which had been sent in search of them, and beat her off after a night action of five hours, the drunken, raving crews fighting naked in the light of the battle-lanterns, with a bucket of rum and a pannikin laid by the tackles of every gun. They ran to Topsail Inlet in North Carolina to refit, and then in the spring they were at the Grand Caicos, ready for a long cruise down the West Indies.

By this time Sharkey and Copley Banks had become very excellent friends, for Sharkey loved a whole-hearted villain, and he loved a man of metal, and it seemed to him that the two met in the captain of the *Ruffling Harry*. It was long before he gave his confidence to him, for cold suspicion lay deep in his character. Never once would he trust himself outside his own ship and away from his own men.

But Copley Banks came often on board the *Happy Delivery*, and joined Sharkey in many of his morose debauches, so that at last any mis-

givings of the latter were set at rest. He knew
nothing of the evil that he had done to his new
boon companion, for of his many victims how
could he remember the woman and the two
boys whom he had slain with such levity so
long ago! When, therefore, he received a
challenge to himself and to his quartermaster for
a carouse upon the last evening of their stay at
the Caicos Bank, he saw no reason to refuse.

A well-found passenger ship had been rifled
the week before, so their fare was of the best,
and after supper five of them drank deeply together. There were the two captains, Birthmark Sweetlocks, Ned Galloway, and Israel
Martin, the old buccaneersman. To wait upon
them was the dumb steward, whose head Sharkey split with his glass, because he had been too
slow in the filling of it.

The quartermaster had slipped Sharkey's pistols away from him, for it was an old joke with
him to fire them cross-handed under the table,
and see who was the luckiest man. It was a
pleasantry which had cost his boatswain his leg,
so now, when the table was cleared, they would
coax Sharkey's weapons away from him on the
excuse of the heat, and lay them out of his
reach.

The Captain's cabin of the *Ruffling Harry*
was in a deck-house upon the poop, and a stern-
chaser gun was mounted at the back of it.

Round shot were racked round the wall, and three great hogsheads of powder made a stand for dishes and for bottles. In this grim room the five pirates sang and roared and drank, while the silent steward still filled up their glasses, and passed the box and the candle round for their tobacco-pipes. Hour after hour the talk became fouler, the voices hoarser, the curses and shoutings more incoherent, until three of the five had closed their blood-shot eyes, and dropped their swimming heads upon the table.

Copley Banks and Sharkey were left face to face, the one because he had drunk the least, the other because no amount of liquor would ever shake his iron nerve or warm his sluggish blood. Behind him stood the watchful steward, for ever filling up his waning glass. From without came the low lapping of the tide, and from over the water a sailor's chanty from the barque.

In the windless tropical night the words came clearly to their ears :

"A trader sailed from Stepney Town,
Wake her up! Shake her up! Try her with the mainsail!
    A trader sailed from Stepney Town
    With a keg full of gold and a velvet gown.
        Ho, the bully Rover Jack,
        Waiting with his yard aback
    Out upon the Lowland Sea."

The two boon companions sat listening in

silence. Then Copley Banks glanced at the steward, and the man took a coil of rope from the shot-rack behind him.

"Captain Sharkey," said Copley Banks, "do you remember the *Duchess of Cornwall*, hailing from London, which you took and sank three years ago off the Statira Shoal?"

"Curse me if I can bear their names in mind," said Sharkey. "We did as many as ten ships a week about that time."

"There were a mother and two sons among the passengers. Maybe that will bring it back to your mind."

Captain Sharkey leant back in thought, with his huge thin beak of a nose jutting upwards. Then he burst suddenly into a high treble, neighing laugh. He remembered it, he said, and he added details to prove it.

"But burn me if it had not slipped from my mind!" he cried. "How came you to think of it?"

"It was of interest to me," said Copley Banks, "for the woman was my wife and the lads were my only sons."

Sharkey stared across at his companion, and saw that the smouldering fire which lurked always in his eyes had burned up into a lurid flame. He read their menace, and he clapped his hands to his empty belt. Then he turned to seize a weapon, but the bight of a rope was cast round him, and in an instant his arms were bound to his side. He fought like a wild cat and screamed for help.

" Ned!" he yelled. " Ned! Wake up! Here's damned villainy! Help, Ned, help!"

But the three men were far too deeply sunk in their swinish sleep for any voice to wake them. Round and round went the rope, until Sharkey was swathed like a mummy from ankle to neck. They propped him stiff and helpless against a powder barrel, and they gagged him with a handkerchief, but his filmy, red-rimmed eyes still looked curses at them. The dumb man chattered in his exultation, and Sharkey winced for the first time when he saw the empty mouth before him. He understood that vengeance, slow and patient, had dogged him long, and clutched him at last.

The two captors had their plans all arranged, and they were somewhat elaborate.

First of all they stove the heads of two of the great powder barrels, and they heaped the contents out upon the table and floor. They piled it round and under the three drunken men, until each sprawled in a heap of it. Then they carried Sharkey to the gun and they triced him sitting over the porthole, with his body about a foot from the muzzle. Wriggle as he would he could not move an inch either to right or left, and the dumb man trussed him up with a sailor's cunning, so that there was no chance that he should work free.

"Now, you bloody devil," said Copley Banks, softly, "you must listen to what I have to say to you, for they are the last words that you will hear. You are my man now, and I have bought you at a price, for I have given all that a man can give here below, and I have given my soul as well.

"To reach you I have had to sink to your level. For two years I strove against it, hoping that some other way might come, but I learnt that there was no other way. I've robbed and I have murdered—worse still, I have laughed and lived with you—and all for the one end. And now my time has come, and you will die as I would have you die, seeing the shadow creeping slowly upon you and the devil waiting for you in the shadow."

Sharkey could hear the hoarse voices of his rovers singing their chanty over the water :

" Where is the trader of Stepney Town ?
Wake her up! Shake her up! Every stick a-bending!
Where is the trader of Stepney Town ?
His gold's on the capstan, his blood's on his gown.
All for bully Rover Jack,
Reaching on the weather tack
Right across the Lowland Sea."

The words came clear to his ear, and just outside he could hear two men pacing backwards and forwards upon the deck. And yet he was helpless, staring down the mouth of the nine-pounder, unable to move an inch or to utter so much as a groan. Again there came the burst of voices from the deck of the barque :

" So it's up and it's over to Stornoway Bay,
Pack it on! Crack it on! Try her with the stun-sails!
It's off on a bowline to Stornoway Bay,
Where the liquor is good and the lasses are gay,
Waiting for their bully Jack,
Watching for him sailing back,
Right across the Lowland Sea."

To the dying pirate the jovial words and rollicking tune made his own fate seem the harsher, but there was no softening in his venomous blue eyes. Copley Banks had brushed away the priming of the gun, and had sprinkled fresh powder over the touch-hole. Then he had taken up the candle and cut it to the length of about an inch. This he placed upon the loose powder at the breach of the gun. Then he scattered powder thickly over the floor beneath, so that when the candle fell at the recoil it must explode the huge pile in which the three drunkards were wallowing.

" You've made others look death in the face, Sharkey," said he ; " now it has come to be your own turn. You and these swine here shall go together ! " He lit the candle-end as he spoke, and blew out the other lights upon the table.

89

Then he passed out with the dumb man, and locked the cabin door upon the outer side. But before he closed it he took an exultant look backwards, and received one last curse from those unconquerable eyes. In the single dim circle of light that ivory-white face, with the gleam of moisture upon the high, bald forehead, was the last that was ever seen of Sharkey.

There was a skiff along side, and in it Copley Banks and the dumb steward made their way to the beach, and looked back upon the brig riding in the moonlight just outside the shadow of the palm trees. They waited and waited, watching that dim light which shone through the stern port. And then at last there came the dull thud of a gun, and an instant later the shattering crash of the explosion. The long, sleek, black barque, the sweep of white sand, and the fringe of nodding, feathery palm trees sprang into dazzling light and back into darkness again. Voices screamed and called upon the bay.

Then Copley Banks, his heart singing within him, touched his companion upon the shoulder, and they plunged together into the lonely jungle of the Caicos.

THE CRIME OF THE BRIG-ADIER

IN all the great hosts of France there was only one officer towards whom the English of Wellington's Army retained a deep, steady, and unchangeable hatred. There were plunderers among the French, and men of violence, gamblers, duellists, and *roués*. All these could be forgiven, for others of their kidney were to be found among the ranks of the English. But one officer of Massena's force had committed a crime which was unspeakable, unheard of, abominable; only to be alluded to with curses late in the evening, when a second bottle had loosened the tongues of men. The news of it was carried back to England, and country gentlemen who knew little of the details of the war grew crimson with passion when they heard of it, and yeomen of the shires raised freckled fists to Heaven and swore. And yet who should be the doer of this dreadful deed but our friend the Brigadier, Etienne Gerard, of the Hussars of Conflans, gay-riding, plume-

tossing, debonnaire, the darling of the ladies
and of the six brigades of light cavalry.

But the strange part of it is that this gallant
gentleman did this hateful thing, and made
himself the most unpopular man in the Peninsula, without ever knowing that he had done
a crime for which there is hardly a name amid
all the resources of our language. He died of
old age, and never once in that imperturbable
self-confidence which adorned or disfigured his
character knew that so many thousand Englishmen would gladly have hanged him with their
own hands. On the contrary, he numbered
this adventure among those other exploits which
he has given to the world, and many a time he
chuckled and hugged himself as he narrated it
to the eager circle who gathered round him in
that humble *café* where, between his dinner and
his dominoes, he would tell, amid tears and
laughter, of that inconceivable Napoleonic past
when France, like an angel of wrath, rose up,
splendid and terrible, before a cowering conti-
nent. Let us listen to him as he tells the
story in his own way and from his own point of
view.

You must know, my friends, said he, that it
was towards the end of the year eighteen hundred and ten that I and Massena and the others
pushed Wellington backwards until we had

hoped to drive him and his army into the Tagus. But when we were still twenty-five miles from Lisbon we found that we were betrayed, for what had this Englishman done but build an enormous line of works and forts at a place called Torres Vedras, so that even we were unable to get through them! They lay across the whole Peninsula, and our army was so far from home that we did not dare to risk a reverse, and we had already learned at Busaco that it was no child's play to fight against these people. What could we do, then, but sit down in front of these lines and blockade them to the best of our power? There we remained for six months, amid such anxieties that Massena said afterwards that he had not one hair which was not white upon his body. For my own part, I did not worry much about our situation, but I looked after our horses, who were in great need of rest and green fodder. For the rest, we drank the wine of the country and passed the time as best we might. There was a lady at Santarem—but my lips are sealed. It is the part of a gallant man to say nothing, though he may indicate that he could say a great deal.

One day Massena sent for me, and I found him in his tent with a great plan pinned upon the table. He looked at me in silence with that single piercing eye of his, and I felt by his expression that the matter was serious. He was nervous and ill at ease, but my bearing seemed to reassure him. It is good to be in contact with brave men.

"Colonel Etienne Gerard," said he, "I have always heard that you are a very gallant and enterprising officer."

It was not for me to confirm such a report, and yet it would be folly to deny it, so I clinked my spurs together and saluted.

"You are also an excellent rider."

I admitted it.

"And the best swordsman in the six brigades of light cavalry."

Massena was famous for the accuracy of his information.

"Now," said he, "if you will look at this plan you will have no difficulty in understanding what it is that I wish you to do. These are the lines of Torres Vedras. You will perceive that they cover a vast space, and you will realize that the English can only hold a position here and there. Once through the lines you have twenty-five miles of open country which lie between them and Lisbon. It is very important to me to learn how Wellington's troops are distributed throughout that space, and it is my wish that you should go and ascertain."

His words turned me cold.

"Sir," said I, "it is impossible that a colonel of light cavalry should condescend to act as a spy."

He laughed and clapped me on the shoulder.

"You would not be a Hussar if you were not a hot-head," said he. "If you will listen you will understand that I have not asked you to act as a spy. What do you think of that horse?"

He had conducted me to the opening of his tent, and there was a Chasseur who led up and down a most admirable creature. He was a dapple grey, not very tall—a little over fifteen hands perhaps—but with the short head and splendid arch of the neck which comes with the Arab blood. His shoulders and haunches were so muscular, and yet his legs so fine, that it thrilled me with joy just to gaze upon him. A fine horse or a beautiful woman, I cannot look at them unmoved, even now when seventy winters have chilled my blood. You can think how it was in the year '10.

"This," said Massena, "is Voltigeur, the swiftest horse in our army. What I desire is that you should start to-night, ride round the lines upon the flank, make your way across the enemy's rear, and return upon the other flank, bringing me news of his dispositions. You will wear a uniform, and will, therefore, if captured, be safe from the death of a spy. It is probable that you will get through the lines un-challenged, for the posts are very scattered. Once through, in daylight you can outride any-thing which you meet, and if you keep off the roads you may escape entirely unnoticed. If you have not reported yourself by to-morrow night, I will understand that you are taken, and I will offer them Colonel Petrie in exchange."

Ah, how my heart swelled with pride and joy as I sprang into the saddle and galloped this grand horse up and down to show the Marshal the mastery which I had of him! He was mag-nificent—we were both magnificent, for Mas-sena clapped his hands and cried out in his de-light. It was not I, but he, who said that a gallant beast deserves a gallant rider. Then, when for the third time, with my panache flying and my dolman streaming behind me, I thun-dered past him, I saw upon his hard old face that he had no longer any doubt that he had chosen the man for his purpose. I drew my sabre, raised the hilt to my lips in salute, and galloped on to my own quarters. Already the news had spread that I had been chosen for a mission, and my little rascals came swarming out of their tents to cheer me. Ah! it brings the tears to my old eyes when I think how proud they were of their Colonel. And I was proud of them also. They deserved a dashing leader.

The night promised to be a stormy one, which was very much to my liking. It was my desire to keep my departure most secret, for it was evident that if the English heard that I had been detached from the army they would naturally conclude that something important was about to happen. My horse was taken, therefore, beyond the picket line, as if for watering, and I followed and mounted him there. I had a map, a compass, and a paper of instructions from the Marshal, and with these in the bosom of my tunic and my sabre at my side, I set out upon my adventure.

A thin rain was falling and there was no moon, so you may imagine that it was not very cheerful. But my heart was light at the thought of the honour which had been done me and the glory which awaited me. This exploit should be one more in that brilliant series which was to change my sabre into a bâton. Ah, how we dreamed, we foolish fellows, young, and drunk with success! Could I have foreseen that night as I rode, the chosen man of sixty thousand, that I should spend my life planting cabbages on a hundred francs a month! Oh, my youth, my hopes, my comrades! But the wheel turns and never stops. Forgive me, my friends, for an old man has his weakness.

My route, then, lay across the face of the high ground of Torres Vedras, then over a streamlet, past a farmhouse which had been burned down and was now only a landmark, then through a forest of young cork oaks, and so to the monastery of San Antonio, which marked the left of the English position. Here I turned south and rode quietly over the downs, for it was at this point that Massena thought that it would be most easy for me to find my way unobserved through the position. I went very slowly, for it was so dark that I could not see my hand in front of me. In such cases I leave my bridle loose and let my horse pick its own way. Voltigeur went confidently forward, and I was very content to sit upon his back and to peer about me, avoiding every light. For three hours we advanced in this cautious way, until it seemed to me that I must have left all danger behind me. I then pushed on more briskly, for I wished to be in the rear of the whole army by daybreak. There are many vineyards in these parts which in winter become open plains, and a horseman finds few difficulties in his way.

But Massena had underrated the cunning of these English, for it appears that there was not one line of defence, but three, and it was the third, which was the most formidable, through which I was at that instant passing. As I rode, elated at my own success, a lantern flashed suddenly before me, and I saw the glint of polished gun-barrels and the gleam of a red coat.

"Who goes there?" cried a voice—such a voice! I swerved to the right and rode like a madman, but a dozen squirts of fire came out of the darkness, and the bullets whizzed all round my ears. That was no new sound to me, my friends, though I will not talk like a foolish conscript and say that I have ever liked it. But at least it had never kept me from thinking clearly, and so I knew that there was nothing for it but to gallop hard and try my luck elsewhere. I rode round the English picket, and then, as I heard nothing more of them, I concluded rightly that I had at last come through their defences. For five miles I rode south, striking a tinder from time to time to look at my pocket compass. And then in an instant—I feel the pang once more as my memory brings back the moment—my horse, without a sob or stagger, fell stone dead beneath me.

I had not known it, but one of the bullets from that infernal picket had passed through his body. The gallant creature had never winced nor weakened, but had gone while life was in him. One instant I was secure on the swiftest, most graceful horse in Massena's army. The next he lay upon his side, worth only the price of his hide, and I stood there that most helpless, most ungainly of creatures, a dismounted Hussar. What could I do with my boots, my spurs, my trailing sabre? I was far inside the enemy's lines. How could I hope to get back again? I am not ashamed to say that I, Etienne Gerard, sat upon my dead horse and sank my face in my hands in my despair. Already the first streaks were whitening the east. In half an hour it would be light. That I should have won my way past every obstacle and then at this last instant be left at the mercy of my enemies, my mission ruined, and myself a prisoner—was it not enough to break a soldier's heart?

But courage, my friends! We have these moments of weakness, the bravest of us; but I have a spirit like a slip of steel, for the more you bend it the higher it springs. One spasm of despair, and then a brain of ice and a heart of fire. All was not yet lost. I who had come through so many hazards would come through this one also. I rose from my horse and considered what had best be done.

And first of all it was certain that I could not get back. Long before I could pass the lines it would be broad daylight. I must hide myself for the day, and then devote the next night to my escape. I took the saddle, holsters, and bridle from poor Voltigeur, and I concealed them among some bushes, so that no

one finding him could know that he was a
French horse. Then, leaving him lying there,
I wandered on in search of some place where I
might be safe for the day. In every direction
I could see camp fires upon the sides of the
hills, and already figures had begun to move
around them. I must hide quickly, or I was
lost.

But where was I to hide ? It was a vineyard
in which I found myself, the poles of the vines
still standing, but the plants gone. There was
no cover there. Besides, I should want some
food and water before another night had come.
I hurried wildly onwards through the waning
darkness, trusting that chance would be my
friend. And I was not disappointed. Chance
is a woman, my friends, and she has her eye
always upon a gallant Hussar.

Well, then, as I stumbled through the vineyard, something loomed in front of me, and I
came upon a great square house with another
long, low building upon one side of it. Three
roads met there, and it was easy to see that this
was the posada, or wine-shop. There was no
light in the windows, and everything was dark
and silent, but, of course, I knew that such
comfortable quarters were certainly occupied,
and probably by some one of importance. I
have learned, however, that the nearer the danger may really be the safer the place, and so I

was by no means inclined to trust myself away from this shelter. The low building was evidently the stable, and into this I crept, for the door was unlatched. The place was full of bullocks and sheep, gathered there, no doubt, to be out of the clutches of marauders. A ladder led to a loft, and up this I climbed, and concealed myself very snugly among some bales of hay upon the top. This loft had a small open window, and I was able to look down upon the front of the inn and also upon the road. There I crouched and waited to see what would happen.

It was soon evident that I had not been mistaken when I had thought that this might be the quarters of some person of importance. Shortly after daybreak an English light dragoon arrived with a despatch, and from then onwards the place was in a turmoil, officers continually riding up and away. Always the same name was upon their lips : " Sir Stapleton—Sir Stapleton." It was hard for me to lie there with a dry moustache and watch the great flagons which were brought out by the landlord to these English officers. But it amused me to look at their fresh-coloured, clean-shaven, careless faces, and to wonder what they would think if they knew that so celebrated a person was lying so near to them. And then, as I lay and watched, I saw a sight which filled me with surprise.

It is incredible the insolence of these English! What do you suppose Milord Wellington had done when he found that Massena had blockaded him and that he could not move his army? I might give you many guesses. You might say that he had raged, that he had despaired, that he had brought his troops together and spoken to them about glory and the fatherland before leading them to one last battle. No, Milord did none of these things. But he sent a fleet ship to England to bring him a number of fox-dogs, and he with his officers settled himself down to chase the fox. It is true what I tell you. Behind the lines of Torres Vedras these mad Englishmen made the fox-chase three days in the week. We had heard of it in the camp, and now I was myself to see that it was true.

For, along the road which I have described, there came these very dogs, thirty or forty of them, white and brown, each with its tail at the same angle, like the bayonets of the Old Guard. My faith, but it was a pretty sight! And behind and amidst them there rode three men with peaked caps and red coats, whom I understood to be the hunters. After them came many horsemen with uniforms of various kinds, stringing along the roads in twos and threes, talking together and laughing. They did not seem to be going above a trot, and it appeared to me that

it must indeed be a slow fox which they hoped
to catch. However, it was their affair, not
mine, and soon they had all passed my window
and were out of sight. I waited and I watched,
ready for any chance which might offer.

Presently an officer, in a blue uniform not
unlike that of our flying artillery, came cantering down the road—an elderly, stout man he
was, with gray side-whiskers. He stopped and
began to talk with an orderly officer of dragoons, who waited outside the inn, and it was
then that I learned the advantage of the English which had been taught me. I could hear
and understand all that was said.

"Where is the meet?" said the officer, and
I thought that he was hungering for his bifstek.
But the other answered him that it was near
Altara, so I saw that it was a place of which he
spoke.

"You are late, Sir George," said the orderly.

"Yes, I had a court-martial. Has Sir Stapleton Cotton gone?"

At this moment a window opened, and a
handsome young man in a very splendid uniform looked out of it.

"Halloa, Murray!" said he. "These cursed
papers keep me, but I will be at your heels."

"Very good, Cotton. I am late already, so
I will ride on."

"You might order my groom to bring round

my horse," said the young general at the window to the orderly below, while the other went on down the road.

The orderly rode away to some outlying stable, and then in a few minutes there came a smart English groom with a cockade in his hat, leading by the bridle a horse—and, oh, my friends, you have never known the perfection to which a horse can attain until you have seen a first-class English hunter. He was superb: tall, broad, strong, and yet as graceful and agile as a deer. Coal black he was in colour, and his neck, and his shoulder, and his quarters, and his fetlocks—how can I describe him all to you ? The sun shone upon him as on polished ebony, and he raised his hoofs in a little, playful dance so lightly and prettily, while he tossed his mane and whinnied with impatience. Never have I seen such a mixture of strength and beauty and grace. I had often wondered how the English Hussars had managed to ride over the Chasseurs of the Guards in the affair at Astorga, but I wondered no longer when I saw the English horses.

There was a ring for fastening bridles at the door of the inn, and the groom tied the horse there while he entered the house. In an instant I had seen the chance which Fate had brought to me. Were I in that saddle I should be better off than when I started. Even Voltigeur could not compare with this magnificent creature. To think is to act with me. In one instant I was down the ladder and at the door of the stable. The next I was out and the bridle was in my hand. I bounded into the saddle. Somebody, the master or the man, shouted wildly behind me. What cared I for his shouts! I touched the horse with my spurs, and he bounded forward with such a spring that only a rider like myself could have sat him. I gave him his head and let him go—it did not matter to me where, so long as we left this inn far behind us. He thundered away across the vineyards, and in a very few minutes I had placed miles between myself and my pursuers. They could no longer tell, in that wild country, in which direction I had gone. I knew that I was safe, and so, riding to the top of a small hill, I drew my pencil and note-book from my pocket and proceeded to make plans of those camps which I could see and to draw the outline of the country.

He was a dear creature upon whom I sat, but it was not easy to draw upon his back, for every now and then his two ears would cock, and he would start and quiver with impatience. At first I could not understand this trick of his, but soon I observed that he only did it when a peculiar noise—" yoy, yoy, yoy "—came from somewhere among the oak woods beneath us.

And then suddenly this strange cry changed into a most terrible screaming, with the frantic blowing of a horn. Instantly he went mad—this horse. His eyes blazed. His mane bristled. He bounded from the earth and bounded again, twisting and turning in a frenzy. My pencil flew one way and my note-book another. And then, as I looked down into the valley, an extraordinary sight met my eyes. The hunt was streaming down it. The fox I could not see, but the dogs were in full cry, their noses down, their tails up, so close together that they might have been one great yellow and white moving carpet. And behind them rode the horsemen —my faith, what a sight! Consider every type which a great army could show: some in hunting dress, but the most in uniforms; blue dragoons, red dragoons, red-trousered hussars, green riflemen, artillery men, gold-slashed lancers, and most of all red, red, red, for the infantry officers ride as hard as the cavalry. Such a crowd, some well mounted, some ill, but all flying along as best they might, the subaltern as good as the general, jostling and pushing, spurring and driving, with every thought thrown to the winds save that they should have the blood of this absurd fox! Truly, they are an extraordinary people, the English!

But I had little time to watch the hunt or to marvel at these islanders, for of all these mad

creatures the very horse upon which I sat was
the maddest. You understand that he was himself a hunter, and that the crying of these dogs
was to him what the call of a cavalry trumpet
in the street yonder would be to me. It thrilled
him. It drove him wild. Again and again he
bounded into the air, and then, seizing the bit
between his teeth, he plunged down the slope
and galloped after the dogs. I swore, and
tugged, and pulled, but I was powerless. This
English General rode his horse with a snaffle
only, and the beast had a mouth of iron. It
was useless to pull him back. One might as
well try to keep a Grenadier from a wine bottle.
I gave it up in despair, and, settling down in
the saddle, I prepared for the worst which could
befall.

What a creature he was! Never have I felt
such a horse between my knees. His great
haunches gathered under him with every stride,
and he shot forward ever faster and faster,
stretched like a greyhound, while the wind beat
in my face and whistled past my ears. I was
wearing our undress jacket, a uniform simple
and dark in itself—though some figures give
distinction to any uniform—and I had taken
the precaution to remove the long panache
from my busby. The result was that, amidst
the mixture of costumes in the hunt, there was
no reason why mine should attract attention, or

why these men, whose thoughts were all with
the chase, should give any heed to me. The
idea that a French officer might be riding with
them was too absurd to enter their minds. I
laughed as I rode, for, indeed, amid all the danger, there was something of comic in the situation.

I have said that the hunters were very un-
equally mounted, and so, at the end of a few
miles, instead of being one body of men, like a
charging regiment, they were scattered over a
considerable space, the better riders well up to
the dogs and the others trailing away behind.
Now, I was as good a rider as any, and my
horse was the best of them all, and so you can
imagine that it was not long before he carried
me to the front. And when I saw the dogs
streaming over the open, and the red-coated
huntsman behind them, and only seven or eight
horsemen between us, then it was that the
strangest thing of all happened, for I, too, went
mad—I, Etienne Gerard! In a moment it
came upon me, this spirit of sport, this desire
to excel, this hatred of the fox. Accursed animal, should he then defy us? Vile robber, his
hour was come! Ah, it is a great feeling, this
feeling of sport, my friends, this desire to tram-
ple the fox under the hoofs of your horse. I
have made the fox-chase with the English. I
have also, as I may tell you some day, fought

the box-fight with the Bustler, of Bristol. And I say to you that this sport is a wonderful thing —full of interest as well as madness.

The farther we went the faster galloped my horse, and soon there were but three men as near the dogs as I was. All thought of fear of discovery had vanished. My brain throbbed, my blood ran hot—only one thing upon earth seemed worth living for, and that was to overtake this infernal fox. I passed one of the horsemen—a Hussar like myself. There were only two in front of me now: the one in a black coat, the other the blue artilleryman whom I had seen at the inn. His grey whiskers streamed in the wind, but he rode magnificently. For a mile or more we kept in this order, and then, as we galloped up a steep slope, my lighter weight brought me to the front. I passed them both, and when I reached the crown I was riding level with the little, hard-faced English huntsman. In front of us were the dogs, and then, a hundred paces beyond them, was a brown wisp of a thing, the fox itself, stretched to the uttermost. The sight of him fired my blood. "Aha, we have you then, assassin!" I cried, and shouted my encouragement to the huntsman. I waved my hand to show him that there was one upon whom he could rely.

And now there were only the dogs between

me and my prey. These dogs, whose duty it
is to point out the game, were now rather a
hindrance than a help to us, for it was hard to
know how to pass them. The huntsman felt
the difficulty as much as I, for he rode behind
them, and could make no progress towards the
fox. He was a swift rider, but wanting in enterprise. For my part, I felt that it would be
unworthy of the Hussars of Conflans if I
could not overcome such a difficulty as this.
Was Etienne Gerard to be stopped by a herd
of fox-dogs? It was absurd. I gave a shout
and spurred my horse.

"Hold hard, sir! Hold hard!" cried the
huntsman.

He was uneasy for me, this good old man,
but I reassured him by a wave and a smile.
The dogs opened in front of me. One or two
may have been hurt, but what would you have?
The egg must be broken for the omelette. I
could hear the huntsman shouting his congratulations behind me. One more effort, and the
dogs were all behind me. Only the fox was in
front.

Ah, the joy and pride of that moment! To
know that I had beaten the English at their
own sport. Here were three hundred all
thirsting for the life of this animal, and yet it
was I who was about to take it. I thought of
my comrades of the light cavalry brigade, of

my mother, of the Emperor, of France. I had brought honour to each and all. Every instant brought me nearer to the fox. The moment for action had arrived, so I unsheathed my sabre. I waved it in the air, and the brave English all shouted behind me.

Only then did I understand how difficult is this fox-chase, for one may cut again and again at the creature and never strike him once. He is small, and turns quickly from a blow. At every cut I heard those shouts of encouragement from behind me, and they spurred me to yet another effort. And then, at last, the supreme moment of my triumph arrived. In the very act of turning I caught him fair with such another back-handed cut as that with which I killed the aide-de-camp of the Emperor of Russia. He flew into two pieces, his head one way and his tail another. I looked back and waved the blood-stained sabre in the air. For the moment I was exalted—superb!

Ah! how I should have loved to have waited to have received the congratulations of these generous enemies. There were fifty of them in sight, and not one who was not waving his hand and shouting. They are not really such a phlegmatic race, the English. A gallant deed in war or in sport will always warm their hearts. As to the old huntsman, he was the nearest to me, and I could see with my

own eyes how overcome he was by what he had
seen. He was like a man paralyzed—his
mouth open, his hand, with outspread fingers,
raised in the air. For a moment my inclina-
tion was to return and to embrace him. But
already the call of duty was sounding in my
ears, and these English, in spite of all the fra-
ternity which exists among sportsmen, would
certainly have made me prisoner. There was
no hope for my mission now, and I had done
all that I could do. I could see the lines of
Massena's camp no very great distance off, for,
by a lucky chance, the chase had taken us in
that direction. I turned from the dead fox,
saluted with my sabre, and galloped away.

But they would not leave me so easily, these
gallant huntsmen. I was the fox now, and the
chase swept bravely over the plain. It was only
at the moment when I started for the camp
that they could have known that I was a
Frenchman, and now the whole swarm of them
were at my heels. We were within gunshot of
our pickets before they would halt, and then
they stood in knots and would not go away, but
shouted and waved their hands at me. No, I
will not think that it was in enmity. Rather
would I fancy that a glow of admiration filled
their breasts, and that their one desire was to
embrace the stranger who had carried himself so
gallantly and well.

THE CROXLEY MASTER

I

M R. ROBERT MONTGOMERY was seated at his desk, his head upon his hands, in a state of the blackest despondency. Before him was the open ledger with the long columns of Dr. Oldacre's prescriptions. At his elbow lay the wooden tray with the labels in various partitions, the cork box, the lumps of twisted sealing-wax, while in front a rank of empty bottles waited to be filled. But his spirits were too low for work. He sat in silence, with his fine shoulders bowed and his head upon his hands.

Outside, through the grimy surgery window over a foreground of blackened brick and slate, a line of enormous chimneys like Cyclopean pillars upheld the lowering, dun-coloured cloud-bank. For six days in the week they spouted smoke, but to-day the furnace fires were banked, for it was Sunday. Sordid and polluting gloom hung over a district blighted and blasted by the greed of man. There was nothing in the sur-

114

roundings to cheer a desponding soul, but it was more than his dismal environment which weighed upon the medical assistant.

His trouble was deeper and more personal. The winter session was approaching. He should be back again at the University completing the last year which would give him his medical degree; but, alas! he had not the money with which to pay his class fees, nor could he imagine how he could procure it. Sixty pounds were wanted to make his career, and it might have been as many thousands for any chance there seemed to be of his obtaining it.

He was roused from his black meditation by the entrance of Dr. Oldacre himself, a large, clean-shaven, respectable man, with a prim manner and an austere face. He had prospered exceedingly by the support of the local Church interest, and the rule of his life was never by word or action to run a risk of offending the sentiment which had made him. His standard of respectability and of dignity was exceedingly high, and he expected the same from his assistants. His appearance and words were always vaguely benevolent. A sudden impulse came over the despondent student. He would test the reality of this philanthropy.

" I beg your pardon, Dr. Oldacre," said he, rising from his chair; " I have a great favour to ask of you."

The doctor's appearance was not encouraging. His mouth suddenly tightened, and his eyes fell.

"Yes, Mr. Montgomery?"

"You are aware, sir, that I need only one more session to complete my course."

"So you have told me."

"It is very important to me, sir."

"Naturally."

"The fees, Dr. Oldacre, would amount to about sixty pounds."

"I am afraid that my duties call me elsewhere, Mr. Montgomery."

"One moment, sir! I had hoped, sir, that perhaps, if I signed a paper promising you interest upon your money, you would advance this sum to me. I will pay you back, sir, I really will. Or, if you like, I will work it off after I am qualified."

The doctor's lips had thinned into a narrow line. His eyes were raised again, and sparkled indignantly.

"Your request is unreasonable, Mr. Montgomery. I am surprised that you should have made it. Consider, sir, how many thousands of medical students there are in this country. No doubt there are many of them who have a difficulty in finding their fees. Am I to provide for them all? Or why should I make an exception in your favour? I am grieved and disappointed, Mr. Montgomery, that you should have put me into the painful position of having to refuse you." He turned upon his heel, and walked with offended dignity out of the surgery.

The student smiled bitterly, and turned to his work of making up the morning prescriptions. It was poor and unworthy work—work which any weakling might have done as well, and this was a man of exceptional nerve and sinew. But, such as it was, it brought him his board and £1 a week, enough to help him during the summer months and let him save a few pounds towards his winter keep. But those class fees! Where were they to come from? He could not save them out of his scanty wage. Dr. Oldacre would not advance them. He saw no way of earning them. His brains were fairly good, but brains of that quality were a drug in the market. He only excelled in his strength; and where was he to find a customer for that? But the ways of Fate are strange, and his customer was at hand.

" Look y'ere !" said a voice at the door.

Montgomery looked up, for the voice was a loud and rasping one. A young man stood at the entrance—a stocky, bull-necked young miner, in tweed Sunday clothes and an aggressive necktie. He was a sinister-looking figure, with dark, insolent eyes, and the jaw and throat of a bulldog.

"Look y'ere!" said he again. "Why hast thou not sent t' medicine oop as thy master ordered?"

Montgomery had become accustomed to the brutal frankness of the Northern worker. At first it had enraged him, but after a time he had grown callous to it, and accepted it as it was meant. But this was something different. It was insolence—brutal, overbearing insolence, with physical menace behind it.

"What name?" he asked coldly.

"Barton. Happen I may give thee cause to mind that name, yoong man. Mak' oop t' wife's medicine this very moment, look ye, or it will be the worse for thee."

Montgomery smiled. A pleasant sense of relief thrilled softly through him. What blessed safety-valve was this through which his jangled nerves might find some outlet. The provocation was so gross, the insult so unprovoked, that he could have none of those qualms which take the edge off a man's mettle. He finished sealing the bottle upon which he was occupied, and he addressed it and placed it carefully in the rack.

"Look here!" said he turning round to the miner, "your medicine will be made up in its turn and sent down to you. I don't allow folk in the surgery. Wait outside in the waiting-room, if you wish to wait at all."

"Yoong man," said the miner, "thou's got to mak' t' wife's medicine here, and now, and quick, while I wait and watch thee, or else happen thou might need some medicine thysel' before all is over."

" I shouldn't advise you to fasten a quarrel upon me." Montgomery was speaking in the hard, staccato voice of a man who is holding himself in with difficulty. " You'll save trouble if you'll go quietly. If you don't you'll be hurt. Ah, you would? Take it, then!"

The blows were almost simultaneous—a savage swing which whistled past Montgomery's ear, and a straight drive which took the workman on the chin. Luck was with the assistant. That single whizzing uppercut, and the way in which it was delivered, warned him that he had a formidable man to deal with. But if he had underrated his antagonist, his antagonist had also underrated him, and had laid himself open to a fatal blow.

The miner's head had come with a crash against the corner of the surgery shelves, and he had dropped heavily onto the ground. There he lay with his bandy legs drawn up and his hands thrown abroad, the blood trickling over the surgery tiles.

" Had enough ? " asked the assistant, breathing fiercely through his nose.

But no answer came. The man was insensible. And then the danger of his position came upon Montgomery, and he turned as white as his antagonist. A Sunday, the immaculate Dr. Oldacre with his pious connection, a savage brawl with a patient ; he would irretrievably lose his situation if the facts came out. It was not much of a situation, but he could not get another without a reference, and Oldacre might refuse him one. Without money for his classes, and without a situation—what was to become of him ? It was absolute ruin.

But perhaps he could escape exposure after all. He seized his insensible adversary, dragged him out into the centre of the room, loosened his collar, and squeezed the surgery sponge over his face. He sat up at last with a gasp and a scowl.

" Domn thee, thou's spoilt my necktie," said he, mopping up the water from his breast.

" I'm sorry I hit you so hard," said Montgomery, apologetically.

" Thou hit me hard ! I could stan' such fly-flappin' all day. 'Twas this here press that cracked my pate for me, and thou art a looky man to be able to boast as thou hast outed me. And now I'd be obliged to thee if thou wilt give me t' wife's medicine."

Montgomery gladly made it up and handed it to the miner.

"You are weak still," said he. "Won't you stay awhile and rest?"

"T' wife wants her medicine," said the man, and lurched out at the door.

The assistant, looking after him, saw him rolling with an uncertain step down the street, until a friend met him, and they walked on arm-in-arm. The man seemed in his rough Northern fashion to bear no grudge, and so Montgomery's fears left him. There was no reason why the doctor should know anything about it. He wiped the blood from the floor, put the surgery in order, and went on with his interrupted task, hoping that he had come scathless out of a very dangerous business.

Yet all day he was aware of a sense of vague uneasiness, which sharpened into dismay when, late in the afternoon, he was informed that three gentlemen had called and were waiting for him in the surgery. A coroner's inquest, a descent of detectives, an invasion of angry relatives—all sorts of possibilities rose to scare him. With tense nerves and a rigid face he went to meet his visitors.

They were a very singular trio. Each was known to him by sight; but what on earth the three could be doing together, and, above all, what they could expect from *him*, was a most inexplicable problem.

The first was Sorley Wilson, the son of the owner of the Nonpareil Coalpit. He was a young blood of twenty, heir to a fortune, a keen sportsman, and down for the Easter Vacation from Magdalene College. He sat now upon the edge of the surgery table, looking in thoughtful silence at Montgomery, and twisting the ends of his small, black, waxed moustache.

The second was Purvis, the publican, owner of the chief beershop, and well known as the local bookmaker. He was a coarse, clean-shaven man, whose fiery face made a singular contrast with his ivory-white bald head. He had shrewd, light-blue eyes with foxy lashes, and he also leaned forward in silence from his chair, a fat, red hand upon either knee, and stared critically at the young assistant.

So did the third visitor, Fawcett, the horse-breaker, who leaned back, his long, thin legs, with their box-cloth riding-gaiters, thrust out in front of him, tapping his protruding teeth with his riding-whip, with anxious thought in every line of his rugged, bony face. Publican, exquisite, and horsebreaker were all three equally silent, equally earnest, and equally critical. Montgomery, seated in the midst of them, looked from one to the other.

" Well, gentlemen ? " he observed, but no answer came.

The position was embarrassing.

" No," said the horsebreaker, at last. " No. It's off. It's nowt."

" Stand oop, lad ; let's see thee standin'." It was the publican who spoke.

Montgomery obeyed. He would learn all about it, no doubt, if he were patient. He stood up and turned slowly round, as if in front of his tailor.

" It's off ! It's off !" cried the horsebreaker. " Why, mon, the Master would break him over his knee."

" Oh, that behanged for a yarn ! " said the young Cantab. " You can drop out if you like, Fawcett, but I'll see this thing through, if I have to do it alone. I don't hedge a penny. I like the cut of him a great deal better than I liked Ted Barton."

" Look at Barton's shoulders, Mr. Wilson."

" Lumpiness isn't always strength. Give me nerve and fire and breed. That's what wins."

" Ay, sir, you have it theer—you have it theer ! " said the fat, red-faced publican, in a thick, suety voice. " It's the same wi' poops. Get 'em clean-bred an' fine, and they'll yark the thick 'uns—yark 'em out o' their skins."

" He's ten good pund on the light side," growled the horsebreaker.

" He's a welter weight, anyhow."

" A hundred and thirty."

" A hundred and fifty, if he's an ounce."

" Well, the master doesn't scale much more than that."

" A hundred and seventy-five."

" That was when he was hog-fat and living high. Work the grease out of him, and I lay there's no great difference between them. Have you been weighed lately, Mr. Montgomery ? "

It was the first direct question which had been asked him. He had stood in the midst of them, like a horse at a fair, and he was just beginning to wonder whether he was more angry or amused.

" I am just eleven stone," said he.

" I said that he was a welter weight."

" But suppose you was trained ? " said the publican. " Wot then ? "

" I am always in training."

" In a manner of speakin', do doubt, he *is* always in trainin'," remarked the horsebreaker. " But trainin' for everyday work ain't the same as trainin' with a trainer ; and I dare bet, with all respec' to your opinion, Mr. Wilson, that there's half a stone of tallow on him at this minute."

The young Cantab put his fingers cn the assistant's upper arm. Then with his other hand on his wrist he bent the forearm sharply, and felt the biceps, as round and hard as a cricket-ball, spring up under his fingers.

" Feel that ! " said he.

The publican and horsebreaker felt it with an air of reverence.

" Good lad ! He'll do yet ! " cried Purvis.

" Gentlemen," said Montgomery, " I think that you will acknowledge that I have been very patient with you. I have listened to all that you have to say about my personal appearance, and now I must really beg that you will have the goodness to tell me what is the matter."

They all sat down in their serious, business-like way.

" That's easy done, Mr. Montgomery," said the fat-voiced publican. " But before sayin' anything, we had to wait and see whether, in a way of speakin', there was any need for us to say anything at all. Mr. Wilson thinks there is. Mr. Fawcett, who has the same right to his opinion, bein' also a backer and one o' the committee, thinks the other way."

" I thought him too light built, and I think so now," said the horsebreaker, still tapping his prominent teeth with the metal head of his riding-whip. " But happen he may pull through ; and he's a fine-made, buirdly young chap, so if you mean to back him, Mr. Wilson———"

" Which I do."

" And you, Purvis ? "

" I ain't one to go back, Fawcett."

" Well, I'll stan' to my share of the purse."

" And well I knew you would," said Purvis, " for it would be somethin' new to find Isaac Fawcett as a spoil-sport. Well, then, we make up the hundred for the stake among us, and the fight stands—always supposin' the young man is willin'."

" Excuse all this rot, Mr. Montgomery," said the University man, in a genial voice. " We've begun at the wrong end, I know, but we'll soon straighten it out, and I hope that you will see your way to falling in with our views. In the first place, you remember the man whom you knocked out this morning? He is Barton—the famous Ted Barton."

" I'm sure, sir, you may well be proud to have outed him in one round," said the publican. " Why, it took Morris, the ten-stone-six champion, a deal more trouble than that before he put Barton to sleep. You've done a fine performance, sir, and happen you'll do a finer, if you give yourself the chance."

" I never heard of Ted Barton, beyond seeing the name on a medicine label," said the assistant.

" Well, you may take it from me that he's a slaughterer," said the horsebreaker. " You've taught him a lesson that he needed, for it was always a word and a blow with him, and the word alone was worth five shillin' in a public court. He won't be so ready now to shake his nief in the face of everyone he meets. However, that's neither here nor there."

Montgomery looked at them in bewilderment.

" For goodness sake, gentlemen, tell me what it is you want me to do ! " he cried.

" We want you to fight Silas Craggs, better known as the Master of Croxley."

" But why ? "

" Because Ted Barton was to have fought him next Saturday. He was the champion of the Wilson coal-pits, and the other was the Master of the iron-folk down at the Croxley smelters. We'd matched our man for a purse of a hundred against the Master. But you've queered our man, and he can't face such a battle with a two-inch cut at the back of his head. There's only one thing to be done, sir, and that is for you to take his place. If you can lick Ted Barton you may lick the Master of Croxley ; but if you don't we're done, for there's no one else who is in the same street with him in this district. It's twenty rounds, two-ounce gloves, Queensberry rules, and a decision on points if you fight to the finish."

For a moment the absurdity of the thing

drove every other thought out of Montgomery's head. But then there came a sudden revulsion. A hundred pounds!—all he wanted to complete his education was lying there ready to his hand, if only that hand were strong enough to pick it up. He had thought bitterly that morning that there was no market for his strength, but here was one where his muscle might earn more in an hour than his brains in a year. But a chill of doubt came over him.

"How can I fight for the coal-pits?" said he. "I am not connected with them."

"Eh, lad, but thou art!" cried old Purvis. "We've got it down in writin', and it's clear enough. 'Any one connected with the coal-pits.' Doctor Oldacre is the coal-pit club doctor; thou art his assistant. What more can they want?"

"Yes, that's right enough," said the Cantab. "It would be a very sporting thing of you, Mr. Montgomery, if you would come to our help when we are in such a hole. Of course, you might not like to take the hundred pounds; but I have no doubt that, in the case of your winning, we could arrange that it should take the form of a watch or piece of plate, or any other shape which might suggest itself to you. You see, you are responsible for our having lost our champion, so we really feel that we have a claim upon you."

" Give me a moment, gentlemen. It is very unexpected. I am afraid the doctor would never consent to my going—in fact, I am sure that he would not."

" But he need never know—not before the fight, at any rate. We are not bound to give the name of our man. So long as he is within the weight limits on the day of the fight, that is all that concerns any one."

The adventure and the profit would either of them have attracted Montgomery. The two combined were irresistible.

" Gentlemen," said he, " I'll do it!"

The three sprang from their seats. The publican had seized his right hand, the horse-dealer his left, and the Cantab slapped him on the back.

" Good lad! good lad!" croaked the publican. " Eh, mon, but if thou yark him, thou'll rise in one day from being just a common doctor to the best-known mon 'twixt here and Bradford. Thou art a witherin' tyke, thou art, and no mistake; and if thou beat the Master of Croxley, thou'll find all the beer thou want for the rest of thy life waiting for thee at the Four Sacks."

" It is the most sporting thing I ever heard of in my life," said young Wilson. " By George, sir, if you pull it off, you've got the constituency in your pocket, if you care to

stand. You know the outhouse in my gar-
den?"

"Next the road?"

"Exactly. I turned it into a gymnasium
for Ted Barton. You'll find all you want
there: clubs, punching ball, bars, dumb-bells,
everything. Then you'll want a sparring partner. Ogilvy has been acting for Barton, but
we don't think that he is class enough. Barton
bears you no grudge. He's a good-hearted
fellow, though cross-grained with strangers.
He looked upon you as a stranger this morning, but he says he knows you now. He is
quite ready to spar with you for practice, and
he will come at any hour you will name."

"Thank you; I will let you know the hour,"
said Montgomery; and so the committee departed jubilant upon their way.

The medical assistant sat for a little time in
the surgery turning it over in his mind. He
had been trained originally at the University by
the man who had been middle-weight champion
in his day. It was true that his teacher was
long past his prime, slow upon his feet and
stiff in his joints, but even so he was still a
tough antagonist; but Montgomery had found
at last that he could more than hold his own
with him. He had won the University medal,
and his teacher, who had trained so many students, was emphatic in his opinion that he had

never had one who was in the same class with
him. He had been exhorted to go in for the
Amateur Championships, but he had no particular ambition in that direction. Once he had
put on the gloves with Hammer Tunstall in
a booth at a fair, and had fought three rattling
rounds, in which he had the worst of it, but
had made the prize-fighter stretch himself to
the uttermost. There was his whole record, and
was it enough to encourage him to stand up to
the Master of Croxley ? He had never heard of
the Master before, but then he had lost touch
of the ring during the last few years of hard
work. After all, what did it matter ? If he
won, there was the money, which meant so
much to him. If he lost, it would only mean
a thrashing. He could take punishment without flinching, of that he was certain. If there
were only one chance in a hundred of pulling
it off, then it was worth his while to attempt it.

Dr. Oldacre, new come from church, with an
ostentatious Prayer-book in his kid-gloved
hand, broke in upon his meditation.

"You don't go to service, I observe, Mr.
Montgomery," said he, coldly.

"No, sir ; I have had some business to detain me."

"It is very near to my heart that my house-
hold should set a good example. There are so
few educated people in this district that a great

responsibility devolves upon us. If we do not live up to the highest, how can we expect these poor workers to do so? It is a dreadful thing to reflect that the parish takes a great deal more interest in an approaching glove-fight than in their religious duties."

" A glove-fight, sir?" said Montgomery, guiltily.

" I believe that to be the correct term. One of my patients tells me that it is the talk of the district. A local ruffian, a patient of ours, by the way, is matched against a pugilist over at Croxley. I cannot understand why the law does not step in and stop so degrading an exhibition. It is really a prize-fight."

" A glove fight, you said."

" I am informed that a two-ounce glove is an evasion by which they dodge the law, and make it difficult for the police to interfere. They contend for a sum of money. It seems dreadful and almost incredible—does it not?— to think that such scenes can be enacted within a few miles of our peaceful home. But you will realize, Mr. Montgomery, that while there are such influences for us to counteract, it is very necessary that we should live up to our highest."

The doctor's sermon would have had more ef- fect if the assistant had not once or twice had occasion to test his highest and come upon it at unexpectedly humble elevations. It is always so particularly easy to "compound for sins we're most inclined to by damning those we have no mind to." In any case, Montgomery felt that of all the men concerned in such a fight—promoters, backers, spectators—it is the actual fighter who holds the strongest and most honourable position. His conscience gave him no concern upon the subject. Endurance and courage are virtues, not vices, and brutality is, at least, better than effeminacy.

There was a little tobacco-shop at the corner of the street, where Montgomery got his bird's-eye and also his local information, for the shopman was a garrulous soul, who knew everything about the affairs of the district. The assistant strolled down there after tea and asked, in a casual way, whether the tobacconist had ever heard of the Master of Croxley.

"Heard of him! Heard of him!" the little man could hardly articulate in his astonishment. "Why, sir, he's the first mon o' the district, an' his name's as well known in the West Riding as the winner o' t' Derby. But Lor', sir "—here he stopped and rummaged among a heap of papers. "They are makin' a fuss about him on account o' his fight wi' Ted Barton, and so the *Croxley Herald* has his life an' record, an' here it is, an' thou canst read it for thysel'."

The sheet of the paper which he held up was a lake of print around an islet of illustration. The latter was a coarse wood-cut of a pugilist's head and neck set in a cross-barred jersey. It was a sinister but powerful face, the face of a debauched hero, clean-shaven, strongly eye-browed, keen-eyed, with a huge aggressive jaw and an animal dewlap beneath it. The long, obstinate cheeks ran flush up to the narrow, sinister eyes. The mighty neck came down square from the ears and curved outwards into shoulders, which had lost nothing at the hands of the local artist. Above was written "Silas Craggs," and beneath, " The Master of Crox-ley."

" Thou'll find all about him there, sir," said the tobacconist. " He's a witherin' tyke, he is, and we're proud to have him in the county. If he hadn't broke his leg he'd have been champion of England."

" Broke his leg, has he ? "

" Yes, and it set badly. They ca' him owd K behind his bock, for thot is how his two legs look. But his arms—well, if they was both stropped to a bench, as the sayin' is, I wonder where the champion of England would be then."

" I'll take this with me," said Montgomery ; and putting the paper into his pocket he re-turned home.

It was not a cheering record which he read there. The whole history of the Croxley Master was given in full, his many victories, his few defeats.

" Born in 1857," said the provincial biographer, " Silas Craggs, better known in sporting circles as The Master of Croxley, is now in his fortieth year."

" Hang it, I'm only twenty-three," said Montgomery to himself, and read on more cheerfully.

" Having in his youth shown a surprising aptitude for the game, he fought his way up among his comrades, until he became the recognized champion of the district and won the proud title which he still holds. Ambitious of a more than local fame, he secured a patron, and fought his first fight against Jack Barton, of Birmingham, in May, 1880, at the old Loiterers' Club. Craggs, who fought at ten-stone-two at the time, had the better of fifteen rattling rounds, and gained an award on points against the Midlander. Having disposed of James Dunn, of Rotherhithe, Cameron, of Glasgow, and a youth named Fernie, he was thought so highly of by the fancy that he was matched against Ernest Willox, at that time middle-weight champion of the North of England, and defeated him in a hard-fought battle, knocking him out in the tenth round after a punishing contest. At this period it looked as if the very highest honours of the ring were within the reach of the young Yorkshireman, but he was laid upon the shelf by a most unfortunate accident. The kick of a horse broke his thigh, and for a year he was compelled to rest himself. When he returned to his work the fracture had set badly, and his activity was much impaired. It was owing to this that he was defeated in seven rounds by Willox, the man whom he had previously beaten, and afterwards by James Shaw, of London, though the latter acknowledged that he had found the toughest customer of his career. Undismayed by his reverses, the Master adapted the style of his fighting to his physical disabilities and resumed his career of victory—defeating Norton (the black), Bobby Wilson, and Levy Cohen, the latter a heavy-weight. Conceding two stone, he fought a draw with the famous Billy McQuire, and afterwards, for a purse of fifty pounds, he defeated Sam Hare at the Pelican Club, London. In 1891 a decision was given against him upon a foul when fighting a winning fight against Jim Taylor, the Australian middle-weight, and so mortified was he by the decision, that he withdrew from the ring. Since then he has hardly fought at all save to accommodate any local aspirant who may wish to learn the difference between a bar-room scramble and a scientific contest. The latest of these ambitious souls comes from the Wilson coal-pits, which have undertaken to put up a stake of £100 and back their local champion. There are various rumours afloat as to who their representative is to be, the name of Ted Barton being freely mentioned ; but the betting, which is seven to one on the Master against any untried man, is a fair reflection of the feeling of the community."

Montgomery read it over twice, and it left him with a very serious face. No light matter this which he had undertaken ; no battle with a rough-and-tumble fighter who presumed upon a local reputation. The man's record showed that he was first-class—or nearly so. There were a few points in his favour, and he must make the most of them. There was age— twenty-three against forty. There was an old ring proverb that "Youth will be served," but the annals of the ring offer a great number of exceptions. A hard veteran, full of cool valour and ring-craft, could give ten or fifteen years and a beating to most striplings. He could not rely too much upon his advantage in age. But then there was the lameness ; that must surely count for a great deal. And, lastly, there was the chance that the Master might underrate his opponent, that he might be remiss in his training, and refuse to abandon his usual way of life, if he thought that he had an easy task before him. In a man of his age and habits this seemed very possible. Montgomery prayed that it might be so. Meanwhile, if his opponent were the best man who ever jumped the ropes into a ring, his own duty was clear. He must prepare himself carefully, throw away no chance, and do the very best that he could. But he knew enough to appreciate the difference which exists in boxing, as in every sport, between the amateur and the professional. The coolness, the power of hitting, above all the capability of taking punishment, count for so much. Those specially developed, gutta-percha-like abdominal muscles of the hardened pugilist will take without flinching a blow which would leave another man writhing on the ground. Such things are not to be acquired in a week, but all that could be done in a week should be done.

The medical assistant had a good basis to start from. He was 5 feet 11 inches—tall enough for anything on two legs, as the old ring men used to say—lithe and spare, with the activity of a panther, and a strength which had hardly yet ever found its limitations. His muscular development was finely hard, but his power came rather from that higher nerve-energy which counts for nothing upon a measuring tape. He had the well-curved nose and the widely-opened eye which never yet were seen upon the face of a craven, and behind everything he had the driving force, which came from the knowledge that his whole career was at stake upon the contest. The three backers rubbed their hands when they saw him at work punching the ball in the gymnasium next morning; and Fawcett, the horsebreaker, who had written to Leeds to hedge his bets, sent a wire to cancel the letter, and to lay another fifty at the market price of seven to one.

Montgomery's chief difficulty was to find time for his training without any interference from the doctor. His work took him a large part of the day, but as the visiting was done on foot, and considerable distances had to be traversed, it was a training in itself. For the rest, he punched the swinging ball and worked with the dumb-bells for an hour every morning and evening, and boxed twice a day with Ted Barton in the gymnasium, gaining as much profit as could be got from a rushing, two-handed slogger. Barton was full of admiration for his cleverness and quickness, but doubtful about his strength. Hard hitting was the feature of his own style, and he exacted it from others.

" Lord, sir, that's a turble poor poonch for an eleven-stone man!" he would cry. " Thou wilt have to hit harder than that afore t' Master will know that thou art theer. Ah, thot's better, mon, thot's fine!" he would add, as his opponent lifted him across the room on the end of a right counter. "Thot's how I likes to feel 'em. Happen thou'lt pull through yet." He chuckled with joy when Montgomery knocked him into a corner. "Eh, mon, thou art comin' along grand. Thou hast fair yarked me off my legs. Do it again, lad, do it again!"

The only part of Montgomery's training which came within the doctor's observation was his diet, and that puzzled him considerably.

"You will excuse my remarking, Mr. Montgomery, that you are becoming rather particular in your tastes. Such fads are not to be encouraged in one's youth. Why do you eat toast with every meal?"

"I find that it suits me better than bread, sir."

"It entails unnecessary work upon the cook. I observe, also, that you have turned against potatoes."

"Yes, sir; I think that I am better without them."

"And you no longer drink your beer?"

"No, sir."

"These causeless whims and fancies are very much to be deprecated, Mr. Montgomery. Consider how many there are to whom these very potatoes and this very beer would be most acceptable."

" No doubt, sir. But at present I prefer to do without them."

They were sitting alone at lunch, and the assistant thought that it would be a good opportunity of asking leave for the day of the fight."

" I should be glad if you could let me have leave for Saturday, Doctor Oldacre."

" It is very inconvenient upon so busy a day."

" I should do a double day's work on Friday so as to leave everything in order. I should hope to be back in the evening."

" I am afraid I cannot spare you, Mr. Montgomery."

This was a facer. If he could not get leave he would go without it.

" You will remember, Doctor Oldacre, that when I came to you it was understood that I should have a clear day every month. I have never claimed one. But now there are reasons why I wish to have a holiday upon Saturday."

Doctor Oldacre gave in with a very bad grace.

" Of course, if you insist upon your formal rights, there is no more to be said, Mr. Montgomery, though I feel that it shows a certain indifference to my comfort and the welfare of the practice. Do you still insist ? "

" Yes, sir."

" Very good. Have your way."

The doctor was boiling over with anger, but Montgomery was a valuable assistant—steady, capable, and hard-working—and he could not afford to lose him. Even if he had been prompted to advance those class fees, for which his assistant had appealed, it would have been against his interests to do so, for he did not wish him to qualify, and he desired him to remain in his subordinate position, in which he worked so hard for so small a wage. There was something in the cool insistence of the young man, a quiet resolution in his voice as he claimed his Saturday, which aroused his curiosity.

" I have no desire to interfere unduly with your affairs, Mr. Montgomery, but were you thinking of having a day in Leeds upon Saturday ? "

" No, sir."

" In the country ? "

" Yes, sir."

" You are very wise. You will find a quiet day among the wild flowers a very valuable restorative. Had you thought of any particular direction ? "

" I am going over Croxley way."

" Well, there is no prettier country when once you are past the iron-works. What could be more delightful than to lie upon the Fells, basking in the sunshine, with perhaps some instructive and elevating book as your companion? I should recommend a visit to the ruins of St. Bridget's Church, a very interesting relic of the early Norman era. By the way, there is one objection which I see to your going to Croxley on Saturday. It is upon that date, as I am informed, that that ruffianly glove-fight takes place. You may find yourself molested by the blackguards whom it will attract."

" I will take my chance of that, sir," said the assistant.

On the Friday night, which was the last before the fight, Montgomery's three backers assembled in the gymnasium and inspected their man as he went through some light exercises to keep his muscles supple. He was certainly in splendid condition, his skin shining with health, and his eyes with energy and confidence. The three walked round him and exulted.

" He's simply ripping!" said the undergraduate. " By gad, you've come out of it splendidly. You're as hard as a pebble, and fit to fight for your life."

" Happen he's a trifle on the fine side," said the publican. " Runs a bit light at the loins, to my way of thinkin'."

" What weight to-day? "

" Ten stone eleven," the assistant answered.

"That's only three pund off in a week's trainin'," said the horsebreaker. "He said right when he said that he was in condition. Well, it's fine stuff all there is of it, but I'm none so sure as there is enough." He kept poking his finger into Montgomery, as if he were one of his horses. "I hear that the Master will scale a hundred and sixty odd at the ring-side."

"But there's some of that which he'd like well to pull off and leave behind wi' his shirt," said Purvis. "I hear they've had a rare job to get him to drop his beer, and if it had not been for that great red-headed wench of his they'd never ha' done it. She fair scratted the face off a potman that had brought him a gallon from t' Chequers. They say the hussy is his sparrin' partner, as well as his sweetheart, and that his poor wife is just breakin' her heart over it. Hullo, young 'un, what do you want?"

The door of the gymnasium had opened, and a lad about sixteen, grimy and black with soot and iron, stepped into the yellow glare of the oil-lamp. Ted Barton seized him by the collar.

"See here, thou yoong whelp, this is private, and we want noan o' thy spyin'!"

"But I maun speak to Mr. Wilson."

The young Cantab stepped forward.

"Well, my lad, what is it?"

"It's aboot t' fight, Mr. Wilson, sir. I wanted to tell your mon somethin' aboot t' Maister."

"We've no time to listen to gossip, my boy. We know all about the Master."

"But thou doant, sir. Nobody knows but me and mother, and we thought as we'd like thy mon to know, sir, for we want him to fair bray him."

"Oh, you want the Master fair brayed, do you? So do we. Well, what have you to say?"

"Is this your mon, sir?"

"Well, suppose it is?"

"Then it's him I want to tell aboot it. T' Maister is blind o' the left eye."

"Nonsense!"

"It's true, sir. Not stone blind, but rarely fogged. He keeps it secret, but mother knows, and so do I. If thou slip him on the left side he can't cop thee. Thou'll find it right as I tell thee. And mark him when he sinks his right. 'Tis his best blow, his right upper-cut. T' Maister's finisher, they ca' it at t' works. It's a turble blow, when it do come home."

"Thank you, my boy. This is information worth having about his sight," said Wilson. "How came you to know so much? Who are you?"

"I'm his son, sir."

Wilson whistled.

" And who sent you to us ? "

" My mother. I maun get back to her again."

" Take this half-crown."

" No, sir, I don't seek money in comin' here. I do it——"

" For love? " suggested the publican.

" For hate ! " said the boy, and darted off into the darkness.

" Seems to me t' red-headed wench may do him more harm than good, after all," remarked the publican. " And now," Mr. Montgomery, sir, you've done enough for this evenin', an' a nine hours' sleep is the best trainin' before a battle. Happen this time to-morrow night you'll be safe back again with your £100 in your pocket."

II

WORK was struck at one o'clock at the coal-
pits and the iron-works, and the fight
was arranged for three.   From the Croxley
Furnaces, from Wilson's Coal-pits, from the
Heartsease Mine, from the Dodd Mills, from
the Leverworth Smelters the workmen came
trooping, each with his fox-terrier or his lurcher
at his heels.   Warped with labour and twisted
by toil, bent double by week-long work in the
cramped coal galleries, or half-blinded with years
spent in front of white-hot fluid metal, these
men still gilded their harsh and hopeless lives
by their devotion to sport.   It was their one relief, the only thing which could distract their
mind from sordid surroundings, and give them
an interest beyond the blackened circle which
inclosed them.   Literature, art, science, all these
things were beyond the horizon; but the race,
the football match, the cricket, the fight, these
were things which they could understand, which
they could speculate upon in advance and comment upon afterwards.   Sometimes brutal, some-

times grotesque, the love of sport is still one of
the great agencies which make for the happi-
ness of our people. It lies very deeply in the
springs of our nature, and when it has been educated out, a higher, more refined nature may be
left, but it will not be of that robust British
type which has left its mark so deeply on the
world. Every one of these ruddled workers,
slouching with his dog at his heels to see something of the fight, was a true unit of his race.

It was a squally May day, with bright sun-
bursts and driving showers. Montgomery
worked all morning in the surgery getting his
medicine made up.

" The weather seems so very unsettled, Mr.
Montgomery," remarked the doctor, "that I
am inclined to think that you had better post-
pone your little country excursion until a later
date."

" I am afraid that I must go to-day, sir."

" I have just had an intimation that Mrs.
Potter, at the other side of Angleton, wishes to
see me. It is probable that I shall be there all
day. It will be extremely inconvenient to leave
the house empty so long."

" I am very sorry, sir, but I must go," said
the assistant, doggedly.

The doctor saw that it would be useless to
argue, and departed in the worst of bad tempers upon his mission. Montgomery felt easier

now that he was gone. He went up to his
room, and packed his running-shoes, his fight-
ing-drawers, and his cricket-sash into a handbag.
When he came down Mr. Wilson was waiting
for him in the surgery.

" I hear the doctor has gone."

" Yes ; he is likely to be away all day."

" I don't see that it matters much. It's
bound to come to his ears by to-night."

" Yes; it's serious with me, Mr. Wilson. If
I win, it's all right. I don't mind telling you
that the hundred pounds will make all the difference to me. But if I lose, I shall lose my
situation, for, as you say, I can't keep it secret."

" Never mind. We'll see you through
among us. I only wonder the doctor has not
heard, for it's all over the country that you are
to fight the Croxley Champion. We've had
Armitage up about it already. He's the Master's backer, you know. He wasn't sure that
you were eligible. The Master said he wanted
you whether you were eligible or not. Armitage has money on, and would have made
trouble if he could. But I showed him that you
came within the conditions of the challenge, and
he agreed that it was all right. They think they
have a soft thing on."

" Well, I can only do my best," said Montgomery.

They lunched together; a silent and rather nervous repast, for Montgomery's mind was full of what was before him, and Wilson had himself more money at stake than he cared to lose.

Wilson's carriage and pair were at the door, the horses with blue-and-white rosettes at their ears, which were the colours of the Wilson Coalpits, well known on many a football field. At the avenue gate a crowd of some hundred pitmen and their wives gave a cheer as the carriage passed. To the assistant it all seemed dream-like and extraordinary — the strangest experience of his life, but with a thrill of human action and interest in it which made it passionately absorbing. He lay back in the open carriage and saw the fluttering handkerchiefs from the doors and windows of the miners' cottages. Wilson had pinned a blue-and-white rosette upon his coat, and every one knew him as their [champion. "Good luck, sir! good luck to thee!" they shouted from the roadside. He felt that it was like some unromantic knight riding down to sordid lists, but there was something of chivalry in it all the same. He fought for others as well as for himself. He might fail from want of skill or strength, but deep in his sombre soul he vowed that it should never be for want of heart.

Mr. Fawcett was just mounting into his

high-wheeled, spidery dogcart, with his little
bit of blood between the shafts. He waved
his whip and fell in behind the carriage. They
overtook Purvis, the tomato-faced publican,
upon the road, with his wife in her Sunday
bonnet. They also dropped into the procession, and then, as they traversed the seven
miles of the high-road to Croxley, their two-
horsed, rosetted carriage became gradually the
nucleus of a comet with a loosely radiating
tail. From every side-road came the miners'
carts, the humble, ramshackle traps, black and
bulging, with their loads of noisy, foul-
tongued, open-hearted partisans. They trailed
for a long quarter of a mile behind them—
cracking, whipping, shouting, galloping, swear-
ing. Horsemen and runners were mixed with
the vehicles. And then suddenly a squad of
the Sheffield Yeomanry, who were having
their annual training in those parts, clattered
and jingled out of a field, and rode as an escort to the carriage. Through the dust-clouds
round him Montgomery saw the gleaming
brass helmets, the bright coats, and the tossing
heads of the chargers, the delighted brown
faces of the troopers. It was more dream-like
than ever.

And then, as they approached the monstrous, uncouth line of bottle-shaped buildings
which marked the smelting-works of Croxley,

their long, writhing snake of dust was headed off by another but longer one which wound across their path. The main-road into which their own opened was filled by the rushing current of traps. The Wilson contingent halted until the others should get past. The iron-men cheered and groaned, according to their humour, as they whirled past their antagonist. Rough chaff flew back and forwards like iron nuts and splinters of coal. " Brought him up, then !" " Got t' hearse for to fetch him back ? " " Where's t' owd K-legs ? " " Mon, mon, have thy photograph took—'twill mind thee of what thou used to look !" " He fight ?— he's now't but a half-baked doctor !" " Happen he'll doctor thy Croxley Champion afore he's through wi't."

So they flashed at each other as the one side waited and the other passed. Then there came a rolling murmur swelling into a shout, and a great break with four horses came clattering along, all streaming with salmon-pink ribbons. The driver wore a white hat with pink rosette, and beside him, on the high seat, were a man and a woman—she with her arm round his waist. Montgomery had one glimpse of them as they flashed past : he with a furry cap drawn low over his brow, a great frieze coat, and a pink comforter round his throat ; she brazen, red-headed, bright-coloured, laughing excitedly.

The Master, for it was he, turned as he passed, gazed hard at Montgomery, and gave him a menacing, gap-toothed grin. It was a hard, wicked face, blue-jowled and craggy, with long, obstinate cheeks and inexorable eyes. The break behind was full of patrons of the sport—flushed iron-foremen, heads of departments, managers. One was drinking from a metal flask, and raised it to Montgomery as he passed; and then the crowd thinned, and the Wilson *cortège* with their dragoons swept in at the rear of the others.

The road led away from Croxley, between curving green hills, gashed and polluted by the searchers for coal and iron. The whole country had been gutted, and vast piles of refuse and mountains of slag suggested the mighty chambers which the labor of man had burrowed beneath. On the left the road curved up to where a huge building, roofless and dismantled, stood crumbling and forlorn, with the light shining through the windowless squares.

"That's the old Arrowsmith's factory. That's where the fight is to be," said Wilson. "How are you feeling now?"

"Thank you. I was never better in my life," Montgomery answered.

"By Gad, I like your nerve!" said Wilson, who was himself flushed and uneasy. "You'll give us a fight for our money, come what may.

That place on the right is the office, and that has been set aside as the dressing and weighing-room."

The carriage drove up to it amidst the shouts of the folk upon the hillside. Lines of empty carriages and traps curved down upon the winding road, and a black crowd surged round the door of the ruined factory. The seats, as a huge placard announced, were five shillings, three shillings, and a shilling, with half-price for dogs. The takings, deducting expenses, were to go to the winner, and it was already evident that a larger stake than a hundred pounds was in question. A babel of voices rose from the door. The workers wished to bring their dogs in free. The men scuffled. The dogs barked. The crowd was a whirling, eddying pool surging with a roar up to the narrow cleft which was its only outlet.

The break, with its salmon-coloured streamers and four reeking horses, stood empty before the door of the office; Wilson, Purvis, Fawcett, and Montgomery passed in.

There was a large, bare room inside with square, clean patches upon the grimy walls, where pictures and almanacs had once hung. Worn linoleum covered the floor, but there was no furniture save some benches and a deal table with a ewer and a basin upon it. Two of the corners were curtained off. In the middle of the room was a weighing-chair. A hugely fat man, with a salmon tie and a blue waist-coat with bird's-eye spots, came bustling up to them. It was Armitage, the butcher and grazier, well known for miles round as a warm man, and the most liberal patron of sport in the Riding.

" Well, well," he grunted, in a thick, fussy, wheezy voice, " you have come, then. Got your man ? Got your man ?"

" Here he is, fit and well. Mr. Montgomery, let me present you to Mr. Armitage."

" Glad to meet you, sir. Happy to make your acquaintance. I make bold to say, sir, that we of Croxley admire your courage, Mr. Montgomery, and that our only hope is a fair fight and no favour and the best man win. That's our sentiment at Croxley."

" And it is my sentiment also," said the assistant.

"Well, you can't say fairer than that, Mr. Montgomery. You've taken a large contrac' in hand, but a large contrac' may be carried through, sir, as any one that knows my dealings could testify. The Master is ready to weigh in ! "

" So am I."

" You must weigh in the buff."

" Montgomery looked askance at the tall,

red-headed woman who was standing gazing out of the window.

"That's all right," said Wilson. "Get behind the curtain and put on your fighting-kit."

He did so, and came out the picture of an athlete, in white, loose drawers, canvas shoes, and the sash of a well-known cricket club round his waist. He was trained to a hair, his skin gleaming like silk, and every muscle rippling down his broad shoulders and along his beautiful arms as he moved them. They bunched into ivory knobs, or slid into long, sinuous curves, as he raised or lowered his hands.

"What thinkest thou o' that?" asked Ted Barton, his second, of the woman in the window.

She glanced contemptuously at the young athlete.

"It's but a poor kindness thou dost him to put a thread-paper yoong gentleman like you against a mon as is a mon. Why, my Jock would throttle him wi' one hond lashed behind him."

"Happen he may—happen not," said Barton. "I have but twa pund in the world, but it's on him, every penny, and no hedgin'. But here's t' Maister, and rarely fine he do look."

The prize-fighter had come out from his curtain, a squat, formidable figure, monstrous in chest and arms, limping slightly on his distorted leg. His skin had none of the freshness and clearness of Montgomery's, but was dusky and mottled, with one huge mole amid the mat of tangled black hair which thatched his mighty breast. His weight bore no relation to his strength, for those huge shoulders and great arms, with brown, sledge-hammer fists, would have fitted the heaviest man that ever threw his cap into a ring. But his loins and legs were slight in proportion. Montgomery, on the other hand, was as symmetrical as a Greek statue. It would be an encounter between a man who was specially fitted for one sport, and one who was equally capable of any. The two looked curiously at each other : a bulldog, and a high-bred, clean-limbed terrier, each full of spirit.

" How do you do ? "

" How do ? " The Master grinned again, and his three jagged front teeth gleamed for an instant. The rest had been beaten out of him in twenty years of battle. He spat upon the floor. " We have a rare fine day for't."

" Capital," said Montgomery.

" That's the good feelin' I like," wheezed the fat butcher. " Good lads, both of them !— prime lads !—hard meat an' good bone. There's no ill-feelin'."

" If he downs me, Gawd bless him ! " said
the Master.

" An' if we down him, Gawd help him ! "
interrupted the woman.

" Haud thy tongue, wench ! " said the Master, impatiently. " Who art thou to put in
thy word ? Happen I might draw my hand
across thy face."

The woman did not take the threat amiss.

" Wilt have enough for thy hand to do,"
Jock," said she. " Get quit o' this gradely
man afore thou turn on me."

The lovers' quarrel was interrupted by the
entrance of a new comer, a gentleman with a
fur-collared overcoat and a very shiny top-hat
—a top-hat of a degree of glossiness which is
seldom seen five miles from Hyde Park. This
hat he wore at the extreme back of his head, so
that the lower surface of the brim made a kind
of frame for his high, bald forehead, his keen
eyes, his rugged and yet kindly face. He
bustled in with the quiet air of possession with
which the ring-master enters the circus.

" It's Mr. Stapleton, the referee from London," said Wilson.

" How do you do, Mr. Stapleton ? I was
introduced to you at the big fight at the Corin-
thian Club, in Piccadilly."

" Ah, I dare say," said the other, shaking
hands. " Fact is, I'm introduced to so many

that I can't undertake to carry their names. Wilson, is it? Well, Mr. Wilson, glad to see you. Couldn't get a fly at the station, and that's why I'm late."

" I'm sure, sir," said Armitage, " we should be proud that any one so well known in the boxing world should come down to our little exhibition."

" Not at all. Not at all. Anything in the interests of boxin'. All ready? Men weighed?"

" Weighing now, sir."

" Ah, just as well I should see it done. Seen you before, Craggs. Saw you fight your second battle against Willox. You had beaten him once, but he came back on you. What does the indicator say?—one hundred and sixty-three pounds—two off for the kit—one hundred and sixty-one. Now, my lad, you jump. My goodness, what colours are you wearing?"

" The Anonymi Cricket Club."

" What right have you to wear them? I belong to the club myself."

" So do I."

" You an amateur?"

" Yes, sir."

" And you are fighting for a money prize?"

" Yes."

" I suppose you know what you are doing? You realize that you're a professional pug from this onwards, and that if ever you fight again—— "

" I'll never fight again."

" Happen you won't," said the woman, and the Master turned a terrible eye upon her.

" Well, I suppose you know your own business best. Up you jump. One hundred and fifty-one, minus two, one hundred and forty-nine—twelve pounds difference, but youth and condition on the other scale. Well, the sooner we get to work the better, for I wish to catch the seven o'clock express at Hellifield. Twenty three-minute rounds, with one-minute intervals, and Queensberry rules. Those are the conditions, are they not ? "

" Yes, sir."

" Very good, then, we may go across."

The two combatants had overcoats thrown over their shoulders, and the whole party, backers, fighters, seconds, and the referee, filed out of the room. A police inspector was waiting for them in the road. He had a notebook in his hand—that terrible weapon which awes even the London cabman.

" I must take your names, gentlemen, in case it should be necessary to proceed for breach of peace."

" You don't mean to stop the fight ? " cried Armitage, in a passion of indignation. " I'm Mr. Armitage, of Croxley, and this is Mr. Wilson, and we'll be responsible that all is fair and as it should be.'

" I'll take the names in case it should be necessary to proceed," said the inspector, impassively.

" But you know me well."

" If you was a dook or even a judge it would be all the same," said the inspector. " It's the law, and there's an end. I'll not take upon myself to stop the fight, seeing that gloves are to be used, but I'll take the names of all concerned. Silas Craggs, Robert Montgomery, Edward Barton, James Stapleton, of London. Who seconds Silas Craggs ? "

" I do," said the woman. " Yes, you can stare, but it's my job, and no one else's. Anastasia's the name—four a's."

" Craggs ? "

" Johnson. Anastasia Johnson. If you jug him, you can jug me."

" Who talked of juggin', ye fool ? " growled the Master. " Coom on, Mr. Armitage, for I'm fair sick o' this loiterin'."

The inspector fell in with the procession, and proceeded, as they walked up the hill, to bargain in his official capacity for a front seat, where he could safeguard the interests of the law, and in his private capacity to lay out thirty shillings at seven to one with Mr. Armitage. Through the door they passed, down a narrow lane walled with a dense bank of humanity, up a wooden ladder to a platform, over a rope which was slung waist-high from four corner-stakes, and then Montgomery realized that he was in that ring in which his immediate destiny was to be worked out. On the stake at one corner there hung a blue-and-white streamer. Barton led him across, the overcoat dangling loosely from his shoulders, and he sat down on a wooden stool. Barton and another man, both wearing white sweaters, stood beside him. The so-called ring was a square, twenty feet each way. At the opposite angle was the sinister figure of the Master, with his red-headed woman and a rough-faced friend to look after him. At each corner were metal basins, pitchers of water, and sponges.

During the hubbub and uproar of the entrance Montgomery was too bewildered to take things in. But now there was a few minutes' delay, for the referee had lingered behind, and so he looked quietly about him. It was a sight to haunt him for a lifetime. Wooden seats had been built in, sloping upwards to the tops of the walls. Above, instead of a ceiling, a great flight of crows passed slowly across a square of grey cloud. Right up to the topmost benches the folk were banked—broadcloth in front, corduroys and fustian behind; faces turned everywhere upon him. The grey reek of the pipes filled the building, and the air was pungent with the acrid smell of cheap, strong tobacco. Everywhere among the human faces were to be seen the heads of the dogs. They growled and yapped from the back benches. In that dense mass of humanity one could hardly pick out individuals, but Montgomery's eyes caught the brazen gleam of the helmets held upon the knees of the ten yeomen of his escort. At the very edge of the platform sat the reporters, five of them : three locals, and two all the way from London. But where was the all-important referee ? There was no sign of him, unless he were in the centre of that angry swirl of men near the door.

Mr. Stapleton had stopped to examine the gloves which were to be used, and entered the building after the combatants. He had started to come down that narrow lane with the human walls which led to the ring. But already it had gone abroad that the Wilson champion was a gentleman, and that another gentleman had been appointed as referee. A wave of suspicion passed through the Croxley folk. They would have one of their own people for a referee. They would not have a stranger. His path was stopped as he made for the ring. Excited men flung themselves in front of him ; they waved their fists in his face and cursed him. A woman howled vile names in his ear. Somebody struck at him with an umbrella. "Go thou back to Lunnon. We want noan o' thee. Go thou back!" they yelled.

Stapleton, with his shiny hat cocked backwards, and his large, bulging forehead swelling from under it, looked round him from beneath his bushy brows. He was in the centre of a savage and dangerous mob. Then he drew his watch from his pocket and held it dial upwards in his palm.

"In three minutes," said he, "I will declare the fight off."

They raged round him. His cool face and that aggressive top-hat irritated them. Grimy hands were raised. But it was difficult, somehow, to strike a man who was so absolutely indifferent.

"In two minutes I declare the fight off."

They exploded into blasphemy. The breath of angry men smoked into his placid face. A gnarled, grimy fist vibrated at the end of his nose. "We tell thee we want noan o' thee. Get thou back where thou com'st from."

"In one minute I declare the fight off."

Then the calm persistence of the man conquered the swaying, mutable, passionate crowd.

"Let him through, mon. Happen there'll be no fight after a'."

"Let him through."

" Bill, thou loomp, let him pass. Dost want the fight declared off ? "

" Make room for the referee !—room for the Lunnon referee ! "

And half pushed, half carried, he was swept up to the ring. There were two chairs by the side of it, one for him and one for the time-keeper. He sat down, his hands on his knees, his hat at a more wonderful angle than ever, impassive but solemn, with the aspect of one who appreciates his responsibilities.

Mr. Armitage, the portly butcher, made his way into the ring and held up two fat hands, sparkling with rings, as a signal for silence.

" Gentlemen !" he yelled. And then in a crescendo shriek, "Gentlemen ! "

" And ladies !" cried somebody, for indeed there was a fair sprinkling of women among the crowd. " Speak up, owd man !" shouted another. " What price pork chops ? " cried somebody at the back. Everybody laughed, and the dogs began to bark. Armitage waved his hands amidst the uproar as if he were conducting an orchestra. At last the babel thinned into silence.

" Gentlemen," he yelled, " the match is between Silas Craggs, whom we call the Master of Croxley, and Robert Montgomery, of the Wilson Coal-pits. The match was to be under eleven-eight. When they were weighed just

now Craggs weighed eleven-seven, and Montgomery ten-nine. The conditions of the contest are—the best of twenty three-minute
rounds with two-ounce gloves. Should the
fight run to its full length it will, of course, be
decided upon points. Mr. Stapleton, the well-
known London referee, has kindly consented
to see fair play. I wish to say that Mr. Wilson
and I, the chief backers of the two men, have
every confidence in Mr. Stapleton, and that we
beg that you will accept his rulings without dis-
pute."

He then turned from one combatant to the
other, with a wave of his hand.

III

" MONTGOMERY—Craggs !" said he.
A great hush fell over the huge assembly. Even the dogs stopped yapping ; one might have thought that the monstrous room was empty. The two men had stood up, the small white gloves over their hands. They advanced from their corners and shook hands : Montgomery gravely, Craggs with a smile. Then they fell into position. The crowd gave a long sigh—the intake of a thousand excited breaths. The referee tilted his chair on to its back legs, and looked moodily critical from the one to the other.

It was strength against activity—that was evident from the first. The Master stood stolidly upon his K-leg. It gave him a tremendous pedestal ; one could hardly imagine his being knocked down. And he could pivot round upon it with extraordinary quickness ; but his advance or retreat was ungainly. His frame, however, was so much larger and broader than that of the student, and his brown, massive face looked so resolute and menacing, that the hearts of the Wilson party sank within them. There was one heart, however, which had not done so. It was that of Robert Montgomery.

Any nervousness which he may have had completely passed away now that he had his work before him. Here was something defin-ite—this hard-faced, deformed Hercules to beat, with a career as the price of beating him. He glowed with the joy of action; it thrilled through his nerves. He faced his man with little in-and-out steps, breaking to the left, breaking to the right, feeling his way, while Craggs, with a dull, malignant eye, pivoted slowly upon his weak leg, his left arm half extended, his right sunk low across the mark. Montgomery led with his left, and then led again, getting lightly home each time. He tried again, but the Mas-ter had his counter ready, and Montgomery reeled back from a harder blow than he had given. Anastasia, the woman, gave a shrill cry of encouragement, and her man let fly his right. Montgomery ducked under it, and in an in-stant the two were in each other's arms.

"Break away! Break away!" said the referee.

The Master struck upwards on the break, and shook Montgomery with the blow. Then it was "time." It had been a spirited opening round. The people buzzed into comment and applause. Montgomery was quite fresh, but the hairy chest of the Master was rising and falling. The man passed a sponge over his head, while Anastasia flapped the towel before him. " Good lass ! Good lass ! " cried the crowd, and cheered her.

The men were up again, the Master grimly watchful, Montgomery as alert as a kitten. The Master tried a sudden rush, squattering along with his awkward gait, but coming faster than one would think. The student slipped aside and avoided him. The Master stopped, grinned, and shook his head. Then he motioned with his hand as an invitation to Montgomery to come to him. The student did so and led with his left, but got a swinging right counter in the ribs in exchange. The heavy blow staggered him, and the Master came scrambling in to complete his advantage ; but Montgomery, with his greater activity, kept out of danger until the call of " time." A tame round, and the advantage with the Master.

" T' Maister's too strong for him," said a smelter to his neighbour.

" Ay ; but t'other's a likely lad. Happen we'll see some sport yet. He can joomp rarely."

" But t' Maister can stop and hit rarely.

Happen he'll mak' him joomp when he gets his nief upon him."

They were up again, the water glistening upon their faces. Montgomery led instantly and got his right home with a sounding smack upon the Master's forehead. There was a shout from the colliers, and " Silence ! Order !" from the referee. Montgomery avoided the counter and scored with his left. Fresh applause, and the referee upon his feet in indignation. " No comments, gentlemen, if *you* please, during the rounds."

" Just bide a bit !" growled the Master.

" Don't talk—fight !" said the referee, angrily.

Montgomery rubbed in the point by a flush hit upon the mouth, and the Master shambled back to his corner like an angry bear, having had all the worst of the round.

" Where's thot seven to one ?" shouted Purvis, the publican. " I'll take six to one !"

There were no answers.

" Five to one !" There were givers at that. Purvis booked them in a tattered notebook.

Montgomery began to feel happy. He lay back with his legs outstretched, his back against the corner-post, and one gloved hand upon each rope. What a delicious minute it was between each round. If he could only keep out of harm's way, he must surely wear this man out before the end of twenty rounds. He was so slow that all his strength went for nothing. "You're fightin' a winnin' fight—a winnin' fight," Ted Barton whispered in his ear. "Go canny; tak' no chances; you have him proper."

But the Master was crafty. He had fought so many battles with his maimed limb that he knew how to make the best of it. Warily and slowly he manœuvred round Montgomery, stepping forward and yet again forward until he had imperceptibly backed him into his corner. The student suddenly saw a flash of triumph upon the grim face, and a gleam in the dull, malignant eyes. The Master was upon him. He sprang aside and was on the ropes. The Master smashed in one of his terrible upper-cuts, and Montgomery half broke it with his guard. The student sprang the other way and was against the other converging rope. He was trapped in the angle. The Master sent in another, with a hoggish grunt which spoke of the energy behind it. Montgomery ducked, but got a jab from the left upon the mark. He closed with his man. "Break away! Break away?" cried the referee. Montgomery disengaged, and got a swinging blow on the ear as he did so. It had been a damaging round for him, and the Croxley people were shouting their delight.

"Gentlemen, I will *not* have this noise!"

Stapleton roared. " I have been accustomed to preside at a well-conducted club, and not at a bear-garden." This little man, with the tilted hat and the bulging forehead, dominated the whole assembly. He was like a headmaster among his boys. He glared round him, and nobody cared to meet his eye.

Anastasia had kissed the Master when he resumed his seat. " Good lass. Do't again !" cried the laughing crowd, and the angry Master shook his glove at her, as she flapped her towel in front of him. Montgomery was weary and a little sore, but not depressed. He had learned something. He would not again be tempted into danger.

For three rounds the honours were fairly equal. The student's hitting was the quicker, the Master's the harder. Profiting by his lesson, Montgomery kept himself in the open, and refused to be herded into a corner. Sometimes the Master succeeded in rushing him to the side-ropes, but the younger man slipped away, or closed and then disengaged. The monotonous " Break away ! Break away !" of the referee broke in upon the quick, low patter of rubber-soled shoes, the dull thud of the blows, and the sharp, hissing breath of two tired men.

The ninth round found both of them in fairly good condition. Montgomery's head

was still singing from the blow that he had in
the corner, and one of his thumbs pained him
acutely and seemed to be dislocated. The
Master showed no sign of a touch, but his
breathing was the more laboured, and a long
line of ticks upon the referee's paper showed
that the student had a good show of points.
But one of this iron-man's blows was worth
three of his, and he knew that without the
gloves he could not have stood for three rounds
against him. All the amateur work that he
had done was the merest tapping and flapping
when compared to those frightful blows, from
arms toughened by the shovel and the crowbar.

It was the tenth round, and the fight was
half over. The betting now was only three to
one, for the Wilson champion had held his own
much better than had been expected. But
those who knew the ringcraft as well as the
staying power of the old prize-fighter knew
that the odds were still a long way in his favour.

" Have a care of him ! " whispered Barton,
as he sent his man up to the scratch. " Have
a care ! He'll play thee a trick, if he can."

But Montgomery saw, or imagined he saw,
that his antagonist was tiring. He looked
jaded and listless, and his hands drooped a little
from their position. His own youth and condition were beginning to tell. He sprang in
and brought off a fine left-handed lead. The

Master's return lacked his usual fire. Again Montgomery led, and again he got home. Then he tried his right upon the mark, and the Master guarded it downwards.

" Too low ! Too low ! A foul ! A foul ! " yelled a thousand voices.

The referee rolled his sardonic eyes slowly round. " Seems to me this buildin' is chock-full of referees," said he.

The people laughed and applauded, but their favour was as immaterial to him as their anger.

" No applause, please ! This is not a theatre ! " he yelled.

Montgomery was very pleased with himself. His adversary was evidently in a bad way. He was piling on his points and establishing a lead. He might as well make hay while the sun shone. The Master was looking all abroad. Montgomery popped one upon his blue jowl and got away without a return. And then the Master suddenly dropped both his hands and began rubbing his thigh. Ah ! that was it, was it ? He had muscular cramp.

" Go in ! Go in ! " cried Teddy Barton.

Montgomery sprang wildly forward, and the next instant was lying half senseless, with his neck nearly broken, in the middle of the ring.

The whole round had been a long conspiracy to tempt him within reach of one of those terrible right-hand upper-cuts for which the Master was famous. For this the listless, weary bearing, for this the cramp in the thigh. When Montgomery had sprang in so hotly he had exposed himself to such a blow as neither flesh nor blood could stand. Whizzing up from below with a rigid arm, which put the Master's eleven stone into its force, it struck him under the jaw : he whirled half round, and fell a helpless and half-paralyzed mass. A vague groan and murmur, inarticulate, too excited for words, rose from the great audience. With open mouths and staring eyes they gazed at the twitching and quivering figure.

" Stand back ! Stand right back ! " shrieked the referee, for the Master was standing over his man ready to give him the *coup-de-grâce* as he rose.

" Stand back, Craggs, this instant ! " Stapleton repeated.

The Master sank his hands sulkily and walked backwards to the rope with his ferocious eyes fixed upon his fallen antagonist. The timekeeper called the seconds. If ten of them passed before Montgomery rose to his feet, the fight was ended. Ted Barton wrung his hands and danced about in an agony in his corner.

As if in a dream—a terrible nightmare—the student could hear the voice of the timekeeper —three—four—five—he got up on his hand—

six—seven—he was on his knee, sick, swimming, faint, but resolute to rise. Eight—he was up, and the Master was on him like a tiger, lashing savagely at him with both hands. Folk held their breath as they watched those terrible blows, and anticipated the pitiful end—so much more pitiful where a game but helpless man refuses to accept defeat.

Strangely automatic is the human brain. Without volition, without effort, there shot into the memory of this bewildered, staggering, half-stupefied man the one thing which could have saved him—that blind eye of which the Master's son had spoken. It was the same as the other to look at, but Montgomery remembered that he had said that it was the left. He reeled to the left side, half felled by a drive which lit upon his shoulder. The Master pivoted round upon his leg and was at him in an instant.

" Yark him, lad ! yark him ! " screamed the woman.

" Hold your tongue ! " said the referee.

Montgomery slipped to the left again and yet again ; but the Master was too quick and clever for him. He struck round and got him full on the face as he tried once more to break away. Montgomery's knees weakened under him, and he fell with a groan on the floor. This time he knew that he was done. With bitter agony he realized, as he groped blindly with his hands, that he could not possibly raise himself. Far away and muffled he heard, amid the murmurs of the multitude, the fateful voice of the timekeeper counting off the seconds.

"One—two—three—four—five—six——"

"Time!" said the referee.

Then the pent-up passion of the great assembly broke loose. Croxley gave a deep groan of disappointment. The Wilsons were on their feet, yelling with delight. There was still a chance for them. In four more seconds their man would have been solemnly counted out. But now he had a minute in which to recover. The referee looked round with relaxed features and laughing eyes. He loved this rough game, this school for humble heroes, and it was pleasant to him to intervene as a *Deux ex machinâ* at so dramatic a moment. His chair and his hat were both tilted at an extreme angle; he and the timekeeper smiled at each other. Ted Barton and the other second had rushed out and thrust an arm each under Montgomery's knee, the other behind his loins, and so carried him back to his stool. His head lolled upon his shoulder, but a douche of cold water sent a shiver through him, and he started and looked round him.

"He's a' right!" cried the people round.

" He's a rare brave lad. Good lad! Good
lad!" Barton poured some brandy into his
mouth. The mists cleared a little, and he realized where he was and what he had to do.
But he was still very weak, and he hardly dared
to hope that he could survive another round.

" Seconds out of the ring!" cried the referee. " Time!"

The Croxley Master sprang eagerly off his
stool.

"Keep clear of him! Go easy for a bit,"
said Barton, and Montgomery walked out to
meet his man once more.

He had had two lessons—the one when the
Master got him into his corner, the other when
he had been lured into mixing it up with so
powerful an antagonist. Now he would be
wary. Another blow would finish him; he
could afford to run no risks. The Master was
determined to follow up his advantage, and
rushed at him, slogging furiously right and
left. But Montgomery was too young and
active to be caught. He was strong upon his
legs once more, and his wits had all come back
to him. It was a gallant sight—the line-of-
battleship trying to pour its overwhelming
broadside into the frigate, and the frigate
manœuvring always so as to avoid it. The
Master tried all his ring-craft. He coaxed the
student up by pretended inactivity; he rushed

at him with furious rushes towards the ropes.
For three rounds he exhausted every wile in
trying to get at him. Montgomery during all
this time was conscious that his strength was
minute by minute coming back to him. The
spinal jar from an upper-cut is overwhelming,
but evanescent. He was losing all sense of
it beyond a great stiffness of the neck. For
the first round after his downfall he had been
content to be entirely on the defensive, only
too happy if he could stall off the furious at-
tacks of the Master. In the second he occasionally ventured upon a light counter. In
the third he was smacking back merrily where
he saw an opening. His people yelled their
approval of him at the end of every round.
Even the iron-workers cheered him with that
fine unselfishness which true sport engenders.
To most of them, unspiritual and unimagina-
tive, the sight of this clean-limbed young
Apollo, rising above disaster and holding on
while consciousness was in him to his appointed
task, was the greatest thing their experience
had ever known.

But the Master's naturally morose temper
became more and more murderous at this
postponement of his hopes. Three rounds ago
the battle had been in his hands ; now it was all
to do over again. Round by round his man
was recovering his strength. By the fifteenth

he was strong again in wind and limb. But the vigilant Anastasia saw something which encouraged her.

"That bash in t' ribs is telling on him, Jock," she whispered. "Why else should he be gulping t' brandy? Go in, lad, and thou hast him yet."

Montgomery had suddenly taken the flask from Barton's hand, and had a deep pull at the contents. Then, with his face a little flushed, and with a curious look of purpose, which made the referee stare hard at him, in his eyes, he rose for the sixteenth round.

"Game as a pairtridge!" cried the publican, as he looked at the hard-set face.

"Mix it oop, lad; mix it oop!" cried the iron-men to their Master.

And then a hum of exultation ran through their ranks as they realized that their tougher, harder, stronger man held the vantage, after all.

Neither of the men showed much sign of punishment. Small gloves crush and numb, but they do not cut. One of the Master's eyes was even more flush with his cheek than Nature had made it. Montgomery had two or three livid marks upon his body, and his face was haggard, save for that pink spot which the brandy had brought into either cheek. He rocked a little as he stood opposite his man, and his hands drooped as if he felt the gloves to be an unutterable weight. It was evident that he was spent and desperately weary. If he received one other blow it must surely be fatal to him. If he brought one home, what power could there be behind it, and what chance was there of its harming the colossus in front of him ? It was the crisis of the fight. This round must decide it. " Mix it oop, lad ; mix it oop ! " the iron-men whooped. Even the savage eyes of the referee were unable to restrain the excited crowd.

Now, at last, the chance had come for Montgomery. He had learned a lesson from his more experienced rival. Why should he not play his own game upon him ? He was spent, but not nearly so spent as he pretended. That brandy was to call up his reserves, to let him have strength to take full advantage of the opening when it came. It was thrilling and tingling through his veins, at the very moment when he was lurching and rocking like a beaten man. He acted his part admirably. The Master felt that there was an easy task before him, and rushed in with ungainly activity to finish it once for all. He slap-banged away left and right, boring Montgomery up against the ropes, swinging in his ferocious blows with those animal grunts which told of the vicious energy behind them.

But Montgomery was too cool to fall a victim to any of those murderous upper-cuts. He kept out of harm's way with a rigid guard, an active foot, and a head which was swift to duck. And yet he contrived to present the same appearance of a man who is hopelessly done. The Master, weary from his own shower of blows, and fearing nothing from so weak a man, dropped his hand for an instant, and at that instant Montgomery's right came home.

It was a magnificent blow, straight, clean, crisp, with the force of the loins and the back behind it. And it landed where he had meant it to—upon the exact point of that blue-grained chin. Flesh and blood could not stand such a blow in such a place. Neither valour nor hardihood can save the man to whom it comes. The Master fell backwards, flat, prostrate, striking the ground with so simultaneous a clap that it was like a shutter falling from a wall. A yell which no referee could control broke from the crowded benches as the giant went down. He lay upon his back, his knees a little drawn up, his huge chest panting. He twitched and shook, but could not move. His feet pawed convulsively once or twice. It was no use. He was done. " Eight—nine—ten ! " said the timekeeper, and the roar of a thousand voices, with a deafening clap like the broadside

of a ship, told that the Master of Croxley was
the Master no more.

Montgomery stood half dazed, looking down
at the huge, prostrate figure. He could hardly
realize that it was indeed all over. He saw the
referee motion towards him with his hand. He
heard his name bellowed in triumph from every
side. And then he was aware of some one
rushing towards him ; he caught a glimpse of a
flushed face and an aureole of flying red hair,
a gloveless fist struck him between the eyes,
and he was on his back in the ring beside his
antagonist, while a dozen of his supporters
were endeavouring to secure the frantic Anastasia. He heard the angry shouting of the
referee, the screaming of the furious woman,
and the cries of the mob. Then something
seemed to break like an over-stretched banjo-
string, and he sank into the deep, deep, mist-
girt abyss of unconsciousness.

The dressing was like a thing in a dream,
and so was a vision of the Master with the grin
of a bulldog upon his face, and his three teeth
amiably protruded. He shook Montgomery
heartily by the hand.

" I would have been rare pleased to shake
thee by the throttle, lad, a short while syne,"
said he. " But I bear no ill-feelin' again' thee.
It was a rare poonch that brought me down—
I have not had a better since my second fight

wi' Billy Edwards in '89. Happen thou might think o' goin' further wi' this business. If thou dost, and want a trainer, there's not much inside t' ropes as I don't know. Or happen thou might like to try it wi' me old style and bare knuckles. Thou hast but to write to t' iron-works to find me."

But Montgomery disclaimed any such ambition. A canvas bag with his share—one hundred and ninety sovereigns—was handed to him, of which he gave ten to the Master, who also received some share of the gate-money.

Then, with young Wilson escorting him on one side, Purvis on the other, and Fawcett carrying his bag behind, he went in triumph to his carriage, and drove amid a long roar, which lined the highway like a hedge for the seven miles, back to his starting-point.

" It's the greatest thing I ever saw in my life. By George, it's ripping!" cried Wilson, who had been left in a kind of ecstasy by the events of the day. " There's a chap over Barnsley way who fancies himself a bit. Let us spring you on him, and let him see what he can make of you. We'll put up a purse—won't we, Purvis? You shall never want a backer."

" At his weight," said the publican, " I'm behind him, I am, for twenty rounds, and no age, country, or color barred."

" So am I!" cried Fawcett; " middle-weight

champion of the world, that's what he is—here, in the same carriage with us. "

But Montgomery was not to be beguiled.

" No ; I have my own work to do now."

" And what may that be ? "

" I'll use this money to get my medical degree."

" Well, we've plenty of doctors, but you're the only man in the Riding that could smack the Croxley Master off his legs. However, I suppose you know your own business best. When you're a doctor, you'd best come down into these parts, and you'll always find a job waiting for you at the Wilson Coal-pits."

Montgomery had returned by devious ways to the surgery. The horses were smoking at the door, and the doctor was just back from his long journey. Several patients had called in his absence, and he was in the worst of tempers.

" I suppose I should be glad that you have come back at all, Mr. Montgomery ! " he snarled. " When next you elect to take a holiday, I trust it will not be at so busy a time."

" I am sorry, sir, that you should have been inconvenienced."

" Yes, sir, I have been exceedingly inconvenienced." Here, for the first time, he looked hard at the assistant. " Good heavens, Mr.

Montgomery, what have you been doing with your left eye ? "

It was where Anastasia had lodged her protest.

Montgomery laughed. " It is nothing, sir," said he.

"And you have a livid mark under your jaw. It is, indeed, terrible that my representative should be going about in so disreputable a condition. How did you receive these injuries ? "

" Well, sir, as you know, there was a little glove-fight to-day over at Croxley."

"And you got mixed up with that brutal crowd ? "

" I *was* rather mixed up with them."

"And who assaulted you ? "

" One of the fighters."

" Which of them ? "

" The Master of Croxley."

" Good heavens ! Perhaps you interfered with him ? "

" Well, to tell the truth, I did a little."

" Mr. Montgomery, in such a practice as mine, intimately associated as it is with the highest and most progressive elements of our small community, it is impossible——"

But just then the tentative bray of a cornet-player searching for his keynote jarred upon their ears, and an instant later the Wilson Colliery brass band was in full cry with, " See the

Conquering Hero Comes," outside the surgery
window. There was a banner waving, and a
shouting crowd of miners.

"What is it? What does it mean?" cried
the angry doctor.

"It means, sir, that I have, in the only way
which was open to me, earned the money which
is necessary for my education. It is my duty,
Doctor Oldacre, to warn you that I am about
to return to the University, and that you should
lose no time in appointing my successor."

THE "SLAPPING SAL"

IT was in the days when France's power was already broken upon the seas, and when more of her three-deckers lay rotting in the Medway than were to be found in Brest harbour. But her frigates and corvettes still scoured the ocean, closely followed ever by those of her rival. At the uttermost ends of the earth these dainty vessels, with sweet names of girls or of flowers, mangled and shattered each other for the honour of the four yards of bunting which flapped from the end of their gaffs.

It had blown hard in the night, but the wind had dropped with the dawning, and now the rising sun tinted the fringe of the storm-wrack as it dwindled into the west and glinted on the endless crests of the long, green waves. To north and south and west lay a skyline which was unbroken save by the spout of foam when two of the great Atlantic seas dashed each other into spray. To the east was a rocky island, jutting out into craggy points, with a few scat-

tered clumps of palm trees and a pennant of
mist streaming out from the bare, conical hill
which capped it. A heavy surf beat upon the
shore, and, at a safe distance from it, the British
32-gun frigate *Leda*, Captain A. P. Johnson,
raised her black, glistening side upon the crest
of a wave, or swooped down into an emerald
valley, dipping away to the nor'ard under easy
sail. On her snow-white quarter-deck stood a
stiff little brown-faced man, who swept the
horizon with his glass.

" Mr. Wharton ! " he cried, with a voice like
a rusty hinge.

A thin, knock-kneed officer shambled across
the poop to him.

" Yes, sir."

" I've opened the sealed orders, Mr. Wharton."

A glimmer of curiosity shone upon the
meagre features of the first lieutenant. The
Leda had sailed with her consort, the *Dido*,
from Antigua the week before, and the admiral's
orders had been contained in a sealed envelope.

" We were to open them on reaching the
deserted island of Sombriero, lying in north
latitude eighteen, thirty-six, west longitude sixty-
three, twenty-eight. Sombriero bore four miles
to the north-east from our port-bow when the
gale cleared, Mr. Wharton."

The lieutenant bowed stiffly. He and the

captain had been bosom friends from childhood. They had gone to school together, joined the navy together, fought again and again together, and married into each other's families, but so long as their feet were on the poop the iron discipline of the service struck all that was human out of them and left only the superior and the subordinate. Captain Johnson took from his pocket a blue paper, which crackled as he unfolded it.

" The 32-gun frigates *Leda* and *Dido* (Captains A. P. Johnson and James Munro) are to cruise from the point at which these instructions are read to the mouth of the Caribbean Sea, in the hope of encountering the French frigate *La Gloire* (48), which has recently harassed our merchant ships in that quarter. H.M. frigates are also directed to hunt down the piratical craft known sometimes as the *Slapping Sal* and sometimes as the *Hairy Hudson*, which has plundered the British ships as per margin, inflicting barbarities upon their crews. She is a small brig, carrying ten light guns, with one twenty-four pound carronade forward. She was last seen upon the 23rd ult. to the north-east of the island of Sombriero.

" (Signed) JAMES MONTGOMERY
" (*Rear Admiral*).
" H.M.S. *Colossus*, Antigua."

" We appear to have lost our consort," said
Captain Johnson, folding up his instructions
and again sweeping the horizon with his glass.
" She drew away after we reefed down. It
would be a pity if we met this heavy Frenchman without the *Dido*, Mr. Wharton. Eh ? "

The lieutenant twinkled and smiled.

" She has eighteen-pounders on the main and
twelves on the poop, sir," said the captain.
" She carries four hundred to our two hundred
and thirty-one. Captain de Milon is the
smartest man in the French service. Oh,
Bobby boy, I'd give my hopes of my flag to
rub my side up against her ! " He turned on
his heel, ashamed of his momentary lapse.
" Mr. Wharton," said he, looking back sternly
over his shoulder, " get those square sails
shaken out and bear away a point more to the
west."

" A brig on the port-bow," came a voice
from the forecastle.

" A brig on the port-bow," said the lieutenant.

The captain sprang upon the bulwarks and
held on by the mizzen-shrouds, a strange little
figure with flying skirts and puckered eyes.
The lean lieutenant craned his neck and whispered to Smeaton, the second, while officers
and men came popping up from below and
clustered along the weather-rail, shading their

eyes with their hands—for the tropical sun was already clear of the palm trees. The strange brig lay at anchor in the throat of a curving estuary, and it was already obvious that she could not get out without passing under the guns of the frigate. A long, rocky point to the north of her held her in.

" Keep her as she goes, Mr. Wharton," said the captain. " Hardly worth while our clearing for action, Mr. Smeaton, but the men can stand by the guns in case she tries to pass us. Cast loose the bow-chasers and send the small-arm men to the forecastle."

A British crew went to its quarters in those days with the quiet serenity of men on their daily routine. In a few minutes, without fuss or sound ,the sailors were knotted round their guns, the marines were drawn up and leaning on their muskets, and the frigate's bowsprit pointed straight for her little victim.

" Is it the *Slapping Sal*, sir ? "

" I have no doubt of it, Mr. Wharton."

" They don't seem to like the look of us, sir. They've cut their cable and are clapping on sail."

It was evident that the brig meant struggling for her freedom. One little patch of canvas fluttered out above another, and her people could be seen working like madmen in the rig-ging. She made no attempt to pass her antag-

onist, but headed up the estuary. The captain
rubbed his hands.

" She's making for shoal water, Mr. Wharton, and we shall have to cut her out, sir. She's
a footy little brig, but I should have thought a
fore-and-after would have been more handy."

" It was a mutiny, sir."

" Ah, indeed ! "

" Yes, sir, I heard of it at Manilla : a bad
business, sir. Captain and two mates murdered.
This Hudson, or Hairy Hudson, as they call
him, led the mutiny. He's a Londoner, sir,
and a cruel villain as ever walked."

" His next walk will be to Execution Dock,
Mr. Wharton. She seems heavily manned. I
wish I could take twenty topmen out of her, but
they would be enough to corrupt the crew of
the ark, Mr. Wharton."

Both officers were looking through their
glasses at the brig. Suddenly the lieutenant
showed his teeth in a grin, while the captain
flushed a deeper red.

" That's Hairy Hudson on the after-rail,
sir."

" The low, impertinent blackguard ! He'll
play some other antics before we are done with
him. Could you reach him with the long eighteen, Mr. Smeaton ? "

" Another cable length will do it, sir."

The brig yawed as they spoke, and as she

came round a spurt of smoke whiffed out from her quarter. It was a pure piece of bravado, for the gun could scarce carry half-way. Then with a jaunty swing the little ship came into the wind again, and shot round a fresh curve in the winding channel.

" The water's shoaling rapidly, sir, " repeated the second lieutenant.

" There's six fathoms by the chart. "

" Four by the lead, sir. "

" When we clear this point we shall see how we lie. Ha! I thought as much! Lay her to, Mr. Wharton. Now we have got her at our mercy! "

The frigate was quite out of sight of the sea now at the head of this river-like estuary. As she came round the curve the two shores were seen to converge at a point about a mile distant. In the angle, as near shore as she could get, the brig was lying with her broadside towards her pursuer and a wisp of black cloth streaming from her mizzen. The lean lieutenant, who had reappeared upon deck with a cutlass strapped to his side and two pistols rammed into his belt, peered curiously at the ensign.

" Is it the Jolly Rodger, sir? " he asked.

But the captain was furious.

" He may hang where his breeches are hanging before I have done with him! " said he. " What boats will you want, Mr. Wharton? "

" We should do it with the launch and the jolly-boat."

" Take four and make a clean job of it. Pipe away the crews at once, and I'll work her in and help you with the long eighteens."

With a rattle of ropes and a creaking of blocks the four boats splashed into the water. Their crews clustered thickly into them : bare-footed sailors, stolid marines, laughing middies, and in the sheets of each the senior officers with their stern schoolmaster faces. The captain, his elbows on the binnacle, still watched the distant brig. Her crew were tricing up the boarding-netting, dragging round the starboard guns, knocking new portholes for them, and making every preparation for a desperate resist-ance. In the thick of it all a huge man, bearded to the eyes, with a red nightcap upon his head, was straining and stooping and haul-ing. The captain watched him with a sour smile, and then snapping up his glass he turned upon his heel. For an instant he stood staring.

" Call back the boats ! " he cried in his thin, creaking voice. " Clear away for action there ! Cast loose those main-deck guns. Brace back the yards, Mr. Smeaton, and stand by to go about when she has weigh enough."

Round the curve of the estuary was coming a huge vessel. Her great yellow bowsprit and white-winged figure-head were jutting out from

the cluster of palm trees, while high above
them towered three immense masts with the
tricolour flag floating superbly from the mizzen.
Round she came, the deep-blue water creaming
under her fore foot, until her long, curving,
black side, her line of shining copper beneath
and of snow-white hammocks above, and the
thick clusters of men who peered over her
bulwarks, were all in full view. Her lower
yards were slung, her ports triced up, and her
guns run out all ready for action. Lying behind one of the promontories of the island, the
lookout men of the *Gloire* upon the shore had
seen the *cul de sac* into which the British frigate
was headed, so that Captain de Milon had
served the *Leda* as Captain Johnson had the
Slapping Sal.

But the splendid discipline of the British
service was at its best in such a crisis. The
boats flew back; their crews clustered aboard,
they were swung up at the davits and the fall-
ropes made fast. Hammocks were brought up
and stowed, bulkheads sent down, ports and
magazines opened, the fires put out in the galley, and the drums beat to quarters. Swarms
of men set the head-sails and brought the
frigate round, while the gun-crews threw off
their jackets and shirts, tightened their belts,
and ran out their eighteen-pounders, peering
through the open portholes at the stately

Frenchman. The wind was very light. Hardly
a ripple showed itself upon the clear blue
water, but the sails blew gently out as the
breeze came over the wooded banks. The
Frenchman had gone about also, and both
ships were now heading slowly for the sea under fore-and-aft canvas, the *Gloire* a hundred
yards in advance. She luffed up to cross the
Leda's bows, but the British ship came round
also, and the two rippled slowly on in such a
silence that the ringing of the ramrods as the
French marines drove home their charges
clanged quite loudly upon the ear.

" Not much sea-room, Mr. Wharton," remarked the captain.

" I have fought actions in less, sir."

" We must keep our distance and trust to
our gunnery. She is very heavily manned,
and if she got alongside we might find ourselves in trouble."

" I see the shakoes of soldiers aboard of
her."

" Two companies of light infantry from
Martinique. Now we have her ! Hard-a-
port, and let her have it as we cross her stern ! "

The keen eye of the little commander had
seen the surface ripple, which told of a passing
breeze. He had used it to dart across the big
Frenchman and to rake her with every gun as
he passed. But, once past her, the *Leda* had

to come back into the wind to keep out of shoal water. The manœuvre brought her on to the starboard side of the Frenchman, and the trim little frigate seemed to heel right over under the crashing broadside which burst from the gaping ports. A moment later her topmen were swarming aloft to set her topsails and royals, and she strove to cross the *Gloire's* bows and rake her again. The French captain, however, brought his frigate's head round, and the two rode side by side within easy pistol-shot, pouring broadsides into each other in one of those murderous duels which, could they all be recorded, would mottle our charts with blood.

In that heavy tropical air, with so faint a breeze, the smoke formed a thick bank round the two vessels, from which the topmasts only protruded. Neither could see anything of its enemy save the throbs of fire in the darkness, and the guns were sponged and trained and fired into a dense wall of vapour. On the poop and the forecastle the marines, in two little red lines, were pouring in their volleys, but neither they nor the seaman-gunners could see what effect their fire was having. Nor, indeed, could they tell how far they were suffering themselves, for, standing at a gun, one could but hazily see that upon the right and the left. But above the roar of the cannon came the sharper sound of the piping shot, the crashing of riven planks, and the occasional heavy thud as spar or block came hurtling on to the deck. The lieutenants paced up and down the line of guns, while Captain Johnson fanned the smoke away with his cocked hat and peered eagerly out.

" This is rare, Bobby ! " said he, as the lieutenant joined him. Then, suddenly restraining himself, " What have we lost, Mr. Wharton ? "

" Out maintopsail yard and our gaff, sir."

" Where's the flag ? "

" Gone overboard, sir."

" They'll think we've struck ! Lash a boat's ensign on the starboard arm of the mizzen cross-jack-yard."

" Yes, sir."

A round shot dashed the binnacle to pieces between them. A second knocked two marines into a bloody, palpitating mash. For a moment the smoke rose, and the English captain saw that his adversary's heavier metal was producing a horrible effect. The *Leda* was a shattered wreck. Her deck was strewed with corpses. Several of her portholes were knocked into one, and one of her eighteen-pounder guns had been thrown right back on to her breech, and pointed straight up to the sky. The thin line of marines still loaded and fired, but half the guns were silent, and their crews were piled thickly round them.

" Stand by to repel boarders ! " yelled the captain.

" Cutlasses, lads, cutlasses ! " roared Wharton.

" Hold your volley till they touch ! " cried the captain of marines.

The huge loom of the Frenchman was seen bursting through the smoke. Thick clusters of boarders hung upon her sides and shrouds. A final broadside leapt from her ports, and the mainmast of the *Leda*, snapping short off a few feet above the deck, spun into the air and crashed down upon the port guns, killing ten men and putting the whole battery out of action. An instant later the two ships scraped together, and the starboard bower anchor of the *Gloire* caught the mizzen-chains of the *Leda* upon the port side. With a yell the black swarm of boarders steadied themselves for a spring.

But their feet were never to reach that blood-stained deck. From somewhere there came a well-aimed whiff of grape, and another, and another. The English marines and seamen, waiting with cutlass and musket behind the silent guns, saw with amazement the dark masses thinning and shredding away. At the same time the port broadside of the Frenchman burst into a roar.

" Clear away the wreck ! " roared the captain. " What the devil are they firing at ? "

" Get the guns clear ! " panted the lieutenant.   " We'll do them yet, boys."

The wreckage was torn and hacked and splintered until first one gun and then another roared
into action again.   The Frenchman's anchor
had been cut away, and the *Leda* had worked
herself free from that fatal hug.   But now, suddenly, there was a scurry up the shrouds of the
Gloire, and a hundred Englishmen were shouting themselves hoarse : " They're running !
They're running !   They're running ! "

And it was true.   The Frenchman had ceased
to fire, and was intent only upon clapping on
every sail that he could carry.   But that shouting hundred could not claim it all as their own.
As the smoke cleared it was not difficult to see
the reason.   The ships had gained the mouth
of the estuary during the fight, and there, about
four miles out to sea, was the *Leda's* consort
bearing down under full sail to the sound of the
guns.   Captain de Milon had done his part for
one day, and presently the *Gloire* was drawing
off swiftly to the north, while the *Dido* was
bowling along at her skirts, rattling away with
her bow-chasers, until a headland hid them both
from view.

But the *Leda* lay sorely stricken, with her
mainmast gone, her bulwarks shattered, her
mizzen-topmast and gaff shot away, her sails
like a beggar's rags, and a hundred of her crew

dead and wounded. Close beside her a mass of wreckage floated upon the waves. It was the stern-post of a mangled vessel, and across it, in white letters on a black ground, was printed, " *The Slapping Sal.*"

" By the Lord ! it was the brig that saved us!" cried Mr. Wharton. " Hudson brought her into action with the Frenchman, and was blown out of the water by a broadside ! "

The little captain turned on his heel and paced up and down the deck. Already his crew were plugging the shot-holes, knotting and splicing and mending. When he came back, the lieutenant saw a softening of the stern lines about his eyes and mouth.

" Are they all gone ? "

" Every man. They must have sunk with the wreck. "

The two officers looked down at the sinister name, and at the stump of wreckage which floated in the discoloured water. Something black washed to and fro beside a splintered gaff and a tangle of halliards. It was the outrageous ensign, and near it a scarlet cap was floating.

" He was a villain, but he was a Briton ! " said the captain, at last. " He lived like a dog, but, by God, he died like a man ! "

THE LORD OF CHÂTEAU NOIR

IT was in the days when the German armies had broken their way across France, and when the shattered forces of the young Republic had been swept away to the north of the Aisne and to the south of the Loire. Three broad streams of armed men had rolled slowly but irresistibly from the Rhine, now meandering to the north, now to the south, dividing, coalescing, but all uniting to form one great lake round Paris. And from this lake there welled out smaller streams, one to the north, one southward to Orleans, and a third westward to Normandy. Many a German trooper saw the sea for the first time when he rode his horse girth-deep into the waves at Dieppe.

Black and bitter were the thoughts of Frenchmen when they saw this weal of dishonour slashed across the fair face of their country. They had fought and they had been overborne. That swarming cavalry, those countless footmen, the masterful guns—they had tried and

tried to make head against them. In battalions
their invaders were not to be beaten ; but man
to man, or ten to ten, they were their equals.
A brave Frenchman might still make a single
German rue the day that he had left his own
bank of the Rhine. Thus, unchronicled amid
the battles and the sieges, there broke out another war, a war of individuals, with foul murder upon the one side and brutal reprisal on
the other.

Colonel von Gramm, of the 24th Posen Infantry, had suffered severely during this new
development. He commanded in the little
Norman town of Les Andelys, and his out-
posts stretched amid the hamlets and farm-
houses of the district round. No French force
was within fifty miles of him, and yet morning
after morning he had to listen to a black report
of sentries found dead at their posts, or of forag-
ing parties which had never returned. Then the
Colonel would go forth in his wrath, and farm-
steadings would blaze and villages tremble ; but
next morning there was still that same dismal
tale to be told. Do what he might, he could
not shake off his invisible enemies. And yet,
it should not have been so hard, for from certain signs in common, in the plan and in the
deed, it was certain that all these outrages came
from a single source.

Colonel von Gramm had tried violence and

it had failed. Gold might be more successful. He published it abroad over the countryside that five hundred francs would be paid for information. There was no response. Then eight hundred. The peasants were incorruptible. Then, goaded on by a murdered corporal, he rose to a thousand, and so bought the soul of François Rejane, farm labourer, whose Norman avarice was a stronger passion than his French hatred.

"You say that you know who did these crimes?" asked the Prussian Colonel, eyeing with loathing the blue-bloused, rat-faced creature before him.

"Yes, Colonel."

"And it was—— ?"

"Those thousand francs, Colonel——"

"Not a sou until your story has been tested. Come! Who is it who has murdered my men?"

"It is Count Eustace of Château Noir."

"You lie!" cried the Colonel, angrily. "A gentleman and a nobleman could not have done such crimes."

The peasant shrugged his shoulders.

"It is evident to me that you do not know the Count. It is this way, Colonel. What I tell you is the truth, and I am not afraid that you should test it. The Count of Château Noir is a hard man: even at the best time he was a hard man. But of late he has been terrible. It was his son's death, you know. His son was under Douay, and he was taken, and then in escaping from Germany he met his death. It was the Count's only child, and indeed we all think that it has driven him mad. With his peasants he follows the German armies. I do not know how many he has killed, but it is he who cuts the cross upon the foreheads, for it is the badge of his house."

It was true. The murdered sentries had each had a saltire cross slashed across their brows, as by a hunting-knife. The Colonel bent his stiff back and ran his forefinger over the map which lay upon the table.

"The Château Noir is not more than four leagues," he said.

"Three and a kilomètre, Colonel."

"You know the place?"

"I used to work there."

Colonel von Gramm rang the bell.

"Give this man food and detain him," said he to the sergeant.

"Why detain me, Colonel? I can tell you no more."

"We shall need you as guide."

"As guide! But the Count? If I were to fall into his hands? Ah, Colonel——"

The Prussian commander waved him away.

"Send Captain Baumgarten to me at once," said he.

The officer who answered the summons was a man of middle age, heavy-jawed, blue-eyed, with a curving yellow moustache, and a brick-red face which turned to an ivory white where his helmet had sheltered it. He was bald, with a shining, tightly-stretched scalp, at the back of which, as in a mirror, it was a favourite mess-joke of the subalterns to trim their moustaches. As a soldier he was slow, but reliable and brave. The Colonel could trust him where a more dashing officer might be in danger.

"You will proceed to Château Noir to-night, Captain," said he. "A guide has been provided. You will arrest the Count and bring him back. If there is an attempt at rescue, shoot him at once."

"How many men shall I take, Colonel?"

"Well, we are surrounded by spies, and our only chance is to pounce upon him before he knows that we are on the way. A large force will attract attention. On the other hand, you must not risk being cut off."

"I might march north, Colonel, as if to join General Goeben. Then I could turn down this road which I see upon your map, and get to Château Noir before they could hear of us. In that case, with twenty men———"

" Very good, Captain. I hope to see you with your prisoner to-morrow morning."

It was a cold December night when Captain Baumgarten marched out of Les Andelys with his twenty Poseners, and took the main road to the north-west. Two miles out he turned suddenly down a narrow, deeply-rutted track, and made swiftly for his man. A thin, cold rain was falling, swishing among the tall poplar trees and rustling in the fields on either side. The Captain walked first with Moser, a veteran sergeant, beside him. The sergeant's wrist was fastened to that of the French peasant, and it had been whispered in his ear that in case of an ambush the first bullet fired would be through his head. Behind them the twenty infantry-men plodded along through the darkness with their faces sunk to the rain, and their boots squeaking in the soft, wet clay. They knew where they were going and why, and the thought upheld them, for they were bitter at the loss of their comrades. It was a cavalry job, they knew, but the cavalry were all on with the advance, and, besides, it was more fitting that the regiment should avenge its own dead men.

It was nearly eight when they left Les Andelys. At half-past eleven their guide stopped at a place where two high pillars, crowned with some heraldic stonework, flanked a huge iron gate. The wall in which it had been the opening had crumbled away, but the great gate still towered above the brambles and weeds which had overgrown its base. The Prussians made their way round it, and advanced stealthily, under the shadow of a tunnel of oak branches, up the long avenue, which was still cumbered by the leaves of last autumn. At the top they halted and reconnoitred.

The black château lay in front of them. The moon had shone out between two rain-clouds, and threw the old house into silver and shadow. It was shaped like an L, with a low arched door in front, and lines of small windows like the open ports of a man-of-war. Above was a dark roof breaking at the corners into little round overhanging turrets, the whole lying silent in the moonshine, with a drift of ragged clouds blackening the heavens behind it. A single light gleamed in one of the lower windows.

The Captain whispered his orders to his men. Some were to creep to the front door, some to the back. Some were to watch the east, and some the west. He and the sergeant stole on tiptoe to the lighted window.

It was a small room into which they looked, very meanly furnished. An elderly man in the dress of a menial was reading a tattered paper by the light of a guttering candle. He leaned back in his wooden chair with his feet upon a box, while a bottle of white wine stood with a

half-filled tumbler upon a stool beside him.
The sergeant thrust his needle-gun through the
glass, and the man sprang to his feet with a
shriek.

"Silence, for your life! The house is surrounded and you cannot escape. Come round
and open the door, or we will show you no
mercy when we come in."

"For God's sake, don't shoot! I will open
it! I will open it!" He rushed from the
room with his paper still crumpled up in his
hand. An instant later, with a groaning of old
locks and a rasping of bars, the low door swung
open, and the Prussians poured into the stone-
flagged passage.

"Where is Count Eustace de Château
Noir?"

"My master! He is out, sir."

"Out at this time of night? Your life for a
lie!"

"It is true, sir. He is out."

"Where?"

"I do not know."

"Doing what?"

"I cannot tell. No, it is no use your cocking your pistol, sir. You may kill me, but
you cannot make me tell you that which I do
not know."

"Is he often out at this hour?"

"Frequently."

" And when does he come home ? "

" Before daybreak."

Captain Baumgarten rasped out a German oath. He had had his journey for nothing, then. The man's answers were only too likely to be true. It was what he might have expected. But at least he would search the house and make sure. Leaving a picket at the front door and another at the back, the sergeant and he drove the trembling butler in front of them —his shaking candle sending strange, flickering shadows over the old tapestries and the low, oak-raftered ceilings. They searched the whole house, from the huge, stone-flagged kitchen below to the dining-hall on the second floor with its gallery for musicians, and its panelling black with age, but nowhere was there a living creature. Up above in an attic they found Marie, the elderly wife of the butler; but the owner kept no other servants, and of his own presence there was no trace.

It was long, however, before Captain Baumgarten had satisfied himself upon the point. It was a difficult house to search. Thin stairs, which only one man could ascend at a time, connected lines of tortuous corridors. The walls were so thick that each room was cut off from its neighbour. Huge fireplaces yawned in each, while the windows were six feet deep in the wall. Captain Baumgarten stamped with his feet, and tore down curtains, and struck with the pommel of his sword. If there were secret hiding-places, he was not fortunate enough to find them.

" I have an idea," said he, at last, speaking in German to the sergeant. " You will place a guard over this fellow, and make sure that he communicates with no one."

" Yes, Captain."

" And you will place four men in ambush at the front and at the back. It is likely enough that about daybreak our bird may return to the nest."

" And the others, Captain ? "

" Let them have their suppers in the kitchen. This fellow will serve you with meat and wine. It is a wild night, and we shall be better here than on the country road."

" And yourself, Captain ? "

" I will take my supper up here in the dining-hall. The logs are laid and we can light the fire. You will call me if there is any alarm. What can you give me for supper—you ? "

" Alas, monsieur, there was a time when I might have answered, ' What you wish !' but now it is all that we can do to find a bottle of new claret and a cold pullet."

" That will do very well. Let a guard go about with him, sergeant, and let him feel the end of a bayonet if he plays us any tricks."

Captain Baumgarten was an old campaigner. In the Eastern provinces, and before that in Bohemia, he had learned the art of quartering himself upon the enemy. While the butler brought his supper he occupied himself in making his preparations for a comfortable night. He lit the candelabrum of ten candles upon the centre table. The fire was already burning up, crackling merrily, and sending spurts of blue, pungent smoke into the room. The Captain walked to the window and looked out. The moon had gone in again, and it was raining heavily. He could hear the deep sough of the wind and see the dark loom of the trees, all swaying in the one direction. It was a sight which gave a zest to his comfortable quarters, and to the cold fowl and the bottle of wine which the butler had brought up for him. He was tired and hungry after his long tramp, so he threw his sword, his helmet, and his revolver-belt down upon a chair, and fell to eagerly upon his supper. Then, with his glass of wine before him and his cigar between his lips, he tilted his chair back and looked about him.

He sat within a small circle of brilliant light which gleamed upon his silver shoulder-straps, and threw out his terra-cotta face, his heavy eyebrows, and his yellow moustache. But outside that circle things were vague and shadowy in the old dining-hall. Two sides were oak-panelled and two were hung with faded tapestry, across which huntsmen and dogs and stags were still dimly streaming. Above the fireplace were rows of heraldic shields with the blazonings of the family and of its alliances, the fatal saltire cross breaking out on each of them.

Four paintings of old seigneurs of Château Noir faced the fireplace, all men with hawk noses and bold, high features, so like each other that only the dress could distinguish the Crusader from the Cavalier of the Fronde. Captain Baumgarten, heavy with his repast, lay back in his chair looking up at them through the clouds of his tobacco smoke, and pondering over the strange chance which had sent him, a man from the Baltic coast, to eat his supper in the ancestral hall of these proud Norman chieftains. But the fire was hot, and the Captain's eyes were heavy. His chin sank slowly upon his chest, and the ten candles gleamed upon the broad white scalp.

Suddenly a slight noise brought him to his feet. For an instant it seemed to his dazed senses that one of the pictures opposite had walked from its frame. There, beside the table, and almost within arm's length of him, was standing a huge man, silent, motionless, with no sign of life save his fierce, glinting eyes. He was black-haired, olive-skinned, with a pointed tuft of black beard, and a great, fierce nose, towards which all his features seemed to run. His cheeks were wrinkled like a last year's apple, but his sweep of shoulder, and bony, corded hands, told of a strength which was unsapped by age. His arms were folded across his arching chest, and his mouth was set in a fixed smile.

"Pray do not trouble yourself to look for your weapons," he said, as the Prussian cast a swift glance at the empty chair in which they had been laid. "You have been, if you will allow me to say so, a little indiscreet to make yourself so much at home in a house every wall of which is honeycombed with secret passages. You will be amused to hear that forty men were watching you at your supper. Ah! what then?"

Captain Baumgarten had taken a step forward with clenched fists. The Frenchman held up the revolver which he grasped in his right hand, while with the left he hurled the German back into his chair.

"Pray keep your seat," said he. "You have no cause to trouble about your men. They have already been provided for. It is astonishing with these stone floors how little one can hear what goes on beneath. You have been relieved of your command, and have now only to think of yourself. May I ask what your name is?"

"I am Captain Baumgarten, of the 24th Posen Regiment."

"Your French is excellent, though you incline, like most of your countrymen, to turn the 'p' into a 'b.' I have been amused to hear them cry 'avez bitié sur moi!' You know, doubtless, who it is who addresses you."

"The Count of Château Noir."

"Precisely. It would have been a misfortune if you had visited my château and I had been unable to have a word with you. I have had to do with many German soldiers, but never with an officer before. I have much to talk to you about."

Captain Baumgarten sat still in his chair. Brave as he was, there was something in this man's manner which made his skin creep with apprehension. His eyes glanced to right and to left, but his weapons were gone, and in a struggle he saw that he was but a child to this gigantic adversary. The Count had picked up the claret bottle and held it to the light.

"Tut! tut!" said he. "And was this the best that Pierre could do for you? I am ashamed to look you in the face, Captain Baumgarten. We must improve upon this."

He blew a call upon a whistle, which hung

from his shooting-jacket. The old manservant
was in the room in an instant.

"Chambertin from bin 15!" he cried, and
a minute later a grey bottle streaked with cob-
webs was carried in as a nurse bears an infant.
The Count filled two glasses to the brim.

"Drink!" said he. "It is the very best in
my cellars, and not to be matched between
Rouen and Paris. Drink, sir, and be happy!
There are cold joints below. There are two
lobsters fresh from Honfleur. Will you
not venture upon a second and more savoury
supper?"

The German officer shook his head. He
drained the glass, however, and his host filled it
once more, pressing him to give an order for
this or that dainty.

"There is nothing in my house which is not
at your disposal. You have but to say the word.
Well, then, you will allow me to tell you a story
while you drink your wine. I have so longed
to tell it to some German officer. It is about
my son, my only child, Eustace, who was taken
and died in escaping. It is a curious little
story, and I think that I can promise you that
you will never forget it.

"You must know, then, that my boy was in
the artillery, a fine young fellow, Captain Baumgarten, and the pride of his mother. She died
within a week of the news of his death reaching

us. It was brought by a brother officer who was at his side throughout, and who escaped while my lad died. I want to tell you all that he told me.

"Eustace was taken at Weissenburg on the 4th of August. The prisoners were broken up into parties, and sent back into Germany by different routes. Eustace was taken upon the 5th to a village called Lauterburg, where he met with kindness from the German officer in command. This good Colonel had the hungry lad to supper, offered him the best he had, opened a bottle of good wine, as I have tried to do for you, and gave him a cigar from his own case. Might I entreat you to take one from mine?"

The German again shook his head. His horror of his companion had increased as he sat watching the lips that smiled and the eyes that glared.

"The Colonel, as I say, was good to my boy. But, unluckily, the prisoners were moved next day across the Rhine to Ettlingen. They were not equally fortunate there. The officer who guarded them was a ruffian and a villain, Captain Baumgarten. He took a pleasure in humiliating and illtreating the brave men who had fallen into his power. That night, upon my son answering fiercely back to some taunt of his, he struck him in the eye, like this!"

The crash of the blow rang through the

hall. The German's face fell forward, his hand up, and blood oozing through his fingers. The Count settled down in his chair once more.

" My boy was disfigured by the blow, and this villain made his appearance the object of his jeers. By the way, you look a little comical yourself at the present moment, Captain, and your Colonel would certainly say that you had been getting into mischief. To continue, however, my boy's youth and his destitution—for his pockets were empty—moved the pity of a kind-hearted major, and he advanced him ten Napoleons from his own pocket without security of any kind. Into your hands, Captain Baumgarten, I return these ten gold pieces, since I cannot learn the name of the lender. I am grateful from my heart for this kindness shown to my boy.

" The vile tyrant who commanded the escort accompanied the prisoners to Durlach, and from there to Carlsruhe. He heaped every outrage upon my lad, because the spirit of the Château Noir would not stoop to turn away his wrath by feigned submission. Ay, this cowardly villain, whose heart's blood shall yet clot upon this hand, dared to strike my son with his open hand, to kick him, to tear hair from his moustache—to use him thus—and thus—and thus!"

The German writhed and struggled. He

was helpless in the hands of this huge giant whose blows were raining upon him. When at last, blinded and half-senseless he staggered to his feet, it was only to be hurled back again into the great oaken chair. He sobbed in his impotent anger and shame.

"My boy was frequently moved to tears by the humiliation of his position," continued the Count. "You will understand me when I say that it is a bitter thing to be helpless in the hands of an insolent and remorseless enemy. On arriving at Carlsruhe, however, his face, which had been wounded by the brutality of his guard, was bound up by a young Bavarian subaltern who was touched by his appearance. I regret to see that your eye is bleeding so. Will you permit me to bind it with my silk handkerchief?"

He leaned forward, but the German dashed his hand aside.

"I am in your power, you monster!" he cried; "I can endure your brutalities, but not your hypocrisy."

The Count shrugged his shoulders. "I am taking things in their order, just as they occurred," said he. "I was under vow to tell it to the first German officer with whom I could talk *tête-à-tête*. Let me see, I had got as far as the young Bavarian at Carlsruhe. I regret extremely that you will not permit me to use such slight skill in surgery as I possess. At Carlsruhe, my lad was shut up in the old caserne, where he remained for a fortnight. The worst pang of his captivity was that some unmannerly curs in the garrison would taunt him with his position as he sat by his window in the evening. That reminds me, Captain, that you are not quite situated upon a bed of roses yourself, are you, now? You came to trap a wolf, my man, and now the beast has you down with his fangs in your throat. A family man, too, I should judge, by that well-filled tunic. Well, a widow the more will make little matter, and they do not usually remain widows long. Get back into the chair, you dog!"

"Well, to continue my story—at the end of a fortnight my son and his friend escaped. I need not trouble you with the dangers which they ran, or with the privations which they endured. Suffice it that to disguise themselves they had to take the clothes of two peasants, whom they waylaid in a wood. Hiding by day and travelling by night, they had got as far into France as Remilly, and were within a mile—a single mile, Captain—of crossing the German lines when a patrol of Uhlans came right upon them. Ah! it was hard, was it not, when they had come so far and were so near to safety?"

The Count blew a double call upon his whistle, and three hard-faced peasants entered the room.

"These must represent my Uhlans," said he. "Well, then, the Captain in command, finding that these men were French soldiers in civilian dress within the German lines, proceeded to hang them without trial or ceremony. I think, Jean, that the centre beam is the strongest."

The unfortunate soldier was dragged from his chair to where a noosed rope had been flung over one of the huge oaken rafters which spanned the room. The cord was slipped over his head, and he felt its harsh grip round his throat. The three peasants seized the other end, and looked to the Count for his orders. The officer, pale, but firm, folded his arms and stared defiantly at the man who tortured him.

"You are now face to face with death, and I perceive from your lips that you are praying. My son was also face to face with death, and he prayed, also. It happened that a general officer came up, and he heard the lad praying for his mother, and it moved him so—he being himself a father—that he ordered his Uhlans away, and he remained with his aide-de-camp only, beside the condemned men. And when he heard all the lad had to tell, that he was the only child of an old family, and that his mother was in failing health, he threw off the rope as I throw of this, and he kissed him on either cheek, as I kiss you, and he bade him go, as I bid you go, and may every kind wish of that noble General, though it could not stave off the fever which slew my son, descend now upon your head."

And so it was that Captain Baumgarten, disfigured, blinded, and bleeding, staggered out into the wind and the rain of that wild December dawn.

THE STRIPED CHEST

"WHAT do you make of her, Allardyce?" I asked.

My second mate was standing beside me upon the poop, with his short, thick legs astretch, for the gale had left a considerable swell behind it, and our two quarter-boats nearly touched the water with every roll. He steadied his glass against the mizzen-shrouds, and he looked long and hard at this disconsolate stranger every time she came reeling up onto the crest of a roller and hung balanced for a few seconds before swooping down upon the other side. She lay so low in the water that I could only catch an occasional glimpse of a pea-green line of bulwark.

She was a brig, but her mainmast had been snapped short off some ten feet above the deck, and no effort seemed to have been made to cut away the wreckage, which floated, sails and yards, like the broken wing of a wounded gull, upon the water beside her. The foremast was still standing, but the foretopsail was flying loose, and the headsails were streaming out in long white pennons in front of her. Never have I seen a vessel which appeared to have gone through rougher handling.

But we could not be surprised at that, for there had been times during the last three days when it was a question whether our own barque would ever see land again. For thirty-six hours we had kept her nose to it, and if the *Mary Sinclair* had not been as good a seaboat as ever left the Clyde, we could not have gone through. And yet here we were at the end of it with the loss only of our gig and of part of the starboard bulwark. It did not astonish us, however, when the smother had cleared away, to find that others had been less lucky, and that this mutilated brig, staggering about upon a blue sea, and under a cloudless sky, had been left, like a blinded man after a lightning flash, to tell of the terror which is past.

Allardyce, who was a slow and methodical Scotchman, stared long and hard at the little craft, while our seamen lined the bulwark or clustered upon the four shrouds to have a view of the stranger. In latitude 20° and longitude 10°, which were about our bearings, one becomes a little curious as to whom one meets, for one has left the main lines of Atlantic commerce to the north. For ten days we had been sailing over a solitary sea.

"She's derelict, I'm thinking," said the second mate.

I had come to the same conclusion, for I could see no sign of life upon her deck, and there was no answer to the friendly wavings from our seamen. The crew had probably deserted her under the impression that she was about to founder.

"She can't last long," continued Allardyce, in his measured way. "She may put her nose down and her tail up any minute. The water's lipping up to the edge of her rail."

"What's her flag?" I asked.

"I'm trying to make out. It's got all twisted and tangled with the halliards. Yes, I've got it now, clear enough. It's the Brazilian flag, but it's wrong side up."

She had hoisted a signal of distress, then, before her people had abandoned her. Perhaps they had only just gone. I took the mate's glass and looked round over the tumultuous face of the deep blue Atlantic, still veined and starred with white lines and spoutings of foam. But nowhere could I see anything human beyond ourselves.

"There may be living men aboard," said I.

"There may be salvage," muttered the second mate.

"Then we will run down upon her lee side, and lie to."

We were not more than a hundred yards from her when we swung our foreyard aback, and there we were, the barque and the brig, ducking and bowing like two clowns in a dance.

"Drop one of the quarter-boats," said I. "Take four men, Mr. Allardyce, and see what you can learn of her."

But just at that moment my first officer, Mr. Armstrong, came on deck, for seven bells had struck, and it was but a few minutes off his watch.   It would interest me to go myself to this abandoned vessel and to see what there might be aboard of her.   So, with a word to Armstrong, I swung myself over the side, slipped down the falls, and took my place in the sheets of the boat.

It was but a little distance, but it took some time to traverse, and so heavy was the roll, that often, when we were in the trough of the sea, we could not see either the barque which we had left or the brig which we were approaching. The sinking sun did not penetrate down there, and it was cold and dark in the hollows of the waves, but each passing billow heaved us up into the warmth and the sunshine once more. At each of these moments, as we hung upon a white-capped ridge between the two dark valleys, I caught a glimpse of the long, pea-green line, and the nodding foremast of the brig, and I steered so as to come round by her stern, so that we might determine which was the best way of boarding her. As we passed her we saw the name *Nossa Sehnora da Vittoria* painted across her dripping counter.

" The weather side, sir," said the second mate. " Stand ˌby with the boathook, carpenter ! " An instant later we had jumped over the bulwarks, which were hardly higher than our boat, and found ourselves upon the deck of the abandoned vessel.

Our first thought was to provide for our own safety in case—as seemed very probable—the vessel should settle down beneath our feet. With this object two of our men held on to the painter of the boat, and fended her off from the vessel's side, so that she might be ready in case we had to make a hurried retreat. The carpenter was sent to find out how much water there was, and whether it was still gaining, while the other seaman, Allardyce and myself, made a rapid inspection of the vessel and her cargo.

The deck was littered with wreckage and with hen-coops, in which the dead birds were washing about. The boats were gone, with the exception of one, the bottom of which had been stove, and it was certain that the crew had abandoned the vessel. The cabin was in a deck house, one side of which had been beaten in by a heavy sea. Allardyce and I entered it, and found the captain's table as he had left it,

his books and papers—all Spanish or Portu-
guese—scattered over it, with piles of cigarette
ash everywhere. I looked about for the log,
but could not find it.

"As likely as not he never kept one," said
Allardyce. "Things are pretty slack aboard a
South American trader, and they don't do more
than they can help. If there was one it must
have been taken away with him in the boat."

"I should like to take all these books and
papers," said I. "Ask the carpenter how
much time we have."

His report was reassuring. The vessel was
full of water, but some of the cargo was buoy-
ant, and there was no immediate danger of her
sinking. Probably she would never sink, but
would drift about as one of those terrible, un-
marked reefs which have sent so many stout
vessels to the bottom.

"In that case there is no danger in your going below, Mr. Allardyce," said I. "See what
you can make of her, and find out how much
of her cargo may be saved. I'll look through
these papers while you are gone."

The bills of lading, and some notes and letters which lay upon the desk, sufficed to inform
me that the Brazilian brig *Nossa Sehnora da
Vittoria* had cleared from Bahia a month before.
The name of the captain was Texeira, but there
was no record as to the number of the crew.

She was bound for London, and a glance at the bills of lading was sufficient to show me that we were not likely to profit much in the way of salvage. Her cargo consisted of nuts, ginger, and wood, the latter in the shape of great logs of valuable tropical growths. It was these, no doubt, which had prevented the ill-fated vessel from going to the bottom, but they were of such a size as to make it impossible for us to extract them. Besides these, there were a few fancy goods, such as a number of ornamental birds for millinery purposes, and a hundred cases of preserved fruits. And then, as I turned over the papers, I came upon a short note in English, which arrested my attention.

"It is requested," said the note, "that the various old Spanish and Indian curiosities, which came out of the Santarem collection, and which are consigned to Prontfoot and Neuman, of Oxford Street, London, should be put in some place where there may be no danger of these very valuable and unique articles being injured or tampered with. This applies most particularly to the treasure-chest of Don Ramirez di Leyra, which must on no account be placed where any one can get at it."

The treasure-chest of Don Ramirez! Unique and valuable articles! Here was a chance of salvage after all! I had risen to my feet with

the paper in my hand, when my Scotch mate
appeared in the doorway.

"I'm thinking all isn't quite as it should be
aboard of this ship, sir," said he. He was a hard-
faced man, and yet I could see that he had been
startled.

"What's the matter?"

"Murder's the matter, sir. There's a man
here with his brains beaten out."

"Killed in the storm?" said I.

"May be so, sir. But I'll be surprised if
you think so after you have seen him."

"Where is he, then?"

"This way, sir; here in the maindeck
house."

There appeared to have been no accommo-
dation below in the brig, for there was the after-
house for the captain, another by the main
hatchway with the cook's galley attached to it,
and a third in the forecastle for the men. It
was to this middle one that the mate led me.
As you entered, the galley, with its litter of
tumbled pots and dishes, was upon the right,
and upon the left was a small room with two
bunks for the officers. Then beyond there was
a place about twelve feet square, which was littered with flags and spare canvas. All round
the walls were a number of packets done up in
coarse cloth and carefully lashed to the wood-
work. At the other end was a great box,

striped red and white, though the red was so faded and the white so dirty that it was only where the light fell directly upon it that one could see the colouring. The box was, by subsequent measurement, four feet three inches in length, three feet two inches in height, and three feet across—considerably larger than a seaman's chest.

But it was not to the box that my eyes or my thoughts were turned as I entered the storeroom. On the floor, lying across the litter of bunting, there was stretched a small, dark man with a short, curling beard. He lay as far as it was possible from the box, with his feet towards it and his head away. A crimson patch was printed upon the white canvas on which his head was resting, and little red ribbons wreathed themselves round his swarthy neck and trailed away on to the floor, but there was no sign of a wound that I could see, and his face was as placid as that of a sleeping child.

It was only when I stooped that I could perceive his injury, and then I turned away with an exclamation of horror. He had been poleaxed ; apparently by some person standing behind him. A frightful blow had smashed in the top of his head and penetrated deeply into his brain. His face might well be placid. for death must have been absolutely instantaneous, and the position of the wound showed

that he could never have seen the person who
had inflicted it.

" Is that foul play or accident, Captain Barclay ? " asked my second mate, demurely.

" You are quite right, Mr. Allardyce. The
man has been murdered, struck down from
above by a sharp and heavy weapon. But who
was he, and why did they murder him ? "

" He was a common seaman, sir," said the
mate. " You can see that if you look at his
fingers." He turned out his pockets as he
spoke and brought to light a pack of cards,
some tarred string, and a bundle of Brazilian
tobacco.

" Hullo, look at this ! " said he.

It was a large, open knife with a stiff spring
blade which he had picked up from the floor.
The steel was shining and bright, so that we
could not associate it with the crime, and yet
the dead man had apparently held it in his
hand when he was struck down, for it still lay
within his grasp.

" It looks to me, sir, as if he knew he was in
danger, and kept his knife handy," said the
mate. " However, we can't help the poor
beggar now. I can't make out these things
that are lashed to the wall. They seem to be
idols and weapons and curios of all sorts done
up in old sacking."

" That's right," said I. " They are the only

things of value that we are likely to get from the cargo. Hail the barque and tell them to send the other quarter-boat to help us to get the stuff aboard.

While he was away I examined this curious plunder which had come into our possession. The curiosities were so wrapped up that I could only form a general idea as to their nature, but the striped box stood in a good light where I could thoroughly examine it. On the lid, which was clamped and cornered with metal-work, there was engraved a complex coat of arms, and beneath it was a line of Spanish which I was able to decipher as meaning, " The treasure-chest of Don Ramirez di Leyra, Knight of the Order of Saint James, Governor and Captain-General of Terra Firma and of the Province of Veraquas." In one corner was the date 1606, and on the other a large white label, upon which was written in English, " You are earnestly requested, upon no account, to open this box." The same warning was repeated underneath in Spanish. As to the lock, it was a very complex and heavy one of engraved steel, with a Latin motto, which was above a seaman's comprehension.

By the time I had finished this examination of the peculiar box, the other quarter-boat with Mr. Armstrong, the first officer, had come alongside, and we began to carry out and place in her the various curiosities which appeared to be the only objects worth moving from the derelict ship. When she was full I sent her back to the barque, and then Allardyce and I, with the carpenter and one seaman, shifted the striped box, which was the only thing left, to our boat, and lowered it over, balancing it upon the two middle thwarts, for it was so heavy that it would have given the boat a dangerous tilt had we placed it at either end. As to the dead man, we left him where we had found him.

The mate had a theory that, at the moment of the desertion of the ship, this fellow had started plundering, and that the captain in an attempt to preserve discipline, had struck him down with a hatchet or some other heavy weapon. It seemed more probable than any other explanation, and yet it did not entirely satisfy me either. But the ocean is full of mysteries, and we were content to leave the fate of the dead seaman of the Brazilian brig to be added to that long list which every sailor can recall.

The heavy box was slung up by ropes on to the deck of the *Mary Sinclair*, and was carried by four seamen into the cabin, where, between the table and the after-lockers, there was just space for it to stand. There it remained during supper, and after that meal the mates remained with me, and discussed over a glass of grog the event of the day. Mr. Armstrong was a long, thin, vulture-like man, an excellent seaman, but famous for his nearness and cupidity. Our treasure-trove had excited him greatly, and already he had begun with glistening eyes to reckon up how much it might be worth to each of us when the shares of the salvage came to be divided.

"If the paper said that they were unique, Mr. Barclay, then they may be worth anything that you like to name. You wouldn't believe the sums that the rich collectors give. A thousand pounds is nothing to them. We'll have something to show for our voyage, or I am mistaken."

"I don't think that," said I. "As far as I can see they are not very different from any other South American curios."

"Well, sir, I've traded there for fourteen voyages, and I have never seen anything like that chest before. That's worth a pile of money, just as it stands. But it's so heavy, that surely there must be something valuable inside it. Don't you think that we ought to open it and see?"

"If you break it open you will spoil it, as likely as not," said the second mate.

Armstrong squatted down in front of it, with

his head on one side, and his long, thin nose within a few inches of the lock.

"The wood is oak," said he, "and it has shrunk a little with age. If I had a chisel or a strong-bladed knife I could force the lock back without doing any damage at all."

The mention of a strong-bladed knife made me think of the dead seaman upon the brig.

"I wonder if he could have been on the job when some one came to interfere with him," said I.

"I don't know about that, sir, but I am perfectly certain that I could open the box. There's a screwdriver here in the locker. Just hold the lamp, Allardyce, and I'll have it done in a brace of shakes."

"Wait a bit," said I, for already, with eyes which gleamed with curiosity and with avarice, he was stooping over the lid. "I don't see that there is any hurry over this matter. You've read that card which warns us not to open it. It may mean anything or it may mean nothing, but somehow I feel inclined to obey it. After all, whatever is in it will keep, and if it is valuable it will be worth as much if it is opened in the owner's offices as in the cabin of the *Mary Sinclair*."

The first officer seemed bitterly disappointed at my decision.

"Surely, sir, you are not superstitious about

it," said he, with a slight sneer upon his thin lips. If it gets out of our own hands, and we don't see for ourselves what is inside it, we may be done out of our rights ; besides———"

"That's enough, Mr. Armstrong," said I, abruptly. "You may have every confidence that you will get your rights, but I will not have that box opened to-night."

"Why, the label itself shows that the box has been examined by Europeans," Allardyce added. "Because a box is a treasure-box is no reason that it has treasures inside it now. A good many folk have had a peep into it since the days of the old Governor of Terra Firma."

Armstrong threw the screwdriver down upon the table and shrugged his shoulders.

"Just as you like," said he ; but for the rest of the evening, although we spoke upon many subjects, I noticed that his eyes were continually coming round, with the same expression of curiosity and greed, to the old striped box.

And now I come to that portion of my story which fills me even now with a shuddering horror when I think of it. The main cabin had the rooms of the officers round it, but mine was the farthest away from it at the end of the little passage which led to the companion. No regular watch was kept by me, except in cases of emergency, and the three mates divided the watches among them. Armstrong had the middle watch, which ends at four in the morning, and he was relieved by Allardyce. For my part I have always been one of the soundest of sleepers, and it is rare for anything less than a hand upon my shoulder to arouse me.

And yet I was aroused that night, or rather in the early gray of the morning. It was just half-past four by my chronometer when something caused me to sit up in my berth wide awake and with every nerve tingling. It was a sound of some sort, a crash with a human cry at the end of it, which still jarred upon my ears. I sat listening, but all was now silent. And yet it could not have been imagination, that hideous cry, for the echo of it still rang in my head, and it seemed to have come from some place quite close to me. I sprang from my bunk, and, pulling on some clothes, I made my way into the cabin.

At first I saw nothing unusual there. In the cold, gray light I made out the red-clothed table, the six rotating chairs, the walnut lockers, the swinging barometer, and there, at the end, the big striped chest. I was turning away with the intention of going upon deck and asking the second mate if he had heard anything, when my eyes fell suddenly upon something which projected from under the table. It was the leg of a man—a leg with a long sea-boot upon it. I stooped, and there was a figure sprawling upon his face, his arms thrown forward and his body twisted. One glance told me that it was Armstrong, the first officer, and a second that he was a dead man. For a few moments I stood gasping. Then I rushed on to the deck, called Allardyce to my assistance, and came back with him into the cabin.

Together we pulled the unfortunate fellow from under the table, and as we looked at his dripping head we exchanged glances, and I do not know which was the paler of the two.

" The same as the Spanish sailor," said I.

" The very same. God preserve us! It's that infernal chest! Look at Armstrong's hand! "

He held up the mate's right hand, and there was the screwdriver which he had wished to use the night before.

" He's been at the chest, sir. He knew that I was on deck and you asleep. He knelt down in front of it, and he pushed the lock back with that tool. Then something happened to him, and he cried out so that you heard him."

" Allardyce," I whispered, " what *could* have happened to him ? "

The second mate put his hand upon my sleeve and drew me into his cabin.

" We can talk here, sir, and we don't know who may be listening to us in there. What do you suppose is in that box, Captain Barclay ? "

" I give you my word, Allardyce, that I have no idea."

" Well, I can only find one theory which will fit all the facts. Look at the size of the box. Look at all the carving and metal-work which may conceal any number of holes. Look at the weight of it; it took four men to carry it. On the top of that, remember that two men have tried to open it, and both have come to their end through it. Now, sir, what can it mean except one thing ? "

" You mean there is a man in it ? "

" Of course there is a man in it. You know how it is in these South American States, sir. A man may be President one week and hunted like a dog the next, they are for ever flying for their lives. My idea is that there is some fellow in hiding there, who is armed and desperate, and who will fight to the death before he is taken."

" But his food and drink ? "

" It's a roomy chest, sir, and he may have some provisions stowed away. As to his drink, he had a friend among the crew upon the brig who saw that he had what he needed."

" You think, then, that the label asking people not to open the box was simply written in his interest ? "

" Yes, sir, that is my idea. Have you any other way of explaining the facts ? "

I had to confess that I had not.

"The question is what are we to do?" I asked.

"The man's a dangerous ruffian who sticks at nothing. I'm thinking it wouldn't be a bad thing to put a rope round the chest and tow it alongside for half an hour; then we could open it at our ease. Or if we just tied the box up and kept him from getting any water maybe that would do as well. Or the carpenter could put a coat of varnish over it and stop all the blow-holes."

"Come, Allardyce," said I, angrily. "You don't seriously mean to say that a whole ship's company are going to be terrorized by a single man in a box. If he's there, I'll engage to fetch him out!" I went to my room and came back with my revolver in my hand. "Now, Allardyce," said I. "Do you open the lock, and I'll stand on guard."

"For God's sake, think what you are doing, sir!" cried the mate. "Two men have lost their lives over it, and the blood of one not yet dry upon the carpet."

"The more reason why we should revenge him."

"Well, sir, at least let me call the carpenter. Three are better than two, and he is a good stout man."

He went off in search of him, and I was left

alone with the striped chest in the cabin. I
don't think that I'm a nervous man, but I kept
the table between me and this solid old relic of
the Spanish Main. In the growing light of
morning the red and white striping was beginning to appear, and the curious scrolls and
wreaths of metal and carving which showed the
loving pains which cunning craftsmen had ex-
pended upon it. Presently the carpenter and
the mate came back together, the former with a
hammer in his hand.

" It's a bad business, this, sir," said he, shaking his head, as he looked at the body of the
mate. " And you think there's some one hiding in the box ?"

" There's no doubt about it," said Allardyce,
picking up the screwdriver and setting his jaw
like a man who needs to brace his courage.
I'll drive the lock back if you'll both stand by.
If he rises let him have it on the head with your
hammer, carpenter ! Shoot at once, sir, if he
raises his hand. Now ! "

He had knelt down in front of the striped
chest, and passed the blade of the tool under the
lid. With a sharp snick the lock flew back.
" Stand by ! " yelled the mate, and with a heave
he threw open the massive top of the box. As
it swung up, we all three sprang back, I with
my pistol levelled, and the carpenter with the
hammer above his head. Then, as nothing

happened, we each took a step forward and peeped in. The box was empty.

Not quite empty either, for in one corner was lying an old yellow candlestick, elaborately engraved, which appeared to be as old as the box itself. Its rich yellow tone and artistic shape suggested that it was an object of value. For the rest there was nothing more weighty or valuable than dust in the old striped treasure-chest.

"Well, I'm blessed!" cried Allardyce, staring blankly into it. "Where does the weight come in, then?"

"Look at the thickness of the sides and look at the lid. Why, it's five inches through. And see that great metal spring across it."

"That's for holding the lid up," said the mate. "You see, it won't lean back. What's that German printing on the inside?"

"It means that it was made by Johann Rothstein of Augsburg, in 1606."

"And a solid bit of work, too. But it doesn't throw much light on what has passed, does it, Captain Barclay? That candlestick looks like gold. We shall have something for our trouble after all."

He leant forward to grasp it, and from that moment I have never doubted as to the reality of inspiration, for on the instant I caught him by the collar and pulled him straight again. It

may have been some story of the Middle
Ages which had come back to my mind, or it
may have been that my eye had caught some
red which was not that of rust upon the upper
part of the lock, but to him and to me it will
always seem an inspiration, so prompt and
sudden was my action.

"There's devilry here," said I. "Give me
the crooked stick from the corner."

It was an ordinary walking-cane with a
hooked top. I passed it over the candlestick
and gave it a pull. With a flash a row of
polished steel fangs shot out from below the
upper lid, and the great striped chest snapped
at us like a wild animal. Clang came the huge
lid into its place, and the glasses on the swinging rack sang and tinkled with the shock. The
mate sat down on the edge of the table and
shivered like a frightened horse.

"You've saved my life, Captain Barclay!"
said he.

So this was the secret of the striped treasure-
chest of old Don Ramirez di Leyra, and this
was how he preserved his ill-gotten gains from
the Terra Firma and the Province of Veraquas.
Be the thief ever so cunning he could not tell
that golden candlestick from the other articles
of value, and the instant that he laid hand
upon it the terrible spring was unloosed and
the murderous steel spikes were driven into his

brain, while the shock of the blow sent the victim backwards and enabled the chest to automatically close itself. How many, I wondered, had fallen victims to the ingenuity of the Mechanic of Augsburg. And as I thought of the possible history of that grim striped chest my resolution was very quickly taken.

"Carpenter, bring three men and carry this on deck."

"Going to throw it overboard, sir?"

"Yes, Mr. Allardyce. I'm not superstitious as a rule, but there are some things which are more than a sailor can be called upon to stand."

"No wonder that brig made heavy weather, Captain Barclay, with such a thing on board. The glass is dropping fast, sir, and we are only just in time."

So we did not even wait for the three sailors, but we carried it out, the mate, the carpenter, and I, and we pushed it with our own hands over the bulwarks. There was a white spout of water, and it was gone. There it lies, the striped chest, a thousand fathoms deep, and if, as they say, the sea will some day be dry land, I grieve for the man who finds that old box and tries to penetrate into its secret.

A SHADOW BEFORE

THE 15th of July, 1870, found John Worlington Dodds a ruined gamester of the Stock Exchange. Upon the 17th he was a very opulent man. And yet he had effected the change without leaving the penurious little Irish townlet of Dunsloe, which could have been bought outright for a quarter of the sum which he had earned during the single day that he was within its walls. There is a romance of finance yet to be written, a story of huge forces which are forever waxing and waning, of bold operations, of breathless suspense, of agonized failure, of deep combinations which are baffled by others still more subtle. The mighty debts of each great European Power stand like so many columns of mercury, for ever rising and falling to indicate the pressure upon each. He who can see far enough into the future to tell how that ever-varying column will stand to-morrow is the man who has fortune within his grasp.

John Worlington Dodds had many of the

gifts which lead a speculator to success. He was quick in observing, just in estimating, prompt and fearless in acting. But in finance there is always the element of luck, which, however one may eliminate it, still remains, like the blank at roulette, a constantly present handicap upon the operator. And so it was that Worlington Dodds had come to grief. On the best advices he had dabbled in the funds of a South American Republic in the days before South American Republics had been found out. The Republic defaulted, and Dodds lost his money. He had bulled the shares of a Scotch railway, and a four months' strike had hit him hard. He had helped to underwrite a coffee company in the hope that the public would come along upon the feed and gradually nibble away some of his holding, but the political sky had been clouded and the public had refused to invest. Everything which he had touched had gone wrong, and now, on the eve of his marriage, young, clear-headed, and energetic, he was actually a bankrupt had his creditors chosen to make him one. But the Stock Exchange is an indulgent body. What is the case of one to-day may be that of another to-morrow, and every one is interested in seeing that the stricken man is given time to rise again. So the burden of Worlington Dodds was lightened for him, many shoulders helped to bear it, and he was able to go for a little summer tour into Ireland, for the doctors had ordered him rest and change of air to restore his shaken nervous system. Thus it was that upon the 15th of July, 1870, he found himself at his breakfast in the fly-blown coffee-room of the George Hotel in the market square of Dunsloe.

It is a dull and depressing coffee-room and one which is usually empty, but on this particular day it was as crowded and noisy as that of any London hotel. Every table was occupied, and a thick smell of fried bacon and of fish hung in the air. Heavily-booted men clattered in and out, spurs jingled, riding-crops were stacked in corners, and there was a general atmosphere of horse. The conversation, too, was of nothing else. From every side Worlington Dodds heard of yearlings, of windgalls, of roarers, of spavins, of cribsuckers, of a hundred other terms which were as unintelligible to him as his own Stock Exchange jargon would have been to the company. He asked the waiter for the reason of it all, and the waiter was an astonished man that there should be any one in this world who did not know it.

"Shure it's the Dunsloe horse-fair, your honour—the greatest horse-fair in all Oireland. It lasts for a wake, and the folk come from far an' near—from England an' Scotland an' iverywhere. If you look out of the winder, your honour, you'll see the horses, and it's asy your honour's conscience must be, or you wouldn't slape so sound that the cratures didn't rouse you with their clatter."

Dodds had a recollection that he had heard a confused murmur, which had interwoven itself with his dreams—a sort of steady rhythmic beating and clanking—and now, when he looked through the window, he saw the cause of it. The square was packed with horses from end to end—grays, bays, browns, blacks, chestnuts—young ones and old, fine ones and coarse, horses of every conceivable sort and size. It seemed a huge function for so small a town, and he remarked as much to the waiter.

" Well, you see, your honour, the horses don't live in the town, an' they don't vex their heads how small it is. But it's in the very centre of the horse-bradin' districts of Oireland, so where should they come to be sould if it wasn't to Dunsloe ? "

The waiter had a telegram in his hand, and he turned the address to Worlington Dodds.

" Shure I niver heard such a name, sorr. Maybe you could tell me who owns it ? "

Dodds looked at the envelope. Strellenhaus was the name.

" No, I don't know," said he. " I never

heard it before. It's a foreign name. Perhaps if you were——"

But at that moment a little round-faced, ruddy-cheeked gentleman, who was breakfasting at the next table, leaned forward and interrupted him.

" Did you say a foreign name, sir ? " said he.

" Strellenhaus is the name."

" I am Mr. Strellenhaus—Mr. Julius Strellenhaus of Liverpool. I was expecting a telegram. Thank you very much."

He sat so near that Dodds, without any wish to play the spy, could not help to some extent overlooking him as he opened the envelope. The message was a very long one. Quite a wad of melon-tinted paper came out from the tawny envelope. Mr. Strellenhaus arranged the sheets methodically upon the table-cloth in front of him, so that no eye but his own could see them. Then he took out a note-book, and, with an anxious face, he began to make entries in it, glancing first at the telegram and then at the book, and writing apparently one letter or figure at a time. Dodds was interested, for he knew exactly what the man was doing. He was working out a cypher. Dodds had often done it himself. And then suddenly the little man turned very pale, as if the full purport of the message had been a shock to him. Dodds had done that also, and his sympathies were all with his neighbour. Then the stranger rose, and, leaving his breakfast untasted, he walked out of the room.

" I'm thinkin' that the gintleman has had bad news, sorr," said the confidential waiter.

" Looks like it," Dodds answered ; and at that moment his thoughts were suddenly drawn off into another direction.

The boots had entered the room with a telegram in his hand.

" Where's Mr. Mancune ? " said he to the waiter.

" Well, there are some quare names about. What was it you said ? "

" Mr. Mancune," said the boots, glancing round him. " Ah, there he is ! " and he handed the telegram to a gentleman who was sitting reading the paper in a corner.

Dodds's eyes had already fallen upon this man, and he had wondered vaguely what he was doing in such company. He was a tall, white-haired, eagle-nosed gentleman, with a waxed moustache and a carefully pointed beard —an aristocratic type which seemed out of its element among the rough, hearty, noisy dealers who surrounded him. This, then, was Mr. Mancune, for whom the second telegram was intended.

As he opened it, tearing it open with a feverish haste, Dodds could perceive that it was as bulky as the first one. He observed also, from the delay in reading it, that it was also in some sort of cypher. The gentleman did not write down any translation of it, but he sat for some time with his nervous, thin fingers twitching amongst the hairs of his white beard, and his shaggy brows bent in the deepest and most absorbed attention whilst he mastered the meaning of it. Then he sprang suddenly to his feet, his eyes flashed, his cheeks flushed, and in his excitement he crumpled the message up in his hand. With an effort he mastered his emotion, put the paper into his pocket, and walked out of the room.

This was enough to excite a less astute and imaginative man than Worlington Dodds. Was there any connection between these two messages, or was it merely a coincidence? Two men with strange names receive two telegrams within a few minutes of each other, each of a considerable length, each in cypher, and each causing keen emotion to the man who received it. One turned pale. The other sprang excitedly to his feet. It might be a coincidence, but it was a very curious one. If it was not a coincidence, then what could it mean? Were they confederates who pretended to work apart, but who each received identical orders from some person at a distance? That was possible, and yet there were difficulties in the way. He puzzled and puzzled, but could find no satisfactory solution to the problem. All breakfast he was turning it over in his mind.

When breakfast was over he sauntered out into the market square, where the horse sale was already in progress. The yearlings were being sold first—tall, long-legged, skittish, wild-eyed creatures, who had run free upon the upland pastures, with ragged hair and towsey manes, but hardy, inured to all weathers, and with the makings of splendid hunters and steeple-chasers when corn and time had brought them to maturity. They were largely of thoroughbred blood, and were being bought by English dealers, who would invest a few pounds now on what they might sell for fifty guineas in a year, if all went well. It was legitimate speculation, for the horse is a delicate creature, he is afflicted with many ailments, the least accident may destroy his value, he is a certain expense and an uncertain profit, and for one who comes safely to maturity several may bring no return at all. So the English horse-dealers took their risks as they bought up the shaggy Irish yearlings. One man with a ruddy face and a yellow overcoat took them by the dozen, with as much *sang froid* as if they had been oranges, entering each bargain in a bloated note-book. He bought forty or fifty during the time that Dodds was watching him.

"Who is that?" he asked his neighbour, whose spurs and gaiters showed that he was likely to know.

The man stared in astonishment at the stranger's ignorance.

"Why, that's Jim Holloway, the great Jim Holloway," said he; then, seeing by the blank look upon Dodds's face that even this information had not helped him much, he went into details. "Sure he's the head of Holloway and Morland, of London," said he. "He's the buying partner, and he buys cheap; and the other stays at home and sells, and he sells dear. He owns more horses than any man in the world, and asks the best money for them. I dare say you'll find that half of what are sold at the Dunsloe fair this day will go to him, and he's got such a purse that there's not a man who can bid against him."

Worlington Dodds watched the doings of the great dealer with interest. He had passed on now to the two-year-olds and three-year-olds, full-grown horses, but still a little loose in the limb and weak in the bone. The London buyer was choosing his animals carefully, but having chosen them, the vigour of his competition drove all other bidders out of it. With a careless nod he would run the figure up five pounds at a time, until he was left in possession of the field. At the same time he was a shrewd observer, and when, as happened more than once, he believed that some one was bidding against him simply in order to run him up, the head would cease suddenly to nod, the note-book would be closed with a snap, and the intruder would be left with a purchase which he did not desire upon his hands. All Dodds's business instincts were aroused by the tactics of this great operator, and he stood in the crowd watching with the utmost interest all that occurred.

It is not to buy young horses, however, that the great dealers come to Ireland, and the real business of the fair commenced when the four and five-year-olds were reached ; the full-grown, perfect horses at their prime and ready for any work or any fatigue. Seventy magnificent creatures had been brought down by a single breeder, a comfortable-looking, keen-eyed, ruddy-cheeked gentleman who stood beside the salesman and whispered cautions and precepts into his ear.

"That's Flynn of Kildare," said Dodds's informant. " Jack Flynn has brought down that string of horses, and the other large string over yonder belongs to Tom Flynn, his brother. The two of them together are the two first breeders in Ireland."

A crowd had gathered in front of the horses. By common consent a place had been made for

Mr. Holloway, and Dodds could catch a glimpse of his florid face and yellow covert-coat in the front rank. He had opened his note-book and was tapping his teeth reflectively with his pencil as he eyed the horses.

" You'll see a fight now between the first seller and the first buyer in the country," said Dodds's acquaintance. " They are a beautiful string, anyhow. I shouldn't be surprised if he didn't average five-and-thirty pound apiece for the lot as they stand."

The salesman had mounted upon a chair, and his keen, clean-shaven face overlooked the crowd. Mr. Jack Flynn's grey whiskers were at his elbow, and Mr. Holloway immediately in front.

" You've seen these horses, gentlemen," said the salesman, with a backward sweep of his hand towards the line of tossing heads and streaming manes. " When you know that they are bred by Mr. Jack Flynn, at his place in Kildare, you will have a guarantee of their quality. They are the best that Ireland can produce, and in this class of horse the best that Ireland can produce are the best in the world, as every riding man knows well. Hunters or carriage horses, all warranted sound and bred from the best stock. There are seventy in Mr. Jack Flynn's string, and he bids me say that if any wholesale dealer would make one bid for the whole lot, to save time, he would have the preference over any purchaser."

There was a pause and a whisper from the crowd in front, with some expressions of discontent. By a single sweep all the small dealers had been put out of it. It was only a long purse which could buy on such a scale as that. The salesman looked round him inquiringly.

"Come, Mr. Holloway," said he, at last. "You didn't come over here for the sake of the scenery. You may travel the country and not see such another string of horses. Give us a starting bid."

The great dealer was still rattling his pencil upon his front teeth.

"Well," said he, at last, "they *are* a fine lot of horses, and I won't deny it. They do you credit, Mr. Flynn, I am sure. All the same, I didn't mean to fill a ship at a single bid in this fashion. I like to pick and choose my horses."

"In that case Mr. Flynn is quite prepared to sell them in smaller lots," said the salesman. "It was rather for the convenience of a wholesale customer that he was prepared to put them all up together. But if no gentleman wishes to bid——"

"Wait a minute," said a voice. "They are very fine horses, these, and I will give you a bid to start you. I will give you twenty pounds each for the string of seventy."

There was a rustle as the crowd all swayed their heads to catch a glimpse of the speaker. The salesman leaned forward.

" May I ask your name, sir ? "

" Strellenhaus—Mr. Strellenhaus of Liverpool."

" It's a new firm," said Dodds's neighbour. " I thought I knew them all, but I never heard of him before."

The salesman's head had disappeared, for he was whispering with the breeder. Now he suddenly straightened himself again.

" Thank you for giving us a lead, sir," said he. " Now gentlemen, you have heard the offer of Mr. Strellenhaus of Liverpool. It will give us a base to start from. Mr. Strellenhaus has offered twenty pounds a head."

" Guineas," said Holloway.

" Bravo, Mr. Holloway ! I knew that you would take a hand. You are not the man to let such a string of horses pass away from you. The bid is twenty guineas a head."

"Twenty-five pounds," said Mr. Strellenhaus.

" Twenty-six."

" Thirty."

It was London against Liverpool, and it was the head of the trade against an outsider. Still, the one man had increased his bids by fives and the other only by ones. Those fives meant determination and also wealth. Holloway had ruled the market so long that the crowd was delighted at finding some one who would stand up to him.

"The bid now stands at thirty pounds a head," said the salesman. "The word lies with you, Mr. Holloway."

The London dealer was glancing keenly at his unknown opponent, and he was asking himself whether this was a genuine rival, or whether it was a device of some sort—an agent of Flynn's, perhaps—for running up the price. Little Mr. Strellenhaus, the same apple-faced gentleman whom Dodds had noticed in the coffee-room, stood looking at the horses with the sharp, quick glances of a man who knows what he is looking for.

"Thirty-one," said Holloway, with the air of a man who has gone to his extreme limit.

"Thirty-two," said Strellenhaus, promptly.

Holloway grew angry at this persistent opposition. His red face flushed redder still.

"Thirty-three!" he shouted.

"Thirty-four," said Strellenhaus.

Holloway became thoughtful, and entered a few figures in his note-book. There were seventy horses. He knew that Flynn's stock was always of the highest quality. With the hunting season coming on he might rely upon sell-

ing them at an average of from forty-five to
fifty. Some of them might carry a heavy
weight and would run to three figures. On the
other hand, there was the feed and keep of
them for three months, the danger of the voyage, the chance of influenza or some of those
other complaints which run through an entire
stable as measles go through a nursery. Deducting all this, it was a question whether at
the present price any profit would be left upon
the transaction. Every pound that he bid
meant seventy out of his pocket. And yet he
could not submit to be beaten by this stranger
without a struggle. As a business matter it
was important to him to be recognized as
the head of his profession. He would make
one more effort if he sacrificed his profit by
doing so.

"At the end of your rope, Mr. Holloway?"
asked the salesman, with the suspicion of a
sneer.

"Thirty-five," cried Holloway, gruffly.

"Thirty-six," said Strellenhaus.

"Then I wish you joy of your bargain,"
said Holloway. "I don't buy at that price, but
I should be glad to sell you some."

Mr. Strellenhaus took no notice of the irony.
He was still looking critically at the horses.
The salesman glanced round him in a perfunc-
tory way.

" Thirty-six pounds bid," said he. " Mr. Jack Flynn's lot is going to Mr. Strellenhaus of Liverpool, at thirty-six pounds a head. Going—going——"

" Forty ! " cried a high, thin, clear voice.

A buzz rose from the crowd, and they were all on tiptoe again, trying to catch a glimpse of this reckless buyer. Being a tall man, Dodds could see over the others, and there at the side of Holloway he saw the masterful nose and aristocratic beard of the second stranger in the coffee-room. A sudden personal interest added itself to the scene. He felt that he was on the verge of something—something dimly seen— which he could himself turn to account. The two men with strange names, the telegrams, the horses—what was underlying it all ?

The salesman was all animation again, and Mr. Jack Flynn was sitting up with his white whiskers bristling and his eyes twinkling. It was the best deal which he had ever made in his fifty years of experience.

" What name, sir ? " asked the salesman.

" Mr. Mancune."

" Address ? "

" Mr. Mancune of Glasgow."

" Thank you for your bid, sir. Forty pounds a head has been bid by Mr. Mancune of Glasgow. Any advance upon forty ? "

" Forty-one," said Strellenhaus.

"Forty-five," said Mancune.

The tactics had changed, and it was the turn of Strellenhaus now to advance by ones, while his rival sprang up by fives. But the former was as dogged as ever.

"Forty-six," said he.

"Fifty!" cried Mancune.

It was unheard of. The most that the horses could possibly average at a retail price was as much as these men were willing to pay whole-sale.

"Two lunatics from Bedlam," whispered the angry Holloway. "If I was Flynn I would see the colour of their money before I went any further."

The same thought had occurred to the sales-man.

"As a mere matter of business, gentlemen," said he, "it is usual in such cases to put down a small deposit as a guarantee of *bona fides*. You will understand how I am placed, and that I have not had the pleasure of doing business with either of you before."

"How much?" asked Strellenhaus, briefly.

"Should we say five hundred?"

"Here is a note for a thousand pounds."

"And here is another," said Mancune.

"Nothing could be more handsome, gentle-men," said the salesman. "It's a treat to see such a spirited competition. The last bid was fifty pounds a head from Mancune. The word lies with you, Mr. Strellenhaus."

Mr. Jack Flynn whispered something to the salesman.

"Quite so! Mr. Flynn suggests, gentlemen, that as you are both large buyers, it would, perhaps, be a convenience to you if he was to add the string of Mr. Tom Flynn, which consists of seventy animals of precisely the same quality, making one hundred and forty in all. Have you any objection, Mr. Mancune?"

"No, sir."

"And you, Mr. Strellenhaus?"

"I should prefer it."

"Very handsome! Very handsome indeed!" murmured the salesman. "Then I understand, Mr. Mancune, that your offer of fifty pounds a head extends to the whole of these horses?"

"Yes, sir."

A long breath went up from the crowd. Seven thousand pounds at one deal. It was a record for Dunsloe.

"Any advance, Mr. Strellenhaus?"

"Fifty-one."

"Fifty-five."

"Fifty-six."

"Sixty."

They could hardly believe their ears. Holloway stood with his mouth open, staring blankly in front of him. The salesman tried hard to look as if such bidding and such prices were nothing unusual. Jack Flynn of Kildare smiled benignly and rubbed his hands together. The crowd listened in dead silence.

"Sixty-one," said Strellenhaus. From the beginning he had stood without a trace of emotion upon his round face, like a little automatic figure which bid by clockwork. His rival was of a more excitable nature. His eyes were shining, and he was for ever twitching at his beard.

"Sixty-five," he cried.

"Sixty-six."

"Seventy."

But the clockwork had run down. No answering bid came from Mr. Strellenhaus.

"Seventy bid, sir."

Mr. Strellenhaus shrugged his shoulders.

"I am buying for another, and I have reached his limit," said he. "If you will permit me to send for instructions——"

"I am afraid, sir, that the sale must proceed."

"Then the horses belong to this gentleman." For the first time he turned towards his rival, and their glances crossed like sword-blades. "It is possible that I may see the horses again."

"I hope so," said Mr. Mancune; and his

white, waxed moustache gave a feline upward bristle.

So, with a bow, they separated. Mr. Strellenhaus walked down to the telegraph-office, where his message was delayed because Mr. Worlington Dodds was already at the end of the wires, for, after dim guesses and vague conjecture, he had suddenly caught a clear view of this coming event which had cast so curious a shadow before it in this little Irish town. Political rumours, names, appearances, telegrams, seasoned horses at any price, there could only be one meaning to it. He held a secret, and he meant to use it.

Mr. Warner, who was the partner of Mr. Worlington Dodds, and who was suffering from the same eclipse, had gone down to the Stock Exchange, but had found little consolation there, for the European system was in a ferment, and rumours of peace and of war were succeeding each other with such rapidity and assurance that it was impossible to know which to trust. It was obvious that a fortune lay either way, for every rumour set the funds fluctuating ; but without special information it was impossible to act, and no one dared to plunge heavily upon the strength of newspaper surmise and the gossip of the street. Warner knew that an hour's work might resuscitate the fallen fortunes of himself and his partner, and

yet he could not afford to make a mistake. He
returned to his office in the afternoon, half inclined to back the chances of peace, for of all
war-scares not one in ten comes to pass. As
he entered the office a telegram lay upon the
table. It was from Dunsloe, a place of which
he had never heard, and was signed by his absent partner. The message was in cypher, but
he soon translated it, for it was short and
crisp.

"I am a bear of everything German and
French. Sell, sell, sell, keep on selling."

For a moment Warner hesitated. What
could Worlington Dodds know at Dunsloe
which was not known in Throgmorton Street?
But he remembered the quickness and decision
of his partner. He would not have sent such
a message without very good grounds. If he
was to act at all he must act at once, so, hard-
ening his heart, he went down to the house,
and, dealing upon that curious system by which
a man can sell what he has not got, and what
he could not pay for if he had it, he disposed
of heavy parcels of French and German securi-
ties. He had caught the market in one of its
little spasms of hope, and there was no lack of
buying until his own persistent selling caused
others to follow his lead, and so brought about
a reaction. When Warner returned to his
offices it took him some hours to work out his

accounts, and he emerged into the streets in the evening with the absolute certainty that the next settling-day would leave him either hopelessly bankrupt or exceedingly prosperous.

It all depended upon Worlington Dodds's information. What could he possibly have found out at Dunsloe?

And then suddenly he saw a newspaper-boy fasten a poster upon a lamp-post, and a little crowd had gathered round it in an instant. One of them waved his hat in the air; another shouted to a friend across the street. Warner hurried up and caught a glimpse of the poster between two craning heads—

"FRANCE DECLARES WAR ON GERMANY."

"By Jove!" cried Warner. "Old Dodds was right, after all."

THE KING OF THE FOXES

IT was after a hunting dinner, and there were
as many scarlet coats as black ones round
the table. The conversation over the cigars
had turned, therefore, in the direction of horses
and horsemen, with reminiscences of phenom-
enal runs where foxes had led the pack from
end to end of a county, and been overtaken at
last by two or three limping hounds and a
huntsman on foot, while every rider in the
field had been pounded. As the port circu-
lated the runs became longer and more apoc-
ryphal, until we had the whips inquiring their
way and failing to understand the dialect of the
people who answered them. The foxes, too,
became more eccentric, and we had foxes up
pollard willows, foxes which were dragged by
the tail out of horses' mangers, and foxes
which had raced through an open front door
and gone to ground in a lady's bonnet-box.
The master had told one or two tall reminiscences, and when he cleared his throat for
another we were all curious, for he was a bit of

an artist in his way and produced his effects in a *crescendo* fashion. His face wore the earnest, practical, severely accurate expression which heralded some of his finest efforts.

" It was before I was master," said he. " Sir Charles Adair had the hounds at that time, and then afterwards they passed to old Lathom, and then to me. It may possibly have been just after Lathom took them over, but my strong impression is that it was in Adair's time. That would be early in the seventies—about seventy-two, I should say.

" The man I mean has moved to another part of the country, but I dare say that some of you can remember him. Danbury was the name—Walter Danbury, or Wat Danbury, as the people used to call him. He was the son of old Joe Danbury, of High Ascombe, and when his father died he came into a very good thing, for his only brother was drowned when the *Magna Charta* foundered, so he inherited the whole estate. It was but a few hundred acres, but it was good arable land, and those were the great days of farming. Besides, it was freehold, and a yeoman farmer without a mortgage was a warmish man before the great fall in wheat came. Foreign wheat and barbed wire—those are the two curses of this country, for the one spoils the farmer's work and the other spoils his play.

"This young Wat Danbury was a very fine fellow, a keen rider, and thorough sportsman, but his head was a little turned at having come, when so young, into a comfortable fortune, and he went the pace for a year or two. The lad had no vice in him, but there was a hard-drinking set in the neighbourhood at that time, and Danbury got drawn in among them ; and, being an amiable fellow who liked to do what his friends were doing, he very soon took to drinking a great deal more than was good for him. As a rule, a man who takes his exercise may drink as much as he likes in the evening, and do himself no very great harm, if he will leave it alone during the day. Danbury had too many friends for that, however, and it really looked as if the poor chap was going to the bad, when a very curious thing happened which pulled him up with such a sudden jerk that he never put his hand upon the neck of a whisky bottle again.

"He had a peculiarity which I have noticed in a good many other men, that though he was always playing tricks with his own health, he was none the less very anxious about it, and was extremely fidgety if ever he had any trivial symptom. Being a tough, open-air fellow, who was always as hard as a nail, it was seldom that there was anything amiss with him ; but at last the drink began to tell, and he woke one morning with his hands shaking and all his nerves tingling like overstretched fiddle-strings. He had been dining at some very wet house the night before, and the wine had, perhaps, been more plentiful than choice; at any rate, there he was, with a tongue like a bath-towel and a head that ticked like an eight-day clock. He was very alarmed at his own condition, and he sent for Doctor Middleton, of Ascombe, the father of the man who practises there now.

" Middleton had been a great friend of old Danbury's, and he was very sorry to see his son going to the devil; so he improved the occasion by taking his case very seriously, and lecturing him upon the danger of his ways. He shook his head and talked about the possibility of *delirium tremens*, or even of mania, if he continued to lead such a life. Wat Danbury was horribly frightened.

" ' Do you think I am going to get anything of the sort?' he wailed.

" ' Well, really, I don't know,' said the doctor, gravely. ' I cannot undertake to say that you are out of danger. Your system is very much out of order. At any time during the day you might have those grave symptoms of which I warn you.'

" ' You think I shall be safe by evening?'

" ' If you drink nothing during the day, and have no nervous symptoms before evening, I think you may consider yourself safe,' the doctor answered. A little fright would, he thought, do his patient good, so he made the most of the matter.

" 'What symptoms may I expect?' asked Danbury.

" 'It generally takes the form of optical delusions.'

" 'I see specks floating all about.'

" 'That is mere biliousness,' said the doctor soothingly, for he saw that the lad was highly strung and he did not wish to overdo it. 'I dare say that you will have no symptoms of the kind, but when they do come they usually take the shape of insects, or reptiles, or curious animals.'

" 'And if I see anything of the kind?'

" 'If you do, you will at once send for me;' and so, with a promise of medicine, the doctor departed.

" Young Wat Danbury rose and dressed and moped about the room feeling very miserable and unstrung, with a vision of the County Asylum for ever in his mind. He had the doctor's word for it that if he could get through to evening in safety he would be all right; but it is not very exhilarating to be waiting for symptoms, and to keep on glancing at your bootjack to see whether it is still a bootjack or whether it has begun to develop antennæ and legs. At last he could stand it no longer, and an overpowering longing for the fresh air and the green grass came over him. Why should he stay indoors when the Ascombe Hunt was meeting within half a mile of him? If he was going to have these delusions which the doctor talked of, he would not have them the sooner nor the worse because he was on horseback in the open. He was sure, too, it would ease his aching head. And so it came about that in ten minutes he was in his hunting-kit, and in ten more he was riding out of his stable-yard with his roan mare Matilda between his knees. He was a little unsteady in his saddle just at first, but the further he went the better he felt, until by the time he reached the meet his head was almost clear, and there was nothing troubling him except those haunting words of the doctor's about the possibility of delusions any time before nightfall.

" But soon he forgot that also, for as he came up the hounds were thrown off, and they drew the Gravel Hanger and afterwards the Hickory Copse. It was just the morning for a scent—no wind to blow it away, no water to wash it out, and just damp enough to make it cling. There was a field of forty, all keen men and good riders, so when they came to the Black Hanger they knew that there would be some sport, for that's a cover which never draws

blank. The woods were thicker in those days
than now, and the foxes were thicker also, and
that great dark oak-grove was swarming with
them. The only difficulty was to make them
break, for it is, as you know, a very close country, and you must coax them out into the open
before you can hope for a run.

"When they came to the Black Hanger the
field took their positions along the cover-side
wherever they thought that they were most
likely to get a good start. Some went in with
the hounds, some clustered at the ends of the
drives, and some kept outside in the hope of
the fox breaking in that direction. Young Wat
Danbury knew the country like the palm of his
hand, so he made for a place where several
drives intersected, and there he waited. He
had a feeling that the faster and the further he
galloped the better he should be, and so he was
chafing to be off. His mare, too, was in the
height of fettle and one of the fastest goers in
the county. Wat was a splendid light-weight
rider—under ten stone with his saddle—and
the mare was a powerful creature, all quarters
and shoulders, fit to carry a lifeguardsman ; and
so it was no wonder that there was hardly a man
in the field who could hope to stay with him.
There he waited and listened to the shouting of
the huntsman and the whips, catching a glimpse
now and then in the darkness of the wood of a

whisking tail, or the gleam of a white-and-tan side amongst the underwood. It was a well-trained pack, and there was not so much as a whine to tell you that forty hounds were working all round you.

" And then suddenly there came one long-drawn yell from one of them, and it was taken up by another, and another, until within a few seconds the whole pack was giving tongue together and running on a hot scent. Danbury saw them stream across one of the drives and disappear upon the other side, and an instant later the three red coats of the hunt-servants flashed after them upon the same line. He might have made a shorter cut down one of the other drives, but he was afraid of heading the fox, so he followed the lead of the huntsman. Right through the wood they went in a bee-line, galloping with their faces brushed by their horses' manes as they stooped under the branches. It's ugly going, as you know, with the roots all wriggling about in the dark-ness, but you can take a risk when you catch an occasional glimpse of the pack running with a breast-high scent ; so in and out they dodged, until the wood began to thin at the edges, and they found themselves in the long bottom where the river runs. It is clear going there upon grassland, and the hounds were running very strong about two hundred yards ahead, keeping parallel with the stream. The field, who had come round the wood instead of going through, were coming hard over the fields upon the left; but Danbury, with the hunt-servants, had a clear lead, and they never lost it. Two of the field got on terms with them: Parson Geddes on a big seventeen-hand bay which he used to ride in those days, and Squire Foley, who rode as a feather-weight, and made his hunters out of cast thoroughbreds from the Newmarket sales; but the others never had a look-in from start to finish, for there was no check and no pulling, and it was clear cross-country racing from start to finish. If you had drawn a line right across the map with a pencil you couldn't go straighter than that fox ran, heading for the South Downs and the sea; and the hounds ran as surely as if they were running to view, and yet from the beginning no one ever saw the fox, and there was never a hallo forrard to tell them that he had been spied. This, however, is not so surprising, for if you've been over that line of country you will know that there are not very many people about.

"There were six of them then in the front row: Parson Geddes, Squire Foley, the hunts-man, two whips, and Wat Danbury, who had forgotten all about his head and the doctor by this time, and had not a thought for anything but the run. All six were galloping just as hard as they could lay hoofs to the ground. One of the whips dropped back, however, as some of the hounds were tailing off, and that brought them down to five. Then Foley's thoroughbred strained herself, as these slim-legged, dainty-fetlocked thoroughbreds will do when the going is rough, and he had to take a back seat. But the other four were still going strong, and they did four or five miles down the river flat at a rasping pace. It had been a wet winter, and the waters had been out a little time before, so there was a deal of sliding and splashing; but by the time they came to the bridge the whole field was out of sight, and these four had the hunt to themselves.

" The fox had crossed the bridge—for foxes do not care to swim a chilly river any more than humans do—and from that point he had streaked away southward as hard as he could tear. It is broken country, rolling heaths, down one slope and up another, and it's hard to say whether the up or the down is the more trying for the horses. This sort of switchback work is all right for a cobby, short-backed, short-legged little horse, but it is killing work for a big, long-striding hunter such as one wants in the Midlands. Anyhow, it was too much for Parson Geddes' seventeen-hand bay, and, though he tried the Irish trick—for he was a rare keen sportsman—of running up the hills by his horse's head, it was all to no use, and he had to give it up. So then there was only the huntsman, the whip, and Wat Danbury—all going strong.

"But the country got worse and worse, and the hills were steeper and more thickly covered in heather and bracken. The horses were over their hocks all the time, and the place was pitted with rabbit-holes; but the hounds were still streaming along, and the riders could not afford to pick their steps. As they raced down one slope, the hounds were always flowing up the opposite one, until it looked like that game where the one figure in falling makes the other one rise. But never a glimpse did they get of the fox, although they knew very well that he must be only a very short way ahead for the scent to lie so strong. And then Wat Danbury heard a crash and a thud at his elbow, and looking round he saw a pair of white cords and top-boots kicking out of a tussock of brambles. The whip's horse had stumbled, and the whip was out of the running. Danbury and the huntsman eased down for an instant; and then, seeing the man staggering to his feet all right, they turned and settled into their saddles once more.

"Joe Clarke, the huntsman, was a famous old rider, known for five counties round; but he reckoned upon his second horse, and the

second horses had all been left many miles behind. However, the one he was riding was
good enough for anything with such a horseman upon his back, and he was going as well
as when he started. As to Wat Danbury, he
was going better. With every stride his own
feelings improved, and the mind of the rider
has its influence upon the mind of the horse.
The stout little roan was gathering its muscular
limbs under it and stretching to the gallop as if
it were steel and whalebone instead of flesh and
blood. Wat had never come to the end of its
powers yet, and to-day he had such a chance of
testing them as he had never had before.

" There was a pasture country beyond the
heather slopes, and for several miles the two
riders were either losing ground as they fumbled
with their crop-handles at the bars of gates, or
gaining it again as they galloped over the fields.
Those were the days before this accursed wire
came into the country, and you could generally
break a hedge where you could not fly it, so
they did not trouble the gates more than they
could help. Then they were down in a hard
lane, where they had to slacken their pace, and
through a farm where a man came shouting
excitedly after them ; but they had no time to
stop and listen to him, for the hounds were on
some ploughland, only two fields ahead. It
was sloping upwards, that ploughland, and the

horses were over their fetlocks in the red, soft soil. When they reached the top they were blowing badly, but a grand valley sloped before them, leading up to the open country of the South Downs. Between, there lay a belt of pine-woods, into which the hounds were streaming, running now in a long, straggling line and shedding one here and one there as they ran. You could see the white-and-tan dots here and there where the limpers were tailing away. But half the pack were still going well, though the pace and distance had both been tremendous —two clear hours now without a check.

" There was a drive through the pinewood— one of those green, slightly-rutted drives where a horse can get the last yard out of itself, for the ground is hard enough to give him clean going and yet springy enough to help him. Wat Danbury got alongside of the huntsman and they galloped together with their stirrup-irons touching, and the hounds within a hundred yards of them.

" ' We have it all to ourselves,' said he.

" ' Yes, sir, we've shook off the lot of 'em this time,' said old Joe Clarke. ' If we get this fox it's worth while 'aving 'im skinned an' stuffed, for 'e's a curiosity 'e is.'

" ' It's the fastest run I ever had in my life !' cried Danbury.

" ' And the fastest that ever I 'ad, an' that

means more,' said the old huntsman. ' But what licks me is that we've never 'ad a look at the beast. 'E must leave an amazin' scent be'ind 'im when these 'ounds can follow 'm like this, and yet none of us have seen 'im when we've 'ad a clear 'alf mile view in front of us.'

" ' I expect we'll have a view of him presently,' said Danbury; and in his mind he added, 'at least, I shall,' for the huntsman's horse was gasping as it ran, and the white foam was pouring down it like the side of a washing-tub.

" They had followed the hounds on to one of the side tracks which led out of the main drive, and that divided into a smaller track still, where the branches switched across their faces as they went and there was barely room for one horse at a time. Wat Danbury took the lead, and he heard the huntsman's horse clumping along heavily behind him, while his own mare was going with less spring than when she had started. She answered to a touch of his crop or spur, however, and he felt that there was something still left to draw upon. And then he looked up, and there was a heavy wooden stile at the end of the narrow track, with a lane of stiff young saplings leading down to it which was far too thick to break through. The hounds were running clear upon the grass-land on the other side, and you were bound either to get over that stile or lose sight of them, for the pace was too hot to let you go round.

" Well, Wat Danbury was not the lad to flinch, and at it he went full split, like a man who means what he is doing. She rose gallantly to it, rapped it hard with her front hoof, shook him on to her withers, recovered herself, and was over. Wat had hardly got back into his saddle when there was a clatter behind him like the fall of a woodstack, and there was the top bar in splinters, the horse on its belly, and the huntsman on hands and knees half a dozen yards in front of him. Wat pulled up for an instant, for the fall was a smasher ; but he saw old Joe spring to his feet and get to his horse's bridle. The horse staggered up, but the moment it put one foot in front of the other Wat saw that it was hopelessly lame—a slipped shoulder and a six-weeks' job. There was nothing he could do, and Joe was shouting to him not to lose the hounds, so off he went again, the one solitary survivor of the whole hunt. When a man finds himself there, he can retire from fox-hunting, for he has tasted the highest which it has to offer. I remember once when I was out with the Royal Surrey—but I'll tell you that story afterwards.

" The pack, or what was left of them, had got a bit ahead during this time ; but he had a clear view of them on the downland, and the mare seemed full of pride at being the only one left, for she was stepping out rarely and tossing her head as she went. There were two miles over the green shoulder of a hill, a rattle down a stony, deep-rutted country lane, where the mare stumbled and nearly came down, a jump over a five-foot brook, a cut through a hazel copse, another dose of heavy ploughland, a couple of gates to open, and then the green, unbroken Downs beyond. 'Well,' said Wat Danbury to himself, 'I'll see this fox run into or I shall see it drowned, for it's all clear going now between this and the chalk cliffs which line the sea.'

" But he was wrong in that, as he speedily discovered. In all the little hollows of the Downs at that part there are plantations of fir-woods, some of which have grown to a good size. You do not see them until you come upon the edge of the valleys in which they lie. Danbury was galloping hard over the short, springy turf, when he came over the lip of one of these depressions, and there was the dark clump of wood lying in front of and beneath him. There were only a dozen hounds still running, and they were just disappearing among the trees. The sunlight was shining straight upon the long, olive-green slopes which curved down towards this wood, and Danbury, who

had the eyes of a hawk, swept them over this
great expanse; but there was nothing moving
upon it. A few sheep were grazing far up on
the right, but there was no other sight of any
living creature. He was certain then that he
was very near to the end, for either the fox
must have gone to ground in the wood or the
hounds' noses must be at his very brush. The
mare seemed to know also what that great
empty sweep of countryside meant, for she
quickened her stride, and a few minutes afterwards Danbury was galloping into the fir-
wood.

" He had come from bright sunshine, but
the wood was very closely planted, and so dim
that he could hardly see to right or to left out
of the narrow path down which he was riding.
You know what a solemn, churchyardy sort of
place a fir-wood is. I suppose it is the absence
of any undergrowth, and the fact that the trees
never move at all. At any rate, a kind of chill
suddenly struck Wat Danbury, and it flashed
through his mind that there had been some
very singular points about this run—its length
and its straightness, and the fact that from the
first find no one had ever caught a glimpse of
the creature. Some silly talk which had been
going round the country about the king of the
foxes—a sort of demon fox, so fast that it could
outrun any pack, and so fierce that they could

do nothing with it if they overtook it—suddenly came back into his mind, and it did not seem so laughable now in the dim fir-wood as it had done when the story had been told over the wine and cigars. The nervousness which had been on him in the morning, and which he had hoped that he had shaken off, swept over him again in an overpowering wave. He had been so proud of being alone, and yet he would have given ten pounds now to have had Joe Clarke's homely face beside him. And then, just at that moment, there broke out from the thickest part of the wood the most frantic hullaballoo that ever he had heard in his life. The hounds had run into their fox.

" Well, you know, or you ought to know, what your duty is in such a case. You have to be whip, huntsman, and everything else if you are the first man up. You get in among the hounds, lash them off, and keep the brush and pads from being destroyed. Of course, Wat Danbury knew all about that, and he tried to force his mare through the trees to the place where all this hideous screaming and howling came from, but the wood was so thick that it was impossible to ride it. He sprang off, therefore, left the mare standing, and broke his way through as best he could with his hunting-lash ready over his shoulder. But as he ran forward he felt his flesh go cold and creepy all over. He had heard hounds run into foxes many times before, but he had never heard such sounds as these. They were not the cries of triumph, but of fear. Every now and then came a shrill yelp of mortal agony. Holding his breath, he ran on until he broke through the interlacing branches and found himself in a little clearing with the hounds all crowding round a patch of tangled bramble at the further end.

" When he first caught sight of them the hounds were standing in a half-circle round this bramble-patch with their backs bristling and their jaws gaping. In front of the brambles lay one of them with his throat torn out, all crimson and white-and-tan. Wat came running out into the clearing, and at the sight of him the hounds took heart again, and one of them sprang with a growl into the bushes. At the same instant, a creature the size of a donkey jumped on to its feet, a huge grey head, with monstrous glistening fangs and tapering fox jaws, shot out from among the branches, and the hound was thrown several feet into the air, and fell howling among the cover. Then there was a clashing snap like a rat-trap closing, and the howls sharpened into a scream and then were still.

" Danbury had been on the look-out for symptoms all day, and now he had found them. He looked once more at the thicket, saw a pair of savage red eyes fixed upon him, and fairly took to his heels. It might only be a passing delusion, or it might be the permanent mania of which the doctor had spoken, but, anyhow, the thing to do was to get back to bed and to quiet, and to hope for the best. He forgot the hounds, the hunt, and everything else in his desperate fears for his own reason. He sprang upon his mare, galloped her madly over the downs, and only stopped when he found himself at a country station. There he left his mare at the inn, and made back for home as quickly as steam would take him. It was evening before he got there, shivering with apprehension and seeing those red eyes and savage teeth at every turn. He went straight to bed and sent for Dr. Middleton.

" 'I've got 'em, doctor,' said he. 'It came about exactly as you said—strange creatures, optical delusions, and everything. All I ask you now is to save my reason.'

" The doctor listened to his story, and was shocked as he heard it.

" 'It appears to be a very clear case,' said he. 'This must be a lesson to you for life.'

" 'Never a drop again if I only come safely through this,' cried Wat Danbury.

" 'Well, my dear boy, if you will stick to

that it may prove a blessing in disguise. But the difficulty in this case is to know where fact ends and fancy begins. You see, it is not as if there was only one delusion. There have been several. The dead dogs, for example, must have been one as well as the creature in the bush.'

" ' I saw it all as clearly as I see you.'

" ' One of the characteristics of this form of delirium is that what you see is even clearer than reality. I was wondering whether the whole run was not a delusion also.'

" Wat Danbury pointed to his hunting-boots still lying upon the floor, flecked with the splashings of two counties.

" ' Hum ! that looks very real, certainly. No doubt, in your weak state, you over-exerted yourself and so brought this attack upon yourself. Well, whatever the cause, our treatment is clear. You will take the soothing mixture which I will send to you, and we shall put two leeches upon your temples to-night to relieve any congestion of the brain.'

" So Wat Danbury spent the night in tossing about and reflecting what a sensitive thing this machinery of ours is, and how very foolish it is to play tricks with what is so easily put out of gear and so difficult to mend. And so he repeated and repeated his oath that this first lesson should be his last, and that from that time forward he would be a sober, hard-working yeoman as his father had been before him. So he lay, tossing and still repentant, when his door flew open in the morning and in rushed the doctor with a newspaper crumpled up in his hand.

" 'My dear boy,' he cried. 'I owe you a thousand apologies. You're the most ill-used lad and I the greatest numskull in the county. Listen to this!' And he sat down upon the side of the bed, flattened out his paper upon his knee, and began to read.

" The paragraph was headed, 'Disaster to the Ascombe Hounds,' and it went on to say that four of the hounds, shockingly torn and mangled, had been found in Winton Fir Wood upon the South Downs. The run had been so severe that half the pack were lamed; but the four found in the wood were actually dead, although the cause of their extraordinary injuries was still unknown. 'So you see,' said the doctor, looking up, 'that I was wrong when I put the dead hounds among the delusions.'

" 'But the cause?' cried Wat.

" 'Well, I think we may guess the cause from an item which has been inserted just as the paper went to press. " Late last night, Mr. Brown, of Smither's Farm, to the east of Hastings, perceived what he imagined to be an enormous dog worrying one of his sheep. He shot the creature, which proves to be a grey Siberian wolf of the variety known as *Lupus Giganticus*. It is supposed to have escaped from some travelling menagerie." '

"That's the story, gentlemen, and Wat Danbury stuck to his good resolutions, for the fright which he had, cured him of all wish to run such a risk again; and he never touches anything stronger than lime-juice—at least, he hadn't before he left this part of the country, five years ago next Lady Day."

THE THREE CORRESPOND-
ENTS

THERE was only the one little feathery
clump of dôm palms in all that great
wilderness of black rocks and orange sand. It
stood high on the bank, and below it the brown
Nile swirled swiftly towards the Ambigole
Cataract, fitting a little frill of foam round each
of the boulders which studded its surface.
Above, out of a naked blue sky, the sun was
beating down upon the sand, and up again
from the sand under the brims of the pith-hats
of the horsemen with the scorching glare of a
blast-furnace. It had risen so high that the
shadows of the horses were no larger than
themselves.

"Whew!" cried Mortimer, mopping his
forehead, "you'd pay five shillings for this at
the hummums."

"Precisely," said Scott. "But you are not
asked to ride twenty miles in a Turkish bath
with a field-glass and a revolver, and a water-
bottle and a whole Christmas-treeful of things

dangling from you. The hot-house at Kew is excellent as a conservatory, but not adapted for exhibitions upon the horizontal bar. I vote for a camp in the palm-grove and a halt until evening."

Mortimer rose on his stirrups and looked hard to the southward. Everywhere were the same black burned rocks and deep orange sand. At one spot only an intermittent line appeared to have been cut through the rugged spurs which ran down to the river. It was the bed of the old railway, long destroyed by the Arabs, but now in process of reconstruction by the advancing Egyptians. There was no other sign of man's handiwork in all that desolate scene.

" It's palm trees or nothing," said Scott.

" Well, I suppose we must ; and yet I grudge every hour until we catch the force up. What *would* our editors say if we were late for the action ? "

" My dear chap, an old bird like you doesn't need to be told that no sane modern general would ever attack until the Press is up."

" You don't mean that," said young Anerley. " I thought we were looked upon as an unmitigated nuisance."

" ' Newspaper correspondents and travelling gentlemen, and all that tribe of useless drones ' —being an extract from Lord Wolseley's ' Soldier's Pocket-Book,'" cried Scott. "We know all about *that*, Anerley;" and he winked behind his blue spectacles. "If there was going to be a battle we should very soon have an escort of cavalry to hurry us up. I've been in fifteen, and I never saw one where they had not arranged for a reporters' table."

"That's very well; but the enemy may be less considerate," said Mortimer.

"They are not strong enough to force a battle."

"A skirmish, then?"

"Much more likely to be a raid upon the rear. In that case we are just where we should be."

"So we are! What a score over Reuter's man up with the advance! Well, we'll outspan and have our tiffin under the palms."

There were three of them, and they stood for three great London dailies. Reuter's was thirty miles ahead; two evening pennies upon camels were twenty miles behind. And among them they represented the eyes and ears of the public—the great silent millions and millions who had paid for everything, and who waited so patiently to know the result of their outlay.

They were remarkable men these body-servants of the Press; two of them already veterans in camps, the other setting out upon his first campaign, and full of deference for his famous comrades.

This first one, who had just dismounted from his bay polo-pony, was Mortimer, of the *Intelligence*—tall, straight, and hawk-faced, with khaki tunic and riding-breeches, drab putties, a scarlet cummerbund, and a skin tanned to the red of a Scotch fir by sun and wind, and mottled by the mosquito and the sand-fly. The other—small, quick, mercurial, with blue-black, curling beard and hair, a fly-switch for ever flicking in his left hand—was Scott, of the *Courier*, who had come through more dangers and brought off more brilliant *coups* than any man in the profession, save the eminent Chandler, now no longer in a condition to take the field. They were a singular contrast, Mortimer and Scott, and it was in their differences that the secret of their close friendship lay. Each dovetailed into the other. The strength of each was in the other's weakness. Together they formed a perfect unit. Mortimer was Saxon—slow, conscientious, and deliberate; Scott was Celtic—quick, happy-go-lucky, and brilliant. Mortimer was the more solid, Scott the more attractive. Mortimer was the deeper thinker, Scott the brighter talker. By a curious coincidence, though each had seen much of warfare, their campaigns had never coincided. Together they covered all recent military history. Scott had done Plevna, the Shipka, the Zulus, Egypt, Suakim ; Mortimer had seen the Boer War, the Chilian, the Bulgaria and Servian, the Gordon relief, the Indian frontier, Brazilian rebellion, and Madagascar. This intimate personal knowledge gave a peculiar flavour to their talk. There was none of the second-hand surmise and conjecture which form so much of our conversation ; it was all concrete and final. The speaker had been there, had seen it, and there was an end of it.

In spite of their friendship there was the keenest professional rivalry between the two men. Either would have sacrificed himself to help his companion, but either would also have sacrificed his companion to help his paper. Never did a jockey yearn for a winning mount as keenly as each of them longed to have a full column in a morning edition whilst every other daily was blank. They were perfectly frank about the matter. Each professed himself ready to steal a march on his neighbour, and each recognized that the other's duty to his employer was far higher than any personal consideration.

The third man was Anerley, of the *Gazette*— young, inexperienced, and rather simple-looking. He had a droop of the lip which some of his more intimate friends regarded as a libel upon his character, and his eyes were so slow and so sleepy that they suggested an affectation.

A leaning towards soldiering had sent him twice to autumn manœuvres, and a touch of colour in his descriptions had induced the proprietors of the *Gazette* to give him a trial as a war-special. There was a pleasing diffidence about his bearing which recommended him to his experienced companions, and if they had a smile sometimes at his guileless ways, it was soothing to them to have a comrade from whom nothing was to be feared. From the day that they left the telegraph-wire behind them at Sarras, the man who was mounted upon a fifteen-guinea thirteen-four Syrian was delivered over into the hands of the owners of the two fastest polo-ponies that ever shot down the Ghezireh ground.

The three had dismounted and led their beasts under the welcome shade. In the brassy, yellow glare every branch above threw so black and solid a shadow that the men involuntarily raised their feet to step over them.

"The palm makes an excellent hat-rack," said Scott, slinging his revolver and his water-bottle over the little upward-pointing pegs which bristle from the trunk. "As a shade-tree, however, it isn't an unqualified success. Curious that in the universal adaptation of means to ends something a little less flimsy could not have been devised for the tropics."

" Like the banyan in India."

"Or the fine hardwood trees in Ashantee, where a whole regiment could picnic under the shade."

"The teak tree isn't bad in Burmah, either. By Jove, the baccy has all come loose in the saddle-bag! That long-cut mixture smokes rather hot for this climate. How about the baggles, Anerley?"

"They'll be here in five minutes."

Down the winding path which curved among the rocks the little train of baggage camels was daintily picking its way. They came mincing and undulating along, turning their heads slowly from side to side with the air of a self-conscious woman. In front rode the three Berberee body-servants upon donkeys, and behind walked the Arab camel-boys. They had been travelling for nine long hours, ever since the first rising of the moon, at the weary camel-drag of two and a half miles an hour, but now they brightened, both beasts and men, at the sight of the grove and the riderless horses. In a few minutes the loads were unstrapped, the animals tethered, a fire lighted, fresh water carried up from the river, and each camel provided with his own little heap of tibbin laid in the centre of the tablecloth, without which no well-bred Arabian will condescend to feed. The dazzling light without, the subdued half-tones within, the green palm-fronds outlined against the deep blue sky, the flitting, silent-footed Arab servants, the crackling of sticks, the reek of a lighting fire, the placid, supercilious heads of the camels, they all come back in their dreams to those who have known them.

Scott was breaking eggs into a pan and rolling out a love-song in his rich, deep voice. Anerley, with his head and arms buried in a deal packing-case, was working his way through strata of tinned soups, bully beef, potted chicken and sardines to reach the jams which lay beneath. The conscientious Mortimer, with his notebook upon his knee, was jotting down what the railway engineer had told him at the line-end the day before. Suddenly he raised his eyes and saw the man himself on his chestnut pony, dipping and rising over the broken ground.

" Hullo ! here's Merryweather ! "

" A pretty lather his pony is in ! He's had her at that hand-gallop for hours, by the look of her. Hullo, Merryweather, hullo ! "

The engineer, a small, compact man with a pointed red beard, had made as though he would ride past their camp without word or halt. Now he swerved, and easing his pony down to a canter, he headed her towards them.

" For God's sake, a drink ! " he croaked. " My tongue is stuck to the roof of my mouth."

Mortimer ran with the water-bottle, Scott

with the whisky-flask, and Anerley with the tin pannikin. The engineer drank until his breath failed him.

"Well, I must be off," said he, striking the drops from his red moustache.

"Any news?"

"A hitch in the railway construction. I must see the General. It's the devil not having a telegraph."

"Anything we can report?" Out came three notebooks.

"I'll tell you after I've seen the General."

"Any dervishes?"

"The usual shaves. Hud-up, Jinny! Goodbye."

With a soft thudding upon the sand and a clatter among the stones the weary pony was off upon her journey once more.

"Nothing serious, I suppose?" said Mortimer, staring after him.

"Deuced serious," cried Scott. "The ham and eggs are burned! No—it's all right—saved, and done to a turn! Pull the box up, Anerley. Come on, Mortimer, stow that notebook! The fork is mightier than the pen just at present. What's the matter with you, Anerley?"

"I was wondering whether what we have just seen was worth a telegram."

"Well, it's for the proprietors to say if it's

worth it. Sordid money considerations are not for us. We must wire about something just to justify our kharki coats and our putties."

"But what is there to say?"

Mortimer's long, austere face broke into a smile over the youngster's innocence. "It's not quite usual in our profession to give each other tips," said he. "However, as my telegram is written, I've no objection to your reading it. You may be sure that I would not show it to you if it were of the slightest importance."

Anerley took up the slip of paper and read—

"Merryweather obstacles stop journey confer General stop nature difficulties later stop rumours dervishes."

"This is very condensed," said Anerley, with wrinkled brows.

"Condensed!" cried Scott. "Why, it's sinfully garrulous. If my old man got a wire like that his language would crack the lampshades. I'd cut out half this; for example, I'd have out 'journey,' and 'nature,' and 'rumours.' But my old man would make a ten-line paragraph of it for all that."

"How?"

"Well, I'll do it myself just to show you. Lend me that stylo." He scribbled for a minute in his notebook. "It works out somewhat on these lines—

"'Mr. Charles H. Merryweather, the eminent railway engineer, who is at present engaged in superintending the construction of the line from Sarras to the front, has met with considerable obstacles to the rapid completion of his important task'—of course the old man knows who Merryweather is, and what he is about, so the word 'obstacles' would suggest all that to him. 'He has to-day been compelled to make a journey of forty miles to the front in order to confer with the General upon the steps which are necessary in order to facilitate the work. Further particulars of the exact nature of the difficulties met with will be made public at a later date. All is quiet upon the line of communications, though the usual persistent rumours of the presence of dervishes in the Eastern desert continue to circulate.—*Our own Correspondent.*'

"How's that?" cried Scott, triumphantly, and his white teeth gleamed suddenly through his black beard. "That's the sort of flapdoodle for the dear old public."

"Will it interest them?"

"Oh, everything interests them. They want to know all about it; and they like to think that there is a man who is getting a hundred a month simply in order to tell it to them."

"It's very kind of you to teach me all this."

" Well, it is a little unconventional, for, after all, we are here to score over each other if we can. There are no more eggs, and you must take it out in jam. Of course, as Mortimer says, such a telegram as this is of no importance one way or another, except to prove to the office that we *are* in the Soudan and not at Monte Carlo. But when it comes to serious work it must be every man for himself."

" Is that quite necessary ? "

" Why, of course it is."

" I should have thought if three men were to combine and to share their news, they would do better than if they were each to act for himself; and they would have a much pleasanter time of it."

The two older men sat with their bread-and-jam in their hands, and an expression of genuine disgust upon their faces.

" We are not here to have a pleasant time," said Mortimer, with a flash through his glasses. " We are here to do our best for our papers. How can they score over each other if we do not do the same. If we all combine we might as well amalgamate with Reuter at once."

" Why, it would take away the whole glory of the profession!" cried Scott. " At present the smartest man gets his stuff first on the wires. What inducement is there to be smart if we all share and share alike."

" And at present the man with the best equipment has the best chance," remarked Mortimer, glancing across at the shot-silk polo ponies and the cheap little Syrian gray. " That is the fair reward of foresight and enterprise. Every man for himself, and let the best man win."

" That's the way to find who the best man is. Look at Chandler. He would never have got his chance if he had not played always off his own bat. You've heard how he pretended to break his leg, sent his fellow-correspondent off for the doctor, and so got a fair start for the telegraph office."

" Do you mean to say that was legitimate ? "

" Everything is legitimate. It's your wits against my wits."

" I should call it dishonourable."

" You may call it what you like. Chandler's paper got the battle and the others didn't. It made Chandler's name."

" Or take Westlake," said Mortimer, cramming the tobacco into his pipe. " Hi, Abdul, you may have the dishes ! Westlake brought his stuff down by pretending to be the Government courier, and using the relays of Government horses. Westlake's paper sold half a million."

" Is that legitimate also," asked Anerley, thoughtfully.

" Why not ? "

" Well, it looks a little like horse-stealing and lying."

" Well, *I* think I should do a little horse-stealing and lying if I could have a column to myself in a London daily. What do you say, Scott? "

" Anything short of manslaughter."

" And I'm not sure that I'd trust you there."

" Well, I don't think I should be guilty of newspaper-man-slaughter. That I regard as a distinct breach of professional etiquette. But if any outsider comes between a highly-charged correspondent and an electric wire, he does it at his peril. My dear Anerley, I tell you frankly that if you are going to handicap yourself with scruples you may just as well be in Fleet Street as in the Soudan. Our life is irregular. Our work has never been systematized. No doubt it will be some day, but the time is not yet. Do what you can and how you can, and be first on the wires ; that's my advice to you ; and also, that when next you come upon a campaign you bring with you the best horse that money can buy. Mortimer may beat me or I may beat Mortimer, but at least we know that between us we have the fastest ponies in the country. We have neglected no chance."

" I am not so certain of that," said Mortimer, slowly. " You are aware, of course, that though a horse beats a camel on twenty miles, a camel beats a horse on thirty."

" What, one of those camels ? " cried Anerley in astonishment.

The two seniors burst out laughing.

" No, no, the real high-bred trotter—the kind of beast the dervishes ride when they make their lightning raids."

" Faster than a galloping horse ? "

" Well, it tires a horse down. It goes the same gait all the way, and it wants neither halt nor drink, and it takes rough ground much better than a horse. They used to have long-distance races at Halfa, and the camel always won at thirty."

" Still, we need not reproach ourselves, Scott, for we are not very likely to have to carry a thirty-mile message. They will have the field telegraph next week."

" Quite so. But at the present moment——"

" I know, my dear chap ; but there is no motion of urgency before the house. Load baggles at five o'clock ; so you have just three hours clear. Any sign of the evening pennies?"

Mortimer swept the northern horizon with his binoculars.

" Not in sight yet."

" They are quite capable of travelling during the heat of the day. Just the sort of thing evening pennies *would* do. Take care of your

match, Anerley. These palm groves go up
like a powder magazine if you set them alight.
Bye-bye." The two men crawled under their
mosquito-nets and sank instantly into the easy
sleep of those whose lives are spent in the
open.

Young Anerley stood with his back against
a palm tree and his briar between his lips,
thinking over the advice which he had received.
After all, they were the heads of the profession,
these men, and it was not for him, the newcomer,
to reform their methods. If they served their
papers in this fashion, then he must do the
same. They had at least been frank and generous in teaching him the rules of the game.
If it was good enough for them it was good
enough for him.

It was a broiling afternoon, and those thin
frills of foam round the black, glistening necks
of the Nile boulders looked delightfully cool
and alluring. But it would not be safe to bathe
for some hours to come. The air shimmered
and vibrated over the baking stretch of sand
and rock. There was not a breath of wind, and
the droning and piping of the insects inclined
one for sleep. Somewhere above a hoopoe was
calling. Anerley knocked out his ashes, and
was turning towards his couch, when his eye
caught something moving in the desert to the
south.

It was a horseman riding towards them as swiftly as the broken ground would permit. A messenger from the army, thought Anerley; and then, as he watched, the sun suddenly struck the man on the side of the head, and his chin flamed into gold. There could not be two horsemen with beards of such a colour. It was Merryweather, the engineer, and he was returning. What on earth was he returning for? He had been so keen to see the General, and yet he was coming back with his mission unaccomplished. Was it that his pony was hopelessly foundered? It seemed to be moving well. Anerley picked up Mortimer's binoculars, and a foam-spattered horse and a weary koorbash-cracking man came cantering up the centre of the field. But there was nothing in his appearance to explain the mystery of his return.

Then as he watched them they dipped down into a hollow and disappeared. He could see that it was one of those narrow khors which led to the river, and he waited, glass in hand, for their immediate reappearance. But minute passed after minute and there was no sign of them. That narrow gully appeared to have swallowed them up. And then with a curious gulp and start he saw a little gray cloud wreathe itself slowly from among the rocks and drift in a long, hazy shred over the desert. In an instant he had torn Scott and Mortimer from their slumbers.

"Get up, you chaps!" he cried. "I believe Merryweather has been shot by dervishes."

"And Reuter not here!" cried the two veterans, exultantly clutching at their note-books. "Merryweather shot! Where? When? How?"

In a few words Anerley explained what he had seen.

"You heard nothing?"

"Nothing."

"Well, a shot loses itself very easily among rocks. By George, look at the buzzards!"

Two large brown birds were soaring in the deep blue heaven. As Scott spoke they circled down and dropped into the little khor.

"That's good enough," said Mortimer, with his nose between the leaves of his book. "'Merryweather headed dervishes stop re-turned stop shot mutilated stop raid communi-cations.' How's that?"

"You think he was headed off?"

"Why else should he return?"

"In that case, if they were out in front of him and others cut him off, there must be sev-eral small raiding-parties."

"I should judge so."

"How about the 'mutilated'?"

"I've fought against Arabs before."

" Where are you off to ? "

" Sarras."

" I think I'll race you in," said Scott.

Anerley stared in astonishment at the absolutely impersonal way in which these men regarded the situation. In their zeal for news it
had apparently never struck them that they,
their camp and their servants, were all in the
lion's mouth. But even as they talked there
came the harsh, importunate rat-tat-tat of an
irregular volley from among the rocks, and the
high, keening whistle of bullets over their heads.
A palm spray fluttered down amongst them.
At the same instant the six frightened servants
came running wildly in for protection.

It was the cool-headed Mortimer who organized the defence, for Scott's Celtic soul was
so aflame at all this " copy " in hand and more
to come, that he was too exuberantly boisterous
for a commander. The other, with his spectacles and his stern face, soon had the servants
in hand.

" *Tali henna! Egri!* What the deuce are
you frightened about ? Put the camels between
the palm trunks. That's right. Now get the
knee-tethers on them. *Quies!* Did you never
hear bullets before ? Now put the donkeys
here. Not much—you don't get my polo-pony
to make a zareba with. Picket the ponies between the grove and the river out of danger's

way. These fellows seem to fire even higher than they did in '85."

"That's got home, anyhow," said Scott, as they heard a soft, splashing thud like a stone in a mud-bank.

"Who's hit, then?"

"The brown camel that's chewing the cud."

As he spoke the creature, its jaw still working, laid its long neck along the ground and closed its large dark eyes.

"That shot cost me fifteen pounds," said Mortimer, ruefully. "How many of them do you make?"

"Four, I think."

"Only four Bezingers, at any rate; there may be some spearmen."

"I think not; it is a little raiding-party of riflemen. By the way, Anerley, you've never been under fire before, have you?"

"Never," said the young pressman, who was conscious of a curious feeling of nervous elation.

"Love and poverty and war, they are all experiences necessary to make a complete life. Pass over those cartridges. This is a very mild baptism that you are undergoing, for behind these camels you are as safe as if you were sitting in the back room of the Authors' Club."

"As safe, but hardly as comfortable," said

Scott. "A long glass of hock and seltzer would be exceedingly acceptable. But oh, Mortimer, what a chance! Think of the General's feelings when he hears that the first action of the war has been fought by the Press column. Think of Reuter, who has been stewing at the front for a week! Think of the evening pennies just too late for the fun! By George, that slug brushed a mosquito off me!"

"And one of the donkeys is hit."

"This is sinful. It will end in our having to carry our own kits to Khartoum."

"Never mind, my boy, it all goes to make copy. I can see the headlines—'Raid on Communications': 'Murder of British Engineer': 'Press Column Attacked.' Won't it be ripping?"

"I wonder what the next line will be?" said Anerley.

"'Our Special Wounded!'" cried Scott, rolling over on to his back. "No harm done," he added, gathering himself up again; "only a chip off my knee. This is getting sultry. I confess that the idea of that back room at the Authors' Club begins to grow upon me."

"I have some diachylon."

"Afterwards will do. We're having 'a 'appy day with Fuzzy on the rush.' I wish he *would* rush."

"They're coming nearer."

"This is an excellent revolver of mine if it didn't throw so devilish high. I always aim at a man's toes if I want to stimulate his digestion. O Lord, there's our kettle gone!"

With a boom like a dinner-gong a Remington bullet had passed through the kettle, and a cloud of steam hissed up from the fire. A wild shout came from the rocks above.

"The idiots think that they have blown us up. They'll rush us now, as sure as fate; then it will be our turn to lead. Got your revolver, Anerley?"

"I have this double-barrelled fowling-piece."

"Sensible man! It's the best weapon in the world at this sort of rough-and-tumble work. What cartridges?"

"Swan-shot."

"That will do all right. I carry this big bore double-barrelled pistol loaded with slugs. You might as well try to stop one of these fellows with a peashooter as with a service revolver."

"There are ways and means," said Scott. "The Geneva Convention does not hold south of the first cataract. It's easy to make a bullet mushroom by a little manipulation of the tip of it. When I was in the broken square at Tamai——"

"Wait a bit," cried Mortimer, adjusting his glasses. "I think they are coming now."

" The time," said Scott, snapping up his watch, " being exactly seventeen minutes past four."

Anerley had been lying behind a camel, staring with an interest which bordered upon fascination at the rocks opposite. Here was a little woolly puff of smoke, and there was another one, but never once had they caught a glimpse of the attackers. To him there was something weird and awesome in these unseen, persistent men who, minute by minute, were drawing closer to them. He had heard them cry out when the kettle was broken, and once, immediately afterwards, an enormously strong voice had roared something which had set Scott shrugging his shoulders.

" They've got to take us first," said he, and Anerley thought his nerve might be better if he did not ask for a translation.

The firing had begun at a distance of some hundred yards, which put it out of the question for them, with their lighter weapons, to make any reply to it. Had their antagonists continued to keep that range the defenders must either have made a hopeless sally or tried to shelter themselves behind their zareba as best they might on the chance that the sound might bring up help. But luckily for them the African had never taken kindly to the rifle, and his primitive instinct to close with his enemy is always too strong for his sense of strategy. They were drawing in, therefore, and now for the first time Anerley caught sight of a face looking at them from over a rock. It was a huge, virile, strong-jawed head of a pure negro type, with silver trinkets gleaming in the ears. The man raised a great arm from behind the rock and shook his Remington at them.

"Shall I fire?" asked Anerley.

"No, no, it is too far; your shot would scatter all over the place."

"It's a picturesque ruffian," said Scott. "Couldn't you kodak him, Mortimer? There's another!"

A fine-featured brown Arab, with a black, pointed beard, was peeping from behind another boulder. He wore the green turban which proclaimed him hadji, and his face showed the keen, nervous exaltation of the religious fanatic.

"They seem a piebald crowd," said Scott.

"That last is one of the real fighting Baggara," remarked Mortimer. "He's a dangerous man."

"He looks pretty vicious. There's another negro!"

"Two more! Dingas, by the look of them. Just the same chaps we get our own black battalions from. As long as they get a fight they don't mind who it's for; but if the idiots had only sense enough to understand, they would know that the Arab is their hereditary enemy, and we their hereditary friends. Look at the silly juggins gnashing his teeth at the very men who put down the slave trade ! "

" Couldn't you explain ? "

" I'll explain with this pistol when he comes a little nearer. Now sit tight, Anerley. They're off ! "

They were indeed. It was the brown man with the green turban who headed the rush. Close at his heels was the negro with the silver ear-rings—a giant of a man, and the other two were only a little behind. As they sprang over the rocks one after the other, it took Anerley back to the school sports when he held the tape for the hurdle-race. It was magnificent, the wild spirit and abandon of it, the flutter of the che-quered galabeeahs, the gleam of steel, the wave of black arms, the frenzied faces, the quick pitter-patter of the rushing feet. The law-abid-ing Briton is so imbued with the idea of the sanctity of human life that it was hard for the young pressman to realize that these men had every intention of killing him, and that he was at perfect liberty to do as much for them. He lay staring as if this were a show and he a spectator.

" Now, Anerley, now ! Take the Arab ! " cried somebody.

He put up the gun and saw the brown fierce

face at the other end of the barrel. He tugged
at the trigger, but the face grew larger and
fiercer with every stride. Again and again he
tugged. A revolver-shot rang out at his elbow,
then another one, and he saw a red spot spring
out on the Arab's brown breast. But he was
still coming on.

"Shoot, you ass, shoot!" screamed Scott.

Again he strained unavailingly at the trigger.
There were two more pistol-shots, and the big
negro had fallen and risen and fallen again.

"Cock it, you fool!" shouted a furious
voice; and at the same instant, with a rush and
flutter, the Arab bounded over the prostrate
camel and came down with his bare feet upon
Anerley's chest. In a dream he seemed to be
struggling frantically with some one upon the
ground, then he was conscious of a tremendous
explosion in his very face, and so ended for him
the first action of the war.

* * * * * *

"Good-bye, old chap. You'll be all right.
Give yourself time." It was Mortimer's voice,
and he became dimly conscious of a long-spec-
tacled face, and of a heavy hand upon his
shoulder.

"Sorry to leave you. We'll be lucky now
if we are in time for the morning editions."
Scott was tightening his girth as he spoke.

" We'll put in our wire that you have been hurt, so your people will know why they don't hear from you. If Reuter or the evening pennies come up, don't give the thing away. Abbas will look after you, and we'll be back tomorrow afternoon. Bye-bye ! "

Anerley heard it all, though he did not feel energy enough to answer. Then, as he watched two sleek brown ponies with their yellow-clad riders dwindling among the rocks, his memory cleared suddenly, and he realized that the first great journalistic chance of his life was slipping away from him. It was a small fight, but it was the first of the war, and the great public at home was all athirst for news. They would have it in the *Courier*; they would have it in the *Intelligence*, and not a word in the *Gazette*. The thought brought him to his feet, though he had to throw his arm around the stem of the palm tree to steady his swimming head.

There was the big black man lying where he had fallen, his huge chest pocked with bullet-marks, every wound rosetted with its circle of flies. The Arab was stretched out within a few yards of him, with two hands clasped over the dreadful thing which had been his head. Across him was lying Anerley's fowling-piece, one barrel discharged, the other at half cock.

" Scott effendi shoot him your gun," said a

voice. It was Abbas, his English-speaking body-servant.

Anerley groaned at the disgrace of it. He had lost his head so completely that he had forgotten to cock his gun; and yet he knew that it was not fear but interest which had so absorbed him. He put his hand up to his head and felt that a wet handkerchief was bound round his forehead.

" Where are the two other dervishes ? "

" They ran away. One got shot in arm."

" What's happened to me ? "

" Effendi got cut on head. Effendi catch bad man by arms, and Scott effendi shoot him. Face burn very bad."

Anerley became conscious suddenly that there was a tingling about his skin and an overpowering smell of burned hair under his nostrils. He put his hand to his moustache. It was gone. His eyebrows too ? He could not find them. His head, no doubt, was very near to the dervish's when they were rolling upon the ground together, and this was the effect of the explosion of his own gun. Well, he would have time to grow some more hair before he saw Fleet Street again. But the cut, perhaps, was a more serious matter. Was it enough to prevent him from getting to the telegraph-office at Sarras ? The only way was to try and see.

But there was only that poor little Syrian gray of his. There it stood in the evening sunshine, with a sunk head and a bent knee, as if its morning's work was still heavy upon it. What hope was there of being able to do thirty-five miles of heavy going upon that? It would be a strain upon the splendid ponies of his companions—and they were the swiftest and most enduring in the country. The most enduring? There was one creature more enduring, and that was a real trotting camel. If he had had one he might have got to the wires first after all, for Mortimer had said that over thirty miles they have the better of any horse. Yes, if he had only had a real trotting camel! And then like a flash came Mortimer's words, "It is the kind of beast that the dervishes ride when they make their lightning raids."

The beasts the dervishes ride! What had these dead dervishes ridden! In an instant he was clambering up the rocks, with Abbas protesting at his heels. Had the two fugitives carried away all the camels, or had they been content to save themselves? The brass gleam from a litter of empty Remington cases caught his eye, and showed where the enemy had been crouching. And then he could have shouted for joy, for there, in the hollow, some little distance off, rose the high, graceful white neck and the elegant head of such a camel as he had never set eyes upon before—a swan-like, beautiful creature, as far from the rough, clumsy baggles as the cart-horse is from the racer.

The beast was kneeling under the shelter of the rocks with its waterskin and bag of doora slung over its shoulders, and its forelegs tethered Arab fashion with a rope round the knees. Anerley threw his leg over the front pommel while Abbas slipped off the cord. Forward flew Anerley towards the creature's neck, then violently backwards, clawing madly at anything which might save him, and then, with a jerk which nearly snapped his loins, he was thrown forward again. But the camel was on its legs now, and the young pressman was safely seated upon one of the fliers of the desert. It was as gentle as it was swift, and it stood oscillating its long neck and gazing round with its large brown eyes, whilst Anerley coiled his legs round the peg and grasped the curved camel-stick which Abbas had handed up to him. There were two bridle-cords, one from the nostril and one from the neck, but he remembered that Scott had said that it was the servant's and not the house-bell which had to be pulled, so he kept his grasp upon the lower. Then he touched the long, vibrating neck with his stick, and in an instant Abbas' farewells seemed to come from far behind him, and the black rocks and yellow sand were dancing past on either side.

It was his first experience of a trotting camel, and at first the motion, although irregular and abrupt, was not unpleasant. Having no stirrup or fixed point of any kind, he could not rise to it, but he gripped as tightly as he could with his knee, and he tried to sway backwards and for-wards as he had seen the Arabs do. It was a large, very concave Makloofa saddle, and he was conscious that he was bouncing about on it with as little power of adhesion as a billiard-ball upon a tea-tray. He gripped the two sides with his hands to hold himself steady. The creature had got into its long, swinging, stealthy trot, its sponge-like feet making no sound upon the hard sand. Anerley leaned back with his two hands gripping hard behind him, and he whooped the creature on.

The sun had already sunk behind the line of black volcanic peaks, which look like huge slag-heaps at the mouth of a mine. The western sky had taken that lovely light-green and pale-pink tint which makes evening beautiful upon the Nile, and the old brown river itself, swirling down amongst the black rocks, caught some shimmer of the colours above. The glare, the heat, and the piping of the insects had all ceased together. In spite of his aching head, Anerley could have cried out for pure physical joy as the swift creature beneath him flew along with him through that cool, invigorating air, with the virile north wind soothing his pringling face.

He had looked at his watch, and now he made a swift calculation of times and distances. It was past six when he had left the camp. Over broken ground it was impossible that he could hope to do more than seven miles an hour—less on bad parts, more on the smooth. His recollection of the track was that there were few smooth and many bad. He would be lucky, then, if he reached Sarras anywhere from twelve to one. Then the messages took a good two hours to go through, for they had to be transcribed at Cairo. At the best he could only hope to have told his story in Fleet Street at two or three in the morning. It was possible that he might manage it, but the chances seemed enormously against him. About three the morning edition would be made up, and his chance gone for ever. The one thing clear was that only the first man at the wires would have any chance at all, and Anerley meant to be first if hard riding could do it. So he tapped away at the bird-like neck, and the creature's long, loose limbs went faster and faster at every tap. Where the rocky spurs ran down to the river, horses would have to go round, while camels might get across, so that Anerley felt that he was always gaining upon his companions.

But there was a price to be paid for the feeling. He had heard of men who had burst when on camel journeys, and he knew that the Arabs swathe their bodies tightly in broad cloth bandages when they prepare for a long march. It had seemed unnecessary and ridiculous when he first began to speed over the level track, but now, when he got on the rocky paths, he understood what it meant. Never for an instant was he at the same angle. Backwards, forwards he swung, with a tingling jar at the end of each sway, until he ached from his neck to his knee. It caught him across the shoulders, it caught him down the spine, it gripped him over the loins, it marked the lower line of his ribs with one heavy, dull throb. He clutched here and there with his hand to try and ease the strain upon his muscles. He drew up his knees, altered his seat, and set his teeth with a grim determination to go through with it should it kill him. His head was splitting, his flayed face smarting, and every joint in his body aching as if it were dislocated. But he forgot all that when, with the rising of the moon, he heard the clinking of horses' hoofs down upon the track by the river, and knew that, unseen by them, he had already got well abreast of his companions. But he was hardly halfway and the time already eleven.

All day the needles had been ticking away

without intermission in the little corrugated
iron hut which served as a telegraph station at
Sarras. With its bare walls and its packing-
case seats it was none the less for the moment
one of the vital spots upon the earth's surface,
and the crisp, importunate ticking might have
come from the world-old clock of Destiny.
Many august people had been at the other
end of those wires, and had communed with
the moist-faced military clerk. A French
Premier had demanded a pledge, and an English marquis had passed on the request to the
General in command, with a question as to how
it would affect the situation. Cipher telegrams
had nearly driven the clerk out of his wits, for
of all crazy occupations the taking of a cipher
message, when you are without the key to the
cipher, is the worst. Much high diplomacy
had been going on all day in the innermost
chambers of European chancellaries, and the
results of it had been whispered into this little
corrugated iron hut. About two in the morning an enormous despatch had come at last to
an end, and the weary operator had opened the
door, and was lighting his pipe in the cool,
fresh air, when he saw a camel plump down in
the dust, and a man, who seemed to be in the
last stage of drunkenness, come rolling towards
him.

"What's the time?" he cried, in a voice

which appeared to be the only sober thing about him.

It was on the clerk's lips to say that it was time that the questioner was in his bed, but it is not safe upon a campaign to be ironical at the expense of kharki-clad men. He contented himself therefore with the bald statement that it was after two.

But no retort that he could have devised could have had a more crushing effect. The voiced turned drunken also, and the man caught at the door-post to uphold him.

"Two o'clock! I'm done after all!" said he. His head was tied up in a bloody handkerchief, his face was crimson, and he stood with his legs crooked as if the pith had all gone out of his back. The clerk began to realize that something out of the ordinary was in the wind.

"How long does it take to get a wire to London?"

"About two hours."

"And it's two now. I could not get it there before four."

"Before three."

"Four."

"No, three."

"But you said two hours."

"Yes, but there's more than an hour's difference in longitude."

"By Heaven, I'll do it yet!" cried Anerley,

and staggering to a packing-case, he began the dictation of his famous despatch.

And so it came about that the *Gazette* had a long column, with headlines like an epitaph, when the sheets of the *Intelligence* and the *Courier* were as blank as the faces of their editors. And so, too, it happened that when two weary men, upon two foundered horses, arrived about four in the morning at the Sarras post-office they looked at each other in silence and departed noiselessly, with the conviction that there are some situations with which the English language is not capable of dealing.

THE NEW CATACOMB

"LOOK here, Burger," said Kennedy, " I
do wish that you would confide in me."
The two famous students of Roman remains
sat together in Kennedy's comfortable room
overlooking the Corso. The night was cold,
and they had both pulled up their chairs to the
unsatisfactory Italian stove which threw out a
zone of stuffiness rather than of warmth. Outside under the bright winter stars lay the
modern Rome, the long, double chain of the
electric lamps, the brilliantly lighted *cafés*, the
rushing carriages, and the dense throng upon
the footpaths. But inside, in the sumptuous
chamber of the rich young English archæologist,
there was only old Rome to be seen. Cracked
and time-worn friezes hung upon the walls,
grey old busts of senators and soldiers with
their fighting heads and their hard, cruel faces
peered out from the corners. On the centre
table, amidst a litter of inscriptions, fragments,
and ornaments, there stood the famous reconstruction by Kennedy of the baths of Caracalla,

which excited such interest and admiration
when it was exhibited in Berlin. Amphoræ
hung from the ceiling, and a litter of curiosities
strewed the rich red Turkey carpet. And of
them all there was not one which was not of
the most unimpeachable authenticity, and of
the utmost rarity and value ; for Kennedy,
though little more than thirty, had a European
reputation in this particular branch of research,
and was, moreover, provided with that long
purse which either proves to be a fatal handicap to the student's energies, or, if his mind
is still true to its purpose, gives him an
enormous advantage in the race for fame.
Kennedy had often been seduced by whim and
pleasure from his studies, but his mind was an
incisive one, capable of long and concentrated
efforts which ended in sharp reactions of sensu-
ous languor. His handsome face, with its
high, white forehead, its aggressive nose, and
its somewhat loose and sensual month, was a
fair index of the compromise between strength
and weakness in his nature.

Of a very different type was his companion,
Julius Burger. He came of a curious blend,
a German father and an Italian mother, with
the robust qualities of the North mingling
strangely with the softer graces of the South.
Blue Teutonic eyes lightened his sun-browned
face, and above them rose a square, massive

forehead, with a fringe of close yellow curls lying round it. His strong, firm jaw was clean-shaven, and his companion had frequently remarked how much it suggested those old Roman busts which peered out from the shadows in the corners of his chamber. Under its bluff German strength there lay always a suggestion of Italian subtlety, but the smile was so honest, and the eyes so frank, that one understood that this was only an indication of his ancestry, with no actual bearing upon his character. In age and in reputation he was on the same level as his English companion, but his life and his work had both been far more arduous. Twelve years before, he had come as a poor student to Rome, and had lived ever since upon some small endowment for research which had been awarded to him by the University of Bonn. Painfully, slowly, and doggedly, with extraordinary tenacity and single-mindedness, he had climbed from rung to rung of the ladder of fame, until now he was a member of the Berlin Academy, and there was every reason to believe that he would shortly be promoted to the Chair of the greatest of German Universities. But the singleness of purpose which had brought him to the same high level as the rich and brilliant Englishman, had caused him in everything outside their work to stand infinitely below him. He had

never found a pause in his studies in which to
cultivate the social graces. It was only when
he spoke of his own subject that his face was
filled with life and soul. At other times he
was silent and embarrassed, too conscious of
his own limitations in larger subjects, and im-
patient of that small talk which is the con-
ventional refuge of those who have no thoughts
to express.

And yet for some years there had been an
acquaintanceship which appeared to be slowly
ripening into a friendship between these two
very different rivals. The base and origin of
this lay in the fact that in their own studies
each was the only one of the younger men who
had knowledge and enthusiasm enough to prop-
erly appreciate the other. Their common interests and pursuits had brought them together,
and each had been attracted by the other's
knowledge. And then gradually something
had been added to this. Kennedy had been
amused by the frankness and simplicity of his
rival, while Burger in turn had been fascinated
by the brilliancy and vivacity which had made
Kennedy such a favourite in Roman society. I
say "had," because just at the moment the
young Englishman was somewhat under a
cloud. A love-affair, the details of which had
never quite come out, had indicated a heartless-
ness and callousness upon his part which

shocked many of his friends. But in the bache-
lor circles of students and artists in which he
preferred to move there is no very rigid code
of honour in such matters, and though a head
might be shaken or a pair of shoulders shrugged
over the flight of two and the return of one, the
general sentiment was probably one of curiosity
and perhaps of envy rather than of reprobation.

" Look here, Burger," said Kennedy, looking hard at the placid face of his companion, " I
do wish that you would confide in me."

As he spoke he waved his hand in the direction of a rug which lay upon the floor. On the
rug stood a long, shallow fruit-basket of the
light wicker-work which is used in the Campaña, and this was heaped with a litter of objects, inscribed tiles, broken inscriptions, cracked
mosaics, torn papyri, rusty metal ornaments,
which to the uninitiated might have seemed to
have come straight from a dustman's bin, but
which a specialist would have speedily recognized as unique of their kind. The pile of
odds and ends in the flat wicker-work basket
supplied exactly one of those missing links of
social development which are of such interest
to the student. It was the German who had
brought them in, and the Englishman's eyes
were hungry as he looked at them.

" I won't interfere with your treasure-trove,
but I should very much like to hear about it,"

he continued, while Burger very deliberately lit a cigar. " It is evidently a discovery of the first importance. These inscriptions will make a sensation throughout Europe."

" For every one here there are a million there ! " said the German. " There are so many that a dozen savants might spend a lifetime over them, and build up a reputation as solid as the castle of St. Angelo."

Kennedy sat thinking with his fine forehead wrinkled and his fingers playing with his long, fair moustache.

"You have given yourself away, Burger ! " said he at last. " Your words can only apply to one thing. You have discovered a new catacomb."

" I had no doubt that you had already come to that conclusion from an examination of these objects."

" Well, they certainly appeared to indicate it, but your last remarks make it certain. There is no place except a catacomb which could contain so vast a store of relics as you describe."

" Quite so. There is no mystery about that. I *have* discovered a new catacomb."

" Where ? "

" Ah, that is my secret, my dear Kennedy. Suffice it that it is so situated that there is not one chance in a million of any one else coming upon it. Its date is different from that of any known catacomb, and it has been reserved for the burial of the highest Christians, so that the remains and the relics are quite different from anything which has ever been seen before. If I was not aware of your knowledge and of your energy, my friend, I would not hesitate, under the pledge of secrecy, to tell you everything about it. But as it is I think that I must certainly prepare my own report of the matter before I expose myself to such formidable competition."

Kennedy loved his subject with a love which was almost a mania—a love which held him true to it, amidst all the distractions which come to a wealthy and dissipated young man. He had ambition, but his ambition was secondary to his mere abstract joy and interest in everything which concerned the old life and history of the city. He yearned to see this new underworld which his companion had discovered.

" Look here, Burger," said he, earnestly. " I assure you that you can trust me most implicitly in the matter. Nothing would induce me to put pen to paper about anything which I see until I have your express permission. I quite understand your feeling and I think it is most natural, but you have really nothing whatever to fear from me. On the other hand, if you don't tell me I shall make a systematic search, and I shall most certainly discover it. In that case, of course, I should make what use I liked of it, since I should be under no obligation to you."

Burger smiled thoughtfully over his cigar.

" I have noticed, friend Kennedy," said he, " that when I want information over any point you are not always so ready to supply it."

" When did you ever ask me anything that I did not tell you ? You remember, for example, my giving you the material for your paper about the temple of the Vestals."

" Ah, well, that was not a matter of much importance. If I were to question you upon some intimate thing would you give me an answer, I wonder ! This new catacomb is a very intimate thing to me, and I should certainly expect some sign of confidence in return."

" What you are driving at I cannot imagine," said the Englishman, " but if you mean that you will answer my question about the catacomb if I answer any question which you may put to me I can assure you that I will certainly do so."

" Well, then," said Burger, leaning luxuriously back in his settee, and puffing a blue tree of cigar-smoke into the air, " tell me all about your relations with Miss Mary Saunderson."

Kennedy sprang up in his chair and glared angrily at his impassive companion.

" What the devil do you mean ? " he cried. " What sort of a question is this? You may mean it as a joke, but you never made a worse one."

" No, I don't mean it as a joke," said Burger, simply. " I am really rather interested in the details of the matter. I don't know much about the world and women and social life and that sort of thing, and such an incident has the fascination of the unknown for me. I know you, and I knew her by sight— I had even spoken to her once or twice. I should very much like to hear from your own lips exactly what it was which occurred between you."

" I won't tell you a word."

" That's all right. It was only my whim to see if you would give up a secret as easily as you expected me to give up my secret of the new catacomb. You wouldn't, and I didn't expect you to. But why should you expect otherwise of me ? There's Saint John's clock striking ten. It is quite time that I was going home."

" No ; wait a bit, Burger," said Kennedy ; " this is really a ridiculous caprice of yours to wish to know about an old love-affair which has burned out months ago. You know we look upon a man who kisses and tells as the greatest coward and villain possible."

"Certainly," said the German, gathering up his basket of curiosities, "when he tells anything about a girl which is previously unknown he must be so. But in this case, as you must be aware, it was a public matter which was the common talk of Rome, so that you are not really doing Miss Mary Saunderson any injury by discussing her case with me. But still, I respect your scruples, and so good night!"

"Wait a bit, Burger," said Kennedy, laying his hand upon the other's arm; "I am very keen upon this catacomb business, and I can't let it drop quite so easily. Would you mind asking me something else in return—something not quite so eccentric this time?"

"No, no; you have refused, and there is an end of it," said Burger, with his basket on his arm. "No doubt you are quite right not to answer, and no doubt I am quite right also—and so again, my dear Kennedy, good night!"

The Englishman watched Burger cross the room, and he had his hand on the handle of the door before his host sprang up with the air of a man who is making the best of that which cannot be helped.

"Hold on, old fellow," said he; "I think you are behaving in a most ridiculous fashion; but still, if this is your condition, I suppose that I must submit to it. I hate saying any-thing about a girl, but, as you say, it is all over Rome, and I don't suppose I can tell you any-thing which you do not know already. What was it you wanted to know?"

The German came back to the stove, and, laying down his basket, he sank into his chair once more.

"May I have another cigar?" said he. "Thank you very much! I never smoke when I work, but I enjoy a chat much more when I am under the influence of tobacco. Now, as regards this young lady, with whom you had this little adventure. What in the world has become of her?"

"She is at home with her own people."

"Oh, really—in England?"

"Yes."

"What part of England—London?"

"No, Twickenham."

"You must excuse my curiosity, my dear Kennedy, and you must put it down to my ignorance of the world. No doubt it is quite a simple thing to persuade a young lady to go off with you for three weeks or so, and then to hand her over to her own family at—what did you call the place?"

"Twickenham."

"Quite so—at Twickenham. But it is something so entirely outside my own experi-

ence that I cannot even imagine how you set
about it. For example, if you had loved this
girl your love could hardly disappear in three
weeks, so I presume that you could not have
loved her at all. But if you did not love her
why should you make this great scandal which
has damaged you and ruined her?"

Kennedy looked moodily into the red eye
of the stove.

"That's a logical way of looking at it, certainly," said he. "Love is a big word, and it
represents a good many different shades of
feeling. I liked her, and—well, you say you've
seen her—you know how charming she could
look. But still I am willing to admit, looking
back, that I could never have really loved
her."

"Then, my dear Kennedy, why did you do
it?"

"The adventure of the thing had a great
deal to do with it."

"What! You are so fond of adventures!"

"Where would the variety of life be without
them? It was for an adventure that I first
began to pay my attentions to her. I've chased
a good deal of game in my time, but there's no
chase like that of a pretty woman. There was
the piquant difficulty of it also, for, as she was
the companion of Lady Emily Rood, it was
almost impossible to see her alone. On the

top of all the other obstacles which attracted me, I learned from her own lips very early in the proceedings that she was engaged."

" Mein Gott! To whom ? "

" She mentioned no names."

" I do not think that any one knows that. So that made the adventure more alluring, did it ? "

" Well, it did certainly give a spice to it. Don't you think so ? "

" I tell you that I am very ignorant about these things."

" My dear fellow, you can remember that the apple you stole from your neighbour's tree was always sweeter than that which fell from your own. And then I found that she cared for me."

" What—at once ? "

" Oh, no ; it took about three months of sapping and mining. But at last I won her over. She understood that my judicial separation from my wife made it impossible for me to do the right thing by her—but she came all the same, and we had a delightful time, as long as it lasted."

" But how about the other man ? "

Kennedy shrugged his shoulders.

" I suppose it is the survival of the fittest," said he. " If he had been the better man she would not have deserted him. Let's drop the subject, for I have had enough of it!"

"Only one other thing. How did you get rid of her in three weeks?"

"Well, we had both cooled down a bit, you understand. She absolutely refused, under any circumstances, to come back to face the people she had known in Rome. Now, of course, Rome is necessary to me, and I was already pining to be back at my work—so there was one obvious cause of separation. Then, again, her old father turned up at the hotel in London, and there was a scene, and the whole thing became so unpleasant that really—though I missed her dreadfully at first—I was very glad to slip out of it. Now, I rely upon you not to repeat anything of what I have said."

"My dear Kennedy, I should not dream of repeating it. But all that you say interests me very much, for it gives me an insight into your way of looking at things, which is entirely different from mine, for I have seen so little of life. And now you want to know about my new catacomb. There's no use my trying to describe it, for you would never find it by that. There is only one thing, and that is for me to take you there."

"That would be splendid."

"When would you like to come?"

"The sooner the better. I am all impatience to see it."

" Well, it is a beautiful night—though a trifle cold. Suppose we start in an hour. We must be very careful to keep the matter to ourselves. If any one saw us hunting in couples they would suspect that there was something going on."

" We can't be too cautious," said Kennedy. " Is it far ? "

" Some miles."

" Not too far to walk ? "

" Oh no, we could walk there easily."

" We had better do so, then. A cabman's suspicions would be aroused if he dropped us both at some lonely spot in the dead of the night."

" Quite so. I think it would be best for us to meet at the Gate of the Appian Way at midnight. I must go back to my lodgings for the matches and candles and things."

" All right, Burger ! I think it is very kind of you to let me into this secret, and I promise you that I will write nothing about it until you have published your report. Good-bye for the present ! You will find me at the Gate at twelve."

The cold, clear air was filled with the musical chimes from that city of clocks as Burger, wrapped in an Italian overcoat, with a lantern hanging from his hand, walked up to the rendezvous. Kennedy stepped out of the shadow to meet him.

" You are ardent in work as well as in love !" said the German, laughing.

" Yes ; I have been waiting here for nearly half an hour."

" I hope you left no clue as to where we were going."

" Not such a fool ! By Jove, I am chilled to the bone ! Come on, Burger, let us warm ourselves by a spurt of hard walking."

Their footsteps sounded loud and crisp upon the rough stone paving of the disappointing road which is all that is left of the most famous highway of the world. A peasant or two going home from the wine-shop, and a few carts of country produce coming up to Rome, were the only things which they met. They swung along, with the huge tombs looming up through the darkness upon each side of them, until they had come as far as the Catacombs of St. Calixtus, and saw against a rising moon the great circular bastion of Cecilia Metella in front of them. Then Burger stopped with his hand to his side.

" Your legs are longer than mine, and you are more accustomed to walking," said he, laughing. " I think that the place where we turn off is somewhere here. Yes, this is it, round the corner of the trattoria. Now, it is a very narrow path, so perhaps I had better go in front and you can follow."

He had lit his lantern, and by its light they were enabled to follow a narrow and devious track which wound across the marshes of the Campaña. The great Aqueduct of old Rome lay like a monstrous caterpillar across the moon-lit landscape, and their road led them under one of its huge arches, and past the circle of crumbling bricks which marks the old arena. At last Burger stopped at a solitary wooden cowhouse, and he drew a key from his pocket.

" Surely your catacomb is not inside a house ! " cried Kennedy.

" The entrance to it is. That is just the safeguard which we have against any one else discovering it."

" Does the proprietor know of it ? "

" Not he. He had found one or two objects which made me almost certain that his house was built on the entrance to such a place. So I rented it from him, and did my excavations for myself. Come in, and shut the door behind you."

It was a long, empty building, with the mangers of the cows along one wall. Burger put his lantern down on the ground, and shaded its light in all directions save one by draping his overcoat round it.

" It might excite remark if any one saw a light in this lonely place," said he. " Just help me to move this boarding."

344

The flooring was loose in the corner, and plank by plank the two savants raised it and leaned it against the wall. Below there was a square aperture and a stair of old stone steps which led away down into the bowels of the earth.

" Be careful ! " cried Burger, as Kennedy, in his impatience, hurried down them. " It is a perfect rabbit's-warren below, and if you were once to lose your way there the chances would be a hundred to one against your ever coming out again. Wait until I bring the light."

" How do you find your own way if it is so complicated ? "

" I had some very narrow escapes at first, but I have gradually learned to go about. There is a certain system to it, but it is one which a lost man, if he were in the dark, could not possibly find out. Even now I always spin out a ball of string behind me when I am going far into the catacomb. You can see for yourself that it is difficult, but every one of these passages divide and subdivide a dozen times before you go a hundred yards."

They had descended some twenty feet from the level of the byre, and they were standing now in a square chamber cut out of the soft tufa. The lantern cast a flickering light, bright below and dim above, over the cracked brown walls. In every direction were the black open-

ings of passages which radiated from this common centre.

" I want you to follow me closely, my
friend," said Burger. " Do not loiter to look
at anything upon the way, for the place to
which I will take you contains all that you can
see, and more. It will save time for us to go
there direct."

He led the way down one of the corridors,
and the Englishman followed closely at his
heels. Every now and then the passage bifur-
cated, but Burger was evidently following some
secret marks of his own, for he neither stopped
nor hesitated. Everywhere along the walls,
packed like the berths upon an emigrant ship,
lay the Christians of old Rome. The yellow
light flickered over the shrivelled features of
the mummies, and gleamed upon rounded
skulls and long, white armbones crossed over
fleshless chests. And everywhere as he passed
Kennedy looked with wistful eyes upon inscriptions, funeral vessels, pictures, vestments,
utensils—all lying as pious hands had placed
them so many centuries ago. It was ap-
parent to him, even in those hurried, passing glances, that this was the earliest and finest
of the catacombs, containing such a storehouse
of Roman remains as had never before come
at one time under the observation of the
student.

"What would happen if the light went out?" he asked, as they hurried onwards.

" I have a spare candle and a box of matches in my pocket. By the way, Kennedy, have you any matches?"

" No; you had better give me some."

" Oh, that is all right. There is no chance of our separating."

" How far are we going? It seems to me that we have walked at least a quarter of a mile."

" More than that, I think. There is really no limit to the tombs—at least, I have never been able to find any. This is a very difficult place, so I think that I will use our ball of string."

He fastened one end of it to a projecting stone and he carried the coil in the breast of his coat, paying it out as he advanced. Kennedy saw that it was no unnecessary precaution, for the passages had become more complex and tortuous than ever, with a perfect network of intersecting corridors. But these all ended in one large circular hall with a square pedestal of tufa topped with a slab of marble at one end of it.

" By Jove!" cried Kennedy in an ecstasy, as Burger swung his lantern over the marble. " It is a Christian altar—probably the first one in existence. Here is the little consecration cross cut upon the corner of it. No doubt this circular space was used as a church."

"Precisely," said Burger. "If I had more time I should like to show you all the bodies which are buried in these niches upon the walls, for they are the early popes and bishops of the Church, with their mitres, their croziers, and full canonicals. Go over to that one and look at it!"

Kennedy went across, and stared at the ghastly head which lay loosely on the shredded and mouldering mitre.

"This is most interesting," said he, and his voice seemed to boom against the concave vault. "As far as my experience goes, it is unique. Bring the lantern over, Burger, for I want to see them all."

But the German had strolled away, and was standing in the middle of a yellow circle of light at the other side of the hall.

"Do you know how many wrong turnings there are between this and the stairs?" he asked. "There are over two thousand. No doubt it was one of the means of protection which the Christians adopted. The odds are two thousand to one against a man getting out, even if he had a light; but if he were in the dark it would, of course, be far more difficult."

"So I should think."

"And the darkness is something dreadful. I

tried it once for an experiment. Let us try it again!" He stooped to the lantern, and in an instant it was as if an invisible hand was squeezed tightly over each of Kennedy's eyes. Never had he known what such darkness was. It seemed to press upon him and to smother him. It was a solid obstacle against which the body shrank from advancing. He put his hands out to push it back from him.

"That will do, Burger," said he. " Let's have the light again."

But his companion began to laugh, and in that circular room the sound seemed to come from every side at once.

"You seem uneasy, friend Kennedy," said he.

" Go on, man, light the candle!" said Kennedy, impatiently.

" It's very strange, Kennedy, but I could not in the least tell by the sound in which direction you stand. Could you tell where I am?"

"No; you seem to be on every side of me."

"If it were not for this string which I hold in my hand I should not have a notion which way to go."

" I dare say not. Strike a light, man, and have an end of this nonsense."

" Well, Kennedy, there are two things which I understand that you are very fond of. The one is an adventure, and the other is an obstacle to surmount. The adventure must be the finding of your way out of this catacomb. The obstacle will be the darkness and the two thousand wrong turns which make the way a little difficult to find. But you need not hurry, for you have plenty of time, and when you halt for a rest now and then, I should like you just to think of Miss Mary Saunderson, and whether you treated her quite fairly."

" You devil, what do you mean ? " roared Kennedy. He was running about in little circles and clasping at the solid blackness with both hands.

" Good-bye," said the mocking voice, and it was already at some distance. " I really do not think, Kennedy, even by your own showing that you did the right thing by that girl. There was only one little thing which you appeared not to know, and I can supply it. Miss Saunderson was engaged to a poor, ungainly devil of a student, and his name was Julius Burger."

There was a rustle somewhere, the vague sound of a foot striking a stone, and then there fell silence upon that old Christian church—a stagnant, heavy silence which closed round Kennedy and shut him in like water round a drowning man.

* * * * * *

Some two months afterwards the following

paragraph made the round of the European Press :—

" One of the most interesting discoveries of recent years is that of the new catacomb in Rome, which lies some distance to the east of the well-known vaults of St. Calixtus. The finding of this important burial-place, which is exceedingly rich in most interesting early Christian remains, is due to the energy and sagacity of Dr. Julius Burger, the young German specialist, who is rapidly taking the first place as an authority upon ancient Rome. Although the first to publish his discovery, it appears that a less fortunate adventurer had anticipated Dr. Burger. Some months ago Mr. Kennedy, the well-known English student, disappeared suddenly from his rooms in the Corso, and it was conjectured that his association with a recent scandal had driven him to leave Rome. It appears now that he had in reality fallen a victim to that fervid love of archæology which had raised him to a distinguished place among living scholars. His body was discovered in the heart of the new catacomb, and it was evident from the condition of his feet and boots that he had tramped for days through the tortuous corridors which make these subterranean tombs so dangerous to explorers. The deceased gentleman had, with inexplicable rashness, made his way into this labyrinth without, as far as can be discovered, taking with him either candles or matches, so that his sad fate was the natural result of his own temerity. What makes the matter more painful is that Dr. Julius Burger was an intimate friend of the deceased. His joy at the extraordinary find which he has been so fortunate as to make has been greatly marred by the terrible fate of his comrade and fellow-worker."

THE DÉBUT OF BIMBASHI JOYCE

IT was in the days when the tide of Mahd-
ism, which had swept in such a flood from
the great Lakes and Darfur to the confines of
Egypt, had at last come to its full, and even
begun, as some hoped, to show signs of a turn.
At its outset it had been terrible. It had en-
gulfed Hicks's army, swept over Gordon and
Khartoum, rolled behind the British forces as
they retired down the river, and finally cast up
a spray of raiding parties as far north as Assouan.
Then it found other channels to east and to
west, to Central Africa and to Abyssinia, and
retired a little on the side of Egypt. For ten
years there ensued a lull, during which the
frontier garrisons looked out upon those distant
blue hills of Dongola. Behind the violet mists
which draped them, lay a land of blood and
horror. From time to time some adventurer
went south towards those haze-girt mountains,
tempted by stories of gum and ivory, but none
ever returned. Once a mutilated Egyptian

and once a Greek woman, mad with thirst and fear, made their way to the lines. They were the only exports of that country of darkness. Sometimes the sunset would turn those distant mists into a bank of crimson, and the dark mountains would rise from that sinister reek like islands in a sea of blood. It seemed a grim symbol in the southern heaven when seen from the fort-capped hills by Wady Halfa.

Ten years of lust in Khartoum, ten years of silent work in Cairo, and then all was ready, and it was time for civilization to take a trip south once more, travelling as her wont is, in an armoured train. Everything was ready, down to the last pack-saddle of the last camel, and yet no one suspected it, for an unconstitutional Government has its advantages. A great administrator had argued, and managed, and cajoled; a great soldier had organized and planned, and made piastres do the work of pounds. And then one night these two master spirits met and clasped hands, and the soldier vanished away upon some business of his own. And just at that very time Bimbashi Hilary Joyce, seconded from the Royal Mallow Fusiliers, and temporarily attached to the Ninth Soudanese, made his first appearance in Cairo.

Napoleon had said, and Hilary Joyce had noted, that great reputations are only to be made in the East. Here he was in the East with four tin cases of baggage, a Wilkinson sword, a Bond's slug-throwing pistol, and a copy of " Green's Introduction to the Study of Arabic." With such a start, and the blood of youth running hot in his veins, everything seemed easy. He was a little frightened of the General, he had heard stories of his sternness to young officers, but with tact and suavity he hoped for the best. So, leaving his effects at Shepheard's Hotel, he reported himself at headquarters.

It was not the General, but the head of the Intelligence Department who received him, the Chief being still absent upon that business which had called him. Hilary Joyce found himself in the presence of a short, thick-set officer, with a gentle voice and a placid expression which covered a remarkably acute and energetic spirit. With that quiet smile and guileless manner he had undercut and outwitted the most cunning of Orientals. He stood, a cigarette between his fingers, looking at the newcomer.

" I heard that you had come. Sorry the Chief isn't here to see you. Gone up to the frontier, you know."

" My regiment is at Wady Halfa. I suppose, sir, that I should report myself there at once ? "

" No ; I was to give you your orders." He

355

led the way to a map upon the wall, and pointed
with the end of his cigarette. " You see this
place. It's the Oasis of Kurkur—a little quiet,
I am afraid, but excellent air. You are to get
out there as quick as possible. You'll find a
company of the Ninth, and half a squadron of
cavalry. You will be in command."

Hilary Joyce looked at the name, printed at
the intersection of two black lines, without
another dot upon the map for several inches
around it.

" A village, sir ? "

" No, a well. Not very good water, I'm
afraid, but you soon get accustomed to natron.
It's an important post, as being at the junction
of two caravan routes. All routes are closed
now, of course, but still you never know who
might come along them."

" We are there, I presume, to prevent raiding ? "

" Well, between you and me, there's really
nothing to raid. You are there to intercept
messengers. They must call at the wells. Of
course you have only just come out, but you
probably understand already enough about the
conditions of this country to know that there
is a great deal of disaffection about, and that
the Khalifa is likely to try and keep in touch
with his adherents. Then, again, Senoussi
lives up that way "—he waved his cigarette to

the westward—" the Khalifa might send a message to him along that route. Anyhow, your
duty is to arrest every one coming along, and
get some account of him before you let him go.
You don't talk Arabic, I suppose?"

" I am learning, sir."

" Well, well, you'll have time enough for
study there. And you'll have a native officer,
Ali something or other, who speaks English,
and can interpret for you. Well, good-bye—
I'll tell the Chief that you reported yourself.
Get on to your post now as quickly as you
can."

Railway to Baliani, the post-boat to Assouan,
and then two days on a camel in the Libyan
Desert with an Ababdeh guide, and three bag-
gage-camels to tie one down to their own
exasperating pace. However, even two and a
half miles an hour mount up in time, and at last,
on the third evening, from the blackened slag-
heap of a hill which is called the Jebel Kurkur,
Hilary Joyce looked down upon a distant
clump of palms, and thought that this cool
patch of green in the midst of the merciless
blacks and yellows was the fairest colour effect
that he had ever seen. An hour later he had
ridden into the little camp, the guard had
turned out to salute him, his native subordinate
had greeted him in excellent English, and he
had fairly entered into his own.

357

It was not an exhilarating place for a lengthy residence. There was one large bowl-shaped, grassy depression sloping down to the three pits of brown and brackish water. There was the grove of palm trees also, beautiful to look upon, but exasperating in view of the fact that Nature has provided her least shady trees on the very spot where shade is needed most. A single widespread acacia did something to restore the balance. Here Hilary Joyce slumbered in the heat, and in the cool he inspected his square-shouldered, spindle-shanked Soudanese, with their cheery black faces and their funny little pork-pie forage caps. Joyce was a martinet at drill, and the blacks loved being drilled, so the Bimbashi was soon popular among them. But one day was exactly like another. The weather, the view, the employment, the food—everything was the same. At the end of three weeks he felt that he had been there for interminable years. And then at last there came something to break the monotony.

One evening as the sun was sinking, Hilary Joyce rode slowly down the old caravan road. It had a fascination for him, this narrow track, winding among the boulders and curving up the nullahs, for he remembered how in the map it had gone on and on, stretching away into the unknown heart of Africa. The countless pads of innumerable camels through many centuries

had beaten it smooth, so that now, unused and
deserted, it still wound away, the strangest of
roads, a foot broad, and perhaps two thousand
miles in length. Joyce wondered as he rode
how long it was since any traveller had jour-
neyed up it from the south, and then he raised
his eyes, and there was a man coming along
the path.

For an instant Joyce thought that it might
be one of his own men, but a second glance as-
sured him that this could not be so. The
stranger was dressed in the flowing robes of an
Arab, and not in the close-fitting khaki of a
soldier. He was very tall, and a high turban
made him seem gigantic. He strode swiftly
along, with head erect, and the bearing of a
man who knows no fear.

Who could he be, this formidable giant coming out of the unknown ? The precursor possibly of a horde of savage spearmen. And
where could he have walked from ? The nearest well was a long hundred miles down the
track. At any rate the frontier post of Kurkur
could not afford to receive casual visitors.
Hilary Joyce whisked round his horse, galloped into camp and gave the alarm. Then,
with twenty horsemen at his back, he rode out
again to reconnoitre.

The man was still coming on in spite of
these hostile preparations. For an instant he

had hesitated when first he saw the cavalry, but escape was out of the question, and he advanced with the air of one who makes the best of a bad job. He made no resistance, and said nothing when the hands of two troopers clutched at his shoulders, but walked quietly between their horses into camp. Shortly afterwards the patrols came in again. There were no signs of any Dervishes. The man was alone. A splendid trotting camel had been found lying dead a little way down the track. The mystery of the stranger's arrival was explained. But why, and whence, and whither?—these were questions for which a zealous officer must find an answer.

Hilary Joyce was disappointed that there were no Dervishes. It would have been a great start for him in the Egyptian army had he fought a little action on his own account. But even as it was, he had a rare chance of impressing the authorities. He would love to show his capacity to the head of the Intelligence, and even more to that grim Chief who never forgot what was smart, or forgave what was slack. The prisoner's dress and bearing showed that he was of importance. Mean men do not ride pure-bred trotting camels. Joyce sponged his head with cold water, drank a cup of strong coffee, put on an imposing official tarboosh instead of his sun-helmet, and formed himself into a court of inquiry and judgment under the acacia tree.

He would have liked his people to have seen him now, with his two black orderlies in waiting, and his Egyptian native officer at his side. He sat behind a camp-table, and the prisoner, strongly guarded, was led up to him. The man was a handsome fellow, with bold grey eyes and a long black beard.

" Why ! " cried Joyce, " the rascal is making faces at me."

A curious contraction had passed over the man's features, but so swiftly that it might have been a nervous twitch. He was now a model of Oriental gravity.

" Ask him who he is, and what he wants ? "

The native officer did so, but the stranger made no reply, save that the same sharp spasm passed once more over his face.

" Well, I'm blessed ! " cried Hilary Joyce. " Of all the impudent scoundrels ! He keeps on winking at me. Who are you, you rascal ? Give an account of yourself ! D'ye hear ? "

But the tall Arab was as impervious to English as to Arabic. The Egyptian tried again and again. The prisoner looked at Joyce with his inscrutable eyes, and occasionally twitched his face at him, but never opened his mouth. The Bimbashi scratched his head in bewilderment.

" Look here, Mahomet Ali, we've got to get some sense out of this fellow. You say there are no papers on him ? "

" No, sir ; we found no papers."

" No clue of any kind ? "

" He has come far, sir. A trotting camel does not die easily. He has come from Dongola, at least."

" Well, we must get him to talk."

" It is possible that he is deaf and dumb."

" Not he. I never saw a man look more all there in my life."

" You might send him across to Assouan."

" And give some one else the credit ! No, thank you. This is my bird. But how are we going to get him to find his tongue ? "

The Egyptian's dark eyes skirted the encampment and rested on the cook's fire.

" Perhaps," said he, " if the Bimbashi thought fit——" He looked at the prisoner and then at the burning wood.

" No, no, it wouldn't do. No, by Jove, that's going too far."

" A very little might do it."

" No, no. It's all very well here, but it would sound just awful if ever it got as far as Fleet Street. But, I say," he whispered, " we might frighten him a bit. There's no harm in that."

" No, sir."

" Tell them to undo the man's galabeeah.
Order them to put a horseshoe in the fire and
make it red-hot."

The prisoner watched the proceedings with
an air which had more of amusement than of
uneasiness. He never winced as the black
sergeant approached with the glowing shoe held
upon two bayonets.

" Will you speak now ? " asked the Bimbashi,
savagely.

The prisoner smiled gently and stroked his
beard.

" Oh, chuck the infernal thing away ! " cried
Joyce, jumping up in a passion. " There's no
use trying to bluff the fellow. He knows we
won't do it. But I *can* and I *will* flog him,
and you tell him from me that if he hasn't
found his tongue by to-morrow morning, I'll
take the skin off his back as sure as my name's
Joyce. Have you said all that ? "

" Yes, sir."

" Well, you can sleep upon it, you beauty,
and a good night's rest may it give you ! "

He adjourned the Court, and the prisoner,
as imperturbable as ever, was led away by the
guard to his supper of rice and water.

Hilary Joyce was a kind-hearted man, and
his own sleep was considerably disturbed by
the prospect of the punishment which he must
inflict next day. He had hopes that the mere

sight of the koorbash and the thongs might prevail over his prisoner's obstinacy. And then, again, he thought how shocking it would be if the man proved to be really dumb after all. The possibility shook him so that he had almost determined by daybreak that he would send the stranger on unhurt to Assouan. And yet what a tame conclusion it would be to the incident! He lay upon his angareeb still debating it when the question suddenly and effectively settled itself. Ali Mahomet rushed into his tent.

"Sir," he cried, "the prisoner is gone!"

"Gone!"

"Yes, sir, and your own best riding camel as well. There is a slit cut in the tent, and he got away unseen in the early morning."

The Bimbashi acted with all energy. Cavalry rode along every track; scouts examined the soft sand of the wadys for signs of the fugitive, but no trace was discovered. The man had utterly disappeared. With a heavy heart Hilary Joyce wrote an official report of the matter and forwarded it to Assouan. Five days later there came a curt order from the Chief that he should report himself there. He feared the worst from the stern soldier, who spared others as little as he spared himself.

And his worst forebodings were realized. Travel-stained and weary, he reported himself

one night at the General's quarters.   Behind a
table piled with papers and strewn with maps
the famous soldier and his Chief of Intelligence
were deep in plans and figures. Their greeting
was a cold one.

"I understand, Captain Joyce," said the
General, "that you have allowed a very important prisoner to slip through your fingers."

"I am sorry, sir."

"No doubt. But that will not mend matters.
Did you ascertain anything about him before
you lost him?"

"No, sir."

"How was that?"

"I could get nothing out of him, sir."

"Did you try?"

"Yes, sir; I did what I could."

"What did you do?"

"Well, sir, I threatened to use physical
force."

"What did he say?"

"He said nothing."

"What was he like?"

"A tall man, sir.   Rather a desperate character, I should think."

"Any way by which we could identify him?"

"A long black beard, sir. Grey eyes. And
a nervous way of twitching his face."

"Well, Captain Joyce," said the General, in
his stern, inflexible voice, "I cannot congratu-

late you upon your first exploit in the Egyptian army. You are aware that every English officer in this force is a picked man. I have the whole British army from which to draw. It is necessary, therefore, that I should insist upon the very highest efficiency. It would be unfair upon the others to pass over any obvious want of zeal or intelligence. You are seconded from the Royal Mallows, I understand ?"

" Yes, sir."

" I have no doubt that your Colonel will be glad to see you fulfilling your regimental duties again."

Hilary Joyce's heart was too heavy for words. He was silent.

" I will let you know my final decision to-morrow morning."

Joyce saluted and turned upon his heel.

" You can sleep upon that, you beauty, and a good night's rest may it give you ! "

Joyce turned in bewilderment. Where had those words been used before ? Who was it who had used them ?

The General was standing erect. Both he and the Chief of the Intelligence were laughing. Joyce stared at the tall figure, the erect bearing, the inscrutable grey eyes.

" Good Lord ! " he gasped.

" Well, well, Captain Joyce, we are quits ! " said the General, holding out his hand. " You gave me a bad ten minutes with that infernal red-hot horseshoe of yours. I've done as much for you. I don't think we can spare you for the Royal Mallows just yet awhile."

"But, sir ; but——!"

"The fewer questions the better, perhaps. But of course it must seem rather amazing. I had a little private business with the Kabbabish. It must be done in person. I did it, and came to your post in my return. I kept on winking at you as a sign that I wanted a word with you alone."

"Yes, yes. I begin to understand."

"I couldn't give it away before all those blacks, or where should I have been the next time I used my false beard and Arab dress? You put me in a very awkward position. But at last I had a word alone with your Egyptian officer, who managed my escape all right."

"He! Mahomet Ali!"

"I ordered him to say nothing. I had a score to settle with you. But we dine at eight, Captain Joyce. We live plainly here, but I think I can do you a little better than you did me at Kurkur."

A FOREIGN OFFICE
ROMANCE

THERE are many folk who knew Alphonse Lacour in his old age. From about the time of the Revolution of '48 until he died in the second year of the Crimean War he was always to be found in the same corner of the Café de Provence, at the end of the Rue St. Honoré, coming down about nine in the evening, and going when he could find no one to talk with. It took some self-restraint to listen to the old diplomatist, for his stories were beyond all belief, and yet he was quick at detecting the shadow of a smile or the slightest little raising of the eyebrows. Then his huge, rounded back would straighten itself, his bulldog chin would project, and his r's would burr like a kettle-drum. When he got as far as "Ah, monsieur r-r-r-rit!" or "Vous ne me cr-r-r-royez pas donc!" it was quite time to remember that you had a ticket for the opera.

There was his story of Talleyrand and the

five oyster-shells, and there was his utterly absurd account of Napoleon's second visit to Ajaccio. Then there was that most circumstantial romance (which he never ventured upon until his second bottle had been uncorked) of the Emperor's escape from St. Helena—how he lived for a whole year in Philadelphia, while Count Herbert de Bertrand, who was his living image, personated him at Longwood. But of all his stories there was none which was more notorious than that of the Koran and the Foreign Office messenger. And yet when Monsieur Otto's memoirs were written it was found that there really was some foundation for old Lacour's incredible statement.

"You must know, monsieur," he would say, "that I left Egypt after Kleber's assassination. I would gladly have stayed on, for I was engaged in a translation of the Koran, and between ourselves I had thoughts at the time of embracing Mahometanism, for I was deeply struck by the wisdom of their views about marriage. They had made an incredible mistake, however, upon the subject of wine, and this was what the Mufti who attempted to convert me could never get over. Then when old Kleber died and Menou came to the top, I felt that it was time for me to go. It is not for me to speak of my own capacities, monsieur, but you will readily understand that the man does not care to be ridden by the mule. I carried my Koran and my papers to London, where Monsieur Otto had been sent by the first Consul to arrange a treaty of peace ; for both nations were very weary of the war, which had already lasted ten years. Here I was most useful to Monsieur Otto on account of my knowledge of the English tongue, and also, if I may say so, on account of my natural capacity. They were happy days during which I lived in the Square of Bloomsbury. The climate of monsieur's country is, it must be confessed, detestable. But then what would you have ? Flowers grow best in the rain. One has but to point to monsieur's fellow-country-women to prove it.

" Well, Monsieur Otto, our Ambassador, was kept terribly busy over that treaty, and all of his staff were worked to death. We had not Pitt to deal with, which was perhaps as well for us. He was a terrible man, that Pitt, and wherever half a dozen enemies of France were plotting together, there was his sharp-pointed nose right in the middle of them. The nation, however, had been thoughtful enough to put him out of office, and we had to do with Monsieur Addington. But Milord Hawkesbury was the Foreign Minister, and it was with him that we were obliged to do our bargaining.

"You can understand that it was no child's play. After ten years of war each nation had got hold of a great deal which had belonged to the other, or to the other's allies. What was to be given back? And what was to be kept? Is this island worth that peninsula? If we do this at Venice, will you do that at Sierra Leone? If we give up Egypt to the Sultan, will you restore the Cape of Good Hope, which you have taken from our allies the Dutch. So we wrangled and wrestled; and I have seen Monsieur Otto come back to the Embassy so exhausted that his secretary and I had to help him from his carriage to his sofa. But at last things adjusted themselves, and the night came round when the treaty was to be finally signed.

"Now you must know that the one great card which we held, and which we played, played, played at every point of the game, was that we had Egypt. The English were very nervous about our being there. It gave us a foot on each end of the Mediterranean, you see. And they were not sure that that wonderful little Napoleon of ours might not make it the base of an advance against India. So whenever Lord Hawkesbury proposed to retain anything, we had only to reply, ' In *that* case, of course, we cannot consent to evacuate Egypt,' and in this way we quickly brought him to reason. It was by the help of Egypt that we gained terms which were remarkably favourable, and especially that we caused the English to consent to give up the Cape of Good Hope; we did not wish your people, monsieur, to have any foothold in South Africa, for history has taught us that the British foothold of one half-century is the British Empire of the next. It is not your army or your navy against which we have to guard, but it is your terrible younger son and your man in search of a career. When we French have a possession across the seas, we like to sit in Paris and to felicitate ourselves upon it. With you it is different. You take your wives and your children and you run away to see what kind of place this may be, and after that we might as well try to take that old Square of Bloomsbury away from you.

"Well, it was upon the first of October that the treaty was finally to be signed. In the morning I was congratulating Monsieur Otto upon the happy conclusion of his labours. He was a little pale shrimp of a man, very quick and nervous, and he was so delighted now at his own success that he could not sit still, but ran about the room chattering and laughing, while I sat on a cushion in the corner, as I had learned to do in the East. Suddenly, in came a messenger with a letter which had been forwarded

from Paris. Monsieur Otto cast his eyes upon
it, and then, without a word, his knees gave way,
and he fell senseless upon the floor. I ran to
him, as did the courier, and between us we carried him to the sofa. He might have been dead
from his appearance, but I could still feel his
heart thrilling beneath my palm.

" ' What is this, then ? ' I asked.

" ' I do not know,' answered the messenger.
'Monsieur Talleyrand told me to hurry as never
man hurried before, and to put this letter into the
hands of Monsieur Otto. I was in Paris at mid-
day yesterday.'

" I know that I am to blame, but I could not
help glancing at the letter, picking it out of the
senseless hand of Monsieur Otto. My God !
the thunderbolt that it was ! I did not faint, but
I sat down beside my chief and I burst into
tears. It was but a few words, but they told
us that Egypt had been evacuated by our troops
a month before. All our treaty was undone
then, and the one consideration which had induced our enemies to give us good terms had
vanished. In twelve hours it would not have
mattered. But now the treaty was not yet
signed. We should have to give up the
Cape. We should have to let England have
Malta. Now that Egypt was gone we had
nothing to offer in exchange.

" But we are not so easily beaten, we Frenchmen. You English misjudge us when you think that because we show emotions which you conceal, that we are therefore of a weak and womanly nature. You cannot read your histories and believe that. Monsieur Otto recovered his senses presently, and we took counsel what we should do.

" ' It is useless to go on, Alphonse,' said he. ' This Englishman will laugh at me when I ask him to sign.'

" ' Courage ! ' I cried ; and then a sudden thought coming into my head—' How do we know that the English will have news of this ? Perhaps they may sign the treaty before they know of it.'

" Monsieur Otto sprang from the sofa and flung himself into my arms.

" ' Alphonse,' he cried, ' you have saved me ! Why should they know about it ? Our news has come from Toulon, to Paris, and thence straight to London. Theirs will come by sea through the straits of Gibraltar. At this moment it is unlikely that anyone in Paris knows of it, save only Talleyrand and the first Consul. If we keep our secret, we may still get our treaty signed.'

" Ah, monsieur, you can imagine the horrible uncertainty in which we spent the day. Never, never shall I forget those slow hours during which we sat together, starting at every distant shout, lest it should be the first sign of the rejoicing which this news would cause in London. Monsieur Otto passed from youth to age in a day. As for me, I find it easier to go out and meet danger than to wait for it. I set forth, therefore, towards evening. I wandered here, and wandered there. I was in the fencing-rooms of Monsieur Angelo, and in the salon-de-boxe of Monsieur Jackson, and in the club of Brooks, and in the lobby of the Chamber of Deputies, but nowhere did I hear any news. Still, it was possible that Milord Hawkesbury had received it himself just as we had. He lived in Harley Street, and there it was that the treaty was to be finally signed that night at eight. I entreated Monsieur Otto to drink two glasses of Burgundy before he went, for I feared lest his haggard face and trembling hands should rouse suspicion in the English minister.

"Well, we went round together in one of the Embassy's carriages, about half-past seven. Monsieur Otto went in alone ; but presently, on excuse of getting his portfolio, he came out again, with his cheeks flushed with joy, to tell me that all was well.

"'He knows nothing,' he whispered. 'Ah, if the next half-hour were over !'

"'Give me a sign when it is settled,' said I.

"'For what reason ?'

" ' Because until then no messenger shall interrupt you. I give you my promise—I, Alphonse Lacour.'

" He clasped my hand in both of his. ' I shall make an excuse to move one of the candles on to the table in the window,' said he, and hurried into the house, whilst I was left waiting beside the carriage.

" Well, if we could but secure ourselves from interruption for a single half-hour the day would be our own. I had hardly begun to form my plans when I saw the lights of a carriage coming swiftly from the direction of Oxford Street. Ah, if it should be the messenger! What could I do? I was prepared to kill him—yes, even to kill him, rather than at this last moment allow our work to be undone. Thousands die to make a glorious war. Why should not one die to make a glorious peace? What though they hurried me to the scaffold? I should have sacrificed myself for my country. I had a little curved Turkish knife strapped to my waist. My hand was on the hilt of it when the carriage which had alarmed me so rattled safely past me.

" But another might come. I must be prepared. Above all, I must not compromise the Embassy. I ordered our carriage to move on, and I engaged what you call a hackney coach. Then I spoke to the driver, and gave him a guinea. He understood that it was a special service.

" ' You shall have another guinea if you do what you are told,' said I.

" ' All right, master,' said he, turning his slow eyes upon me without a trace of excitement or curiosity.

" ' If I enter your coach with another gentleman, you will drive up and down Harley Street and take no orders from any one but me. When I get out, you will carry the other gentleman to Watier's Club in Bruton Street.'

" ' All right, master,' said he again.

" So I stood outside Milord Hawkesbury's house, and you can think how often my eyes went up to that window in the hope of seeing the candle twinkle in it. Five minutes passed, and another five. Oh, how slowly they crept along ! It was a true October night, raw and cold, with a white fog crawling over the wet, shining cobblestones, and blurring the dim oil-lamps. I could not see fifty paces in either direction, but my ears were straining, straining, to catch the rattle of hoofs or the rumble of wheels. It is not a cheering place, monsieur, that Street of Harley, even upon a sunny day. The houses are solid and very respectable over yonder, but there is nothing of the feminine about them. It is a city to be inhabited by males. But on that raw night, amid the damp and the fog, with the anxiety gnawing at my heart, it seemed the saddest, weariest spot in the whole wide world. I paced up and down, slapping my hands to keep them warm, and still straining my ears. And then suddenly out of the dull hum of the traffic down in Oxford Street I heard a sound detach itself, and grow louder and louder, and clearer and clearer with every instant, until two yellow lights came flashing through the fog, and a light cabriolet whirled up to the door of the Foreign Minister. It had not stopped before a young fellow sprang out of it and hurried to the steps, while the driver turned his horse and rattled off into the fog once more.

" Ah, it is in the moment of action that I am best, monsieur. You, who only see me when I am drinking my wine in the Café de Provence, cannot conceive the heights to which I rise. At that moment, when I knew that the fruits of a ten-years' war were at stake, I was magnificent. It was the last French campaign, and I the General and army in one.

" ' Sir,' said I, touching him upon the arm, ' are you the messenger for Lord Hawkesbury ?'

" ' Yes,' said he.

" ' I have been waiting for you half an hour,' said I. ' You are to follow me at once. He is with the French Ambassador.'

" I spoke with such assurance that he never

hesitated for an instant. When he entered the hackney coach and I followed him in, my heart gave such a thrill of joy that I could hardly keep from shouting aloud. He was a poor little creature, this Foreign Office messenger, not much bigger than Monsieur Otto, and I —monsieur can see my hands now, and imagine what they were like when I was seven-and-twenty years of age.

" Well, now that I had him in my coach, the question was what I should do with him. I did not wish to hurt him if I could help it.

" ' This is a pressing business,' said he. ' I have a despatch which I must deliver instantly.'

" Our coach had rattled down Harley Street, but now, in accordance with my instruction, it turned and began to go up again.

" ' Hello ? ' he cried. ' What's this ? '

" ' What then ? ' I asked.

" ' We are driving back. Where is Lord Hawkesbury ? '

" ' We shall see him presently.'

" ' Let me out ! ' he shouted. ' There's some trickery in this. Coachman, stop the coach ! Let me out, I say ! '

" I dashed him back into his seat as he tried to turn the handle of the door. He roared for help. I clapped my palm across his mouth. He made his teeth meet through the side of it. I seized his own cravat and bound it over his lips. He still mumbled and gurgled, but the noise was covered by the rattle of our wheels. We were passing the minister's house, and there was no candle in the window.

"The messenger sat quiet for a little, and I could see the glint of his eyes as he stared at me through the gloom. He was partly stunned, I think, by the force with which I had hurled him into his seat. And also he was pondering, perhaps, what he should do next. Presently he got his mouth partly free from the cravat.

"'You can have my watch and my purse if you will let me go,' said he.

"'Sir,' said I, 'I am as honourable a man as you are yourself.'

"'Who are you, then?'

"'My name is of no importance.'

"'What do you want with me?'

"'It is a bet.'

"'A bet? What d'you mean? Do you understand that I am on the Government service, and that you will see the inside of a jail for this?'

"'That is the bet. That is the sport,' said I.

"'You may find it poor sport before you finish,' he cried. 'What is this insane bet of yours, then?'

"'I have bet,' I answered, 'that I will recite

a chapter of the Koran to the first gentleman whom I should meet in the street.'

" I do not know what made me think of it, save that my translation was always running in my head. He clutched at the door-handle, and again I had to hurl him back into his seat.

" ' How long will it take ? ' he gasped.

" ' It depends on the chapter,' I answered.

" ' A short one, then, and let me go ! '

" ' But is it fair ? ' I argued. ' When I say a chapter I do not mean the shortest chapter, but rather one which should be of average length.'

" ' Help ! help ! help ! ' he squealed, and I was compelled again to adjust his cravat.

" ' A little patience,' said I, ' and it will soon be over. I should like to recite the chapter which would be of most interest to yourself. You will confess that I am trying to make things as pleasant as I can for you ? '

" He slipped his mouth free again.

" ' Quick, then, quick ! ' he groaned.

" ' The Chapter of the Camel ? ' I suggested.

" ' Yes, yes.'

" ' Or that of the Fleet Stallion ? '

" ' Yes, yes. Only proceed ! '

" We had passed the window and there was no candle. I settled down to recite the Chapter of the Stallion to him.

" Perhaps you do not know your Koran very well, monsieur? Well, I knew it by heart then, as I know it by heart now. The style is a little exasperating for any one who is in a hurry. But, then, what would you have? The people in the East are never in a hurry, and it was written for them. I repeated it all with the dignity and solemnity which a sacred book demands, and the young Englishman he wriggled and groaned.

" ' When the horses, standing on three feet and placing the tip of their fourth foot upon the ground, were mustered in front of him in the evening, he said, " I have loved the love of earthly good above the remembrance of things on high, and have spent the time in viewing these horses. Bring the horses back to me." And when they were brought back he began to cut off their legs and '——

" It was at this moment that the young Englishman sprang at me. My God! how little can I remember of the next few minutes! He was a boxer, this shred of a man. He had been trained to strike. I tried to catch him by the hands. Pac, pac, he came upon my nose and upon my eye. I put down my head and thrust at him with it. Pac, he came from be- low. But, ah! I was too much for him. I hurled myself upon him, and he had no place where he could escape from my weight. He

fell flat upon the cushions, and I seated myself upon him with such conviction that the
wind flew from him as from a burst bellows.

"Then I searched to see what there was with
which I could tie him. I drew the strings
from my shoes, and with one I secured his
wrists, and with another his ankles. Then I
tied the cravat round his mouth again, so that
he could only lie and glare at me. When I
had done all this, and had stopped the bleeding of my own nose, I looked out of the
coach, and ah, monsieur, the very first thing
which caught my eyes was that candle,
that dear little candle, glimmering in the
window of the minister. Alone, with these
two hands, I had retrieved the capitula-
tion of an army and the loss of a province.
Yes, monsieur, what Abercrombie and five
thousand men had done upon the beach at
Aboukir was undone by me, single-handed, in
a hackney coach in Harley Street.

"Well, I had no time to lose, for at any
moment Monsieur Otto might be down. I
shouted to my driver, gave him his second
guinea, and allowed him to proceed to Watier's.
For myself, I sprang into our Embassy carriage,
and a moment later the door of the minister
opened. He had himself escorted Monsieur
Otto downstairs, and now so deep was he in
talk that he walked out bareheaded as far as

the carriage. As he stood there by the open door, there came the rattle of wheels, and a man rushed down the pavement.

" ' A despatch of great importance for Milord Hawkesbury ! ' he cried.

" I could see that it was not my messenger, but a second one. Milord Hawkesbury caught the paper from his hand and read it by the light of the carriage lamp. His face, monsieur, was as white as this plate before he had finished.

" ' Monsieur Otto,' he cried, ' we have signed this treaty upon a false understanding. Egypt is in our hands.'

" ' What ! ' cried Monsieur Otto. ' Impossible ! '

" ' It is certain. It fell to Abercrombie last month.'

" ' In that case,' said Monsieur Otto, ' it is very fortunate that the treaty is signed.'

" ' Very fortunate for you, sir,' cried Milord Hawkesbury, and he turned back to the house.

" Next day, monsieur, what they call the Bow Street runners were after me, but they could not run across salt water, and Alphonse Lacour was receiving the congratulations of Monsieur Talleyrand and the first Consul before ever his pursuers had got as far as Dover."

THE END

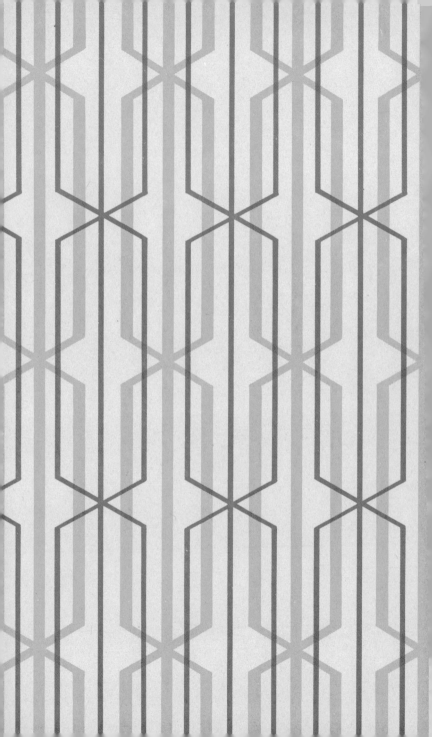